The SUN Will NEVER SET

Lynn ~

Thank you so much for your support! I hope you enjoy the story!

- B

The SUN Will NEVER SET

BETHANY BORGSCHATZ

— Beaver's Pond Press —
Saint Paul, Minnesota

Edited by Wendy Weckwerth
Cover Illustration by Gabrielle Marroquin

ISBN: 978-1-64343-877-1
Library of Congress Catalog Number: 2020915131
Printed in the United States of America
First Printing: 2020
24 23 22 21 20   5 4 3 2 1

Book design by Athena Currier

Beaver's Pond Press
939 Seventh Street West
Saint Paul, MN 55102

(952) 829-8818
www.BeaversPondPress.com

Contact Bethany Borgschatz at www.bethanyborgschatz.com for information about speaking engagements, book club discussions, and interviews.

I once met an elderly lady in a bookstore. When asked by the shop owner about the types of books she likes to read, she replied, "Anything with sex, violence, and mayhem."

My lady, this one is for you.

PROLOGUE

FOUR SHORT MILES FROM THE COAST OF WHAT IS NOW known as the English Channel sits the medieval city of Bayeux—the door to West Francia and a welcoming maiden to seduce the relentless tribes of Norsemen who ravaged the area in the late ninth century. Years before the intricate tapestry telling the story of Bayeux's feats was woven, the events themselves played out on history's stage. One of the of the greatest dynasties the world has ever known would be born from this city's womb. Forth from her would spring warriors, holy men, kings and queens, and conquerors.

Fertile land surrounded the city of Bayeux. The forests harbored an ample supply of wood. The rivers and lakes teemed with fresh water and fish. Wildlife grazed and roamed freely. The earth provided reliable and strong stone. Norsemen raided along the coast for years in search of rich lands to plunder and claim for their own. The pagan invaders had already arrived in Paris, and after a time they succeeded in breaching her walls. In the aftermath, in an effort to nurture peace, the king made a pact with one of the fiercest Norse attackers. The wild warrior known as Rollo defended the realm of West Francia from future Norsemen raids; in return, he gained leadership over the area. However, the agreement didn't impede the

Norseman from carrying out his own attacks on cities in the area entrusted to him. The residents of Bayeux knew the time to defend their city neared with each passing year. They built her walls strong enough to withstand the oncoming hordes that charged her now.

The previous night, from the tops of the walls, the inhabitants of Bayeux's stronghold had surveyed the surrounding farms as they burned. The sparkling glow of tall fires had danced in the night, visible for miles from atop the walls. Despite knowledge of the devastation being wrought, the sight was beautiful to behold. A terrible beauty, yes, but still beauty. Bayeux's walls held through the night. The captive Franks could feel the frustration of the attacking Norsemen. Anxiety grew as morning neared. All who dwelt within the walls knew what would happen once the savages overran the fortress. Fear overwhelmed some of them. They abandoned their posts and their homes to take refuge in the woods to the north.

In the early morning hours, activity around the walls mysteriously stopped. The citizens of Bayeux enjoyed a brief respite. It appeared the Norsemen had given up. The city wall had held! The city gave one last collective sigh of relief before, all at once, the Norsemen, in a new formation, charged with all their numbers at one side of the wall and broke through. The sounds of Frankish terror and Norse delight resounded through the city.

Rollo, a great warrior known for his brutality, led the charge. Though he had calmed in the years after his Christian baptism and his acquisition of land in West Francia, he found himself hungry for more. Bayeux promised riches that would increase his wealth in astounding ways . . . not to mention the stories he'd heard of a beautiful young noblewoman who resided in the city. The time had come for him to take a new wife. An ancient scream escaped his lips as he ran, a battle-ax in each hand, toward the hole in the city's wall.

The Capture of Bayeux

Two young maidens waited in the dark chill, high in the stronghold's tallest tower, which loomed above the center of the city. A heavy wooden door, locked and guarded, stood as their final defense. Lady Myra, daughter of Count Berengar of Bayeux, wrung her hands, her green eyes wide. She couldn't settle herself, even with near-constant pacing. Her handmaiden, the orphan Poppa, stayed with Myra to keep her company and protect her from capture, by any means necessary. Poppa considered what Lord Peter, the steward, had instructed her to do if the Norsemen should break through. She glanced at her late father's sword—still sheathed in its blue velvet case—and then at the pacing young lady. Poppa shivered. She knew she couldn't bring herself to do the task. She sat on the edge of her chair, calculating a way around her orders as her eyes swept the room.

A feather bed large enough for two dominated the tower room, which was decorated with fine imported fashions. A carved bedpost stood at each corner holding back a thick velvet curtain. Myra, who enjoyed her late-morning slumbers, would close them to filter the light from the tall windows on the eastern wall. Poppa entered each morning with a heavy sigh at the thought of opening those curtains and waking her lady.

New tapestries hung from the thick stone walls. Handwoven in the Far East, the tapestries used bright colors to depict scenes of a royal court in a land far away. Ladies paraded and danced with men in the midst of a garden of flowers. Myra loved the romance in the story it told. A large Oriental rug covered the middle of the flagstone floor. It had arrived with the same trader who brought the tapestries. Poppa could still remember him rolling out—with a flourish—his wares on the floor of the great hall below. Myra had wanted them all. Her father had finally acquiesced, though it cost him many volumes of grain.

Two carved wooden chairs sat atop the rug. As Poppa sat in one of them, she remembered happier times when she and Myra sat and shared the latest court gossip, the costly embroidered cushions keeping them comfortable. No matter. All these rich items meant nothing now. The girls had stacked most of the room's heavy objects in front of the large doors in an effort to bar the attackers. All of it would be forfeit if the Norsemen overran the castle. Every last piece would belong to them. Poppa had a sudden impulse to torch it all, leaving the intruders with only ash.

As Poppa's mind wandered, a loud banging erupted from below. The tower walls shook. Poppa remembered a dream from weeks before. She had awakened in the chill of her quarters, shaking with an excited fear from what she'd seen in her slumber. As the banging below grew in intensity, a plot unfolded before her. She quickly assessed and weighed the options. They had no other choice. It was her duty. They would have to move quickly and quietly, so as not to alert the guards.

Poppa hastened to doff her simple dress.

"What are you playing at?" Lady Myra looked at her handmaiden in horror. Her beautiful young face twisted in confusion as her green eyes grew even bigger and brighter.

From floors below them, shouts of battle swelled. Incessant pounding threatened the doors of the stronghold's inner holdfast. Soon the army of Norsemen would break through the last of the city's defenses.

"Quick, my lady, give me your dress," Poppa ordered.

"What?" Myra's eyes searched Poppa in confusion.

Another loud crash sounded from below.

Poppa gaped at the face of her frightened lady and friend. Instinctively she knew Myra's expression mirrored her own. "Hurry, there's little time. We must switch places."

Myra nodded in quick understanding and began tearing at her own gown. They rushed, each fumbling to help the other unfasten and refasten hooks. In moments the pair stood face to face, each wearing the other's clothes: the handmaiden Poppa in rich pink silk and Lady Myra in a simple dress of blue homespun wool. The noise from below crescendoed.

"I cannot let you do this." Lady Myra's fingers began to fret behind her back as she tried to undo the buttons and remove her handmaiden's dress.

"You must." Poppa remained steadfast as she placed her hands over Myra's frenzied fingers. She snatched a cloak from the wardrobe and wrapped it around her lady.

A disastrous crash and the roar of war burst forth from the main hall below. The thunder of countless footsteps followed.

Myra shook.

"Hurry—you must get through the tunnels and to the woods beyond. Remember the area that didn't burn in the night? Start there. It should be safe. Follow the river inland, away from the sea. Use my name if you're stopped by anyone. Say all is lost, and you fled in fear. The Norsemen will be looking for nobility to capture and ransom. They won't bother with a simple peasant girl."

"No. I cannot leave you behind." Large tears filled Myra's eyes and spilled onto her cheeks. They transferred to Poppa's cheeks and hair when they hugged tightly.

Friends and playmates since infancy, they had spent few days apart. Over the years, their bond grew into a sisterhood. When Poppa's father died, Count Berengar had taken her into his household, treating her like another daughter. The thought of separation tied a sickly knot in her stomach.

"It's willed by God. I told you my dream." Poppa looked at her with determination. Her fate was set. She would not and could not falter.

Myra knew her friend's tenacity and stubbornness were unshakable once decided on a plan. Still, she had to try. "Only a dream that spoke of a man, larger than any other, on the other end of a sword point. I cannot leave you to that fate."

"If they come, I'll fight."

"You'll die. Or worse . . . " Myra paused. Her green eyes shone through her tears. She tried desperately to plead with Poppa. "You could come with me."

Poppa shook her head as she placed a hand on each side of Myra's face. "They know the count had a young daughter. They will search for her if they don't find her. We wouldn't get far. Your chances are better if you travel alone. When they make it here, they'll find what they seek."

Poppa hugged her friend one last time. "There's no more time. Go now. Flee!" Poppa shouted and pushed Myra into the hidden passageway. She closed the door. She dropped the rich tapestry back into place, concealing the door.

Below, battle cries mixed with the moans of the dying. Poppa picked up her father's sword and held it fast. The weight felt familiar and sure in her hand. He had bequeathed it to her upon his death. Her father, Bayeux's master-at-arms, had always wanted a son.

Instead, he'd received a daughter—and a wife dead in the birthing bed. Poppa's upbringing had been unique. She was learning swordplay and the art of the hunt while other girls learned to sew and sing. After he died, a new life laid out before her. A life that included dressing in a simple gown every morning. It suited her well, and her beauty soon eclipsed all the other young ladies in the city.

Poppa's hair was a rich dark brown, and her eyes shone with a honeyed brightness. Her skin, normally milky white, glowed from the summer sun. Trim and fit from her ongoing sword practice, her body was lithe and sure. Poppa had received a number of marriage offers. The courtiers agreed that several more attractive offers were withheld because of her unfortunate habit of speaking her mind when a more wise and genteel lady would hold her tongue.

She needed that fiery spirit now. She could hear the rough footfalls of the savages as they climbed the stairs. They would arrive at the door in seconds.

She grabbed a torch in her other hand and waited.

A deafening banging came upon the heavy door. Its force made the dust from the curtains fly up and dance in the morning light shining through leaded glass. Poppa glanced at the finely made furniture blocking the door: a writing desk, two small dressers, and ornate lamps lay in a crisscrossed heap. She desperately hoped the pile would hit the wall and jam the door.

The Norsemen tried to push open the door. Poppa smiled tightly when she saw her plan work. Though she didn't speak their tongue, it was clear the men on the other side were yelling profanities at the restriction. She could see their hands, caked with dirt and blood, pushing hard against the door. Her heart pounded in her chest. It beat in her ears—a rapid pulsing, drums that urged her on. She ran to the crack in the door, which was wide enough to thrust the torch through. The Norsemen on the other side screamed as fire met flesh.

She pulled the torch back. She waited, wide-eyed, to see what would happen next. Abruptly, new sets of hands pushed on the door, and it burst open. The blockage flew in all directions. Poppa jumped back from the flying items and stood in the center of the room. She held her arms outstretched, a torch in one hand and a cold steel blade in the other as she welcomed the intruders with fire and ice. Her lips wore a challenging smile even though she knew the battle was lost. She wouldn't yield without a fight.

The Norsemen had long hair and long beards. They were naked from the waist up, revealing bluish tattoos inked in sharp lines that swirled ancient runes over their skin. Two of them rushed her at the same time, wild smiles on their dirty faces. In a flash of steel and fire, she dropped them to their knees, wounded and burned. A third knocked the torch from her hand. She felt a sharp pain in her left arm where his steel bit into her flesh, which found no protection in the fine pink silk. Reflexively, she stabbed her sword into his belly and pulled it out. With a groan, the body fell at her feet and onto the Oriental rug Myra loved so much. Before she had time to look up, new hands wrapped around her neck, cutting short the wild scream upon her lips.

By the will of these rough hands she moved through the air at a swift speed. Her sword lay abandoned on the floor, the point painted red. Quite suddenly, her back hit the wall, knocking the breath from her lungs. Her eyes closed. She could feel herself pinned between the wall and the man who held her neck. When her eyes opened, the largest man she'd ever seen stood before her. His hand loosened a little, allowing her to breathe but still restricting her movements. She saw his naked chest first. Fresh splatters of blood littered his chest and transferred to her dress as he pressed against her. Blue tattoos covered most of his skin. She followed them from chest to neck until their eyes met. His brown eyes looked heated with a hint of something else—need, possibly, or maybe hunger.

A fierce white scar curved through his left eyebrow, adding to the menace of his expression.

Poppa raised her knee as swiftly as she could and connected with his groin.

He cursed in surprise. His grip loosened, but only for a moment. Then it tightened stronger than before. At last, he laughed aloud. The sound was rich and deep as it hummed through her bones. Tears of frustration stung her vision.

"Please, my lady, do that one more time and I'll—"

"Rollo!" A murderous voice called from behind him.

Poppa looked over her captor's shoulder and saw a bald man whose face was red with blood. Blue tattoos covered one side of his head and face. Eyes of the coldest blue looked at and through her. When he spoke, his foreign words sounded harsh and inelegant to her ears. He wore a determined expression as he nodded to her.

Rollo argued over his shoulder in the same tongue. She watched as he gestured with his free hand to the dead man on the floor. She could feel his anger pulsating through his grip around her neck. She struggled to breathe.

The bald man's hands rose in a placating gesture as he spoke more slowly and calmly. Though she could not understand him, she could tell his words were an effort at reason. Whatever he said must have had the desired effect. Rollo's grip loosened the smallest amount as the men shared a look.

The bald man knelt to help the two wounded men on the floor. They cursed as they limped out. A few more Norsemen came in and carried out the body of the man she'd killed. She regarded them briefly before her gaze returned to the deep brown eyes roving her body. As she watched him, her mind spun with the reality that this was the legendary Rollo.

Rollo of the Norsemen, Robert by Christian baptism, Invader of Paris, Defender of Francia at Rouen, gave her a crooked smile as he leaned in. "One move, princess." His lips touched hers once or twice as he spoke in French, the language of her people. "One move and, by my word, you will regret it. I had a mind to be done with you, but my man tells me one of my kin was captured. I may need you for a trade, so you're safe. For now. Though if anything should happen to Ragnhild . . ."

He smiled wolfishly as he released her neck and lowered her to the floor. He pulled her hands behind her back. Poppa winced as the sword wound on her arm flamed, yet she stayed silent as he bound her wrists tightly with rope. He grasped her bound hands firmly from behind and pushed her out of the room and down the stairs. He paused only once—to retrieve her father's sword, which still dripped with the blood of his kinsmen. She had heard the stories about his large frame that reportedly was so massive he couldn't sit a horse. Though she thought the stories embellished at the time, she could now attest to their truthfulness. He towered above her. He was as large as a bear, but lean. His muscles rippled beneath his skin, making up the bulk of his mass. She could feel the heat from his chest as he held her close to him. He was twice her size, she realized. One of his broad hands eclipsed both of hers beneath their bondage.

She could smell the carnage of battle before they reached the main hall. Once the setting of many lively parties, it was now littered with corpses of the fallen. The stench of blood and death hung in the air. Poppa tried not to lose the contents of her stomach as Rollo guided her through the hall and into the courtyard, where the Norsemen were collecting the bodies of the dead. She saw the lifeless body of Myra's lord father, Count Berengar. Two Norsemen, splattered with dirt and blood, laid the count on the ground. One of the Norsemen unbuckled an axe from his side and lifted it high in the air above the lifeless body.

She gave a whelp of terror at the scene and closed her eyes to stop the tears from falling, but she couldn't close her ears to the thunk of the ax meeting the bone of the count's neck. Stunned by the violence, she quickly turned away from the scene. She allowed Rollo to push her along. He did most of the work for her as they moved across the courtyard. Fatigue started to set in. Her head hung heavily. Her eyes welled with grief. The only hope she could muster was the thought that Myra had gotten away and found the others who'd fled.

On the edge of the stronghold's grounds, still in view of the courtyard, he pushed her into a large tent already erected and furnished. He tied the rope binding her hands to one of the poles in the middle of the tent. Then he turned his back to her and followed the progress of his savage men as they continued to pile the bodies. Her countrymen and his, piled together.

She gasped when the men lit a pyre at the bottom of the pile and the bodies caught fire. Tears rolled down her cheeks. "Those men should be given a Christian burial in the churchyard!"

Rollo's sudden movement made her jump. She recovered quickly, standing her ground and keeping her vision in line with his. "And you should be offered to my men—after I've enjoyed you. So you would do well to hold your tongue."

Poppa clenched her jaw and refused to break eye contact. Rollo gave her a small smirk before he turned to bellow, "Get me a drink! I must quench at least one of my thirsts this day!"

She could feel the many eyes upon her as she stood barefoot in the soft mud and grass. Men and women alike, all warriors, watched her as they drank from their horns and celebrated their victory. Rollo kept his back, covered by a heavy dark fur, to her. She noticed he didn't leave his perch to join the others. Instead, his men came to him but never inside the tent, never past him and closer to her.

The man from before with the cold blue eyes returned, and they talked in hushed silence. His icy stare glanced in her direction often.

Poppa tried to listen in on their conversation, but they spoke in hushed tones, their language unfamiliar. She took this time to note her surroundings. A bed, big enough for two, lay in one corner. As she looked at the plush furs, quilts, and feathered pillows, she realized how weary her body had become. In a normal setting, the bed would be a comfortable, welcoming presence, but now it loomed and threatened as if at fault for what would happen next. She felt her exhaustion grow, and she longed for her own bed in the castle. A bed most likely now spoiled by some Norseman and his prey. She shook with frustration and fear. She let her eyes roam the tent again, hoping the cataloging would distract her. A small writing desk with pieces of parchment strewn on top stood beside the bed. Rolled-up scrolls of various sizes leaned against it. In front of her sat a small table that held a golden bowl filled with water. Rollo had used the water to wash off the dirt and gore of battle. A servant hadn't yet come to empty and refresh it. On the side of the tent opposite the bed, a large wooden table held maps, pawns, more parchment, and other items littered around. Most notably, laid her father's sword, back in its blue velvet sheath.

She felt emboldened by the knowledge of Myra's value in a trade. Poppa wasn't fearful for her own life or her innocence. She waited for the blue-eyed man to leave and for Rollo to finish his third drink before she spoke. "Why do you guard me like a dog, Rollo?" She let his name roll off her tongue. "I'm tied tightly, but there's nowhere for me to run."

She thought of Myra, safe beyond their reach. The success of their ruse brought a smile to her lips.

Rollo moved toward her slowly, his eyes traveling over her, down her, assessing her breasts, the curve of her hips. Under the scrutiny of his gaze, she remembered Myra's smaller frame. The dress she now wore hugged her curves tightly, too tightly. She felt naked under Rollo's gaze. She swallowed hard when his eyes met hers.

He broke the stare as he circled around her. “Do you know what happens to women captives after a battle?”

Rollo moved behind her. His body was so close she could once again feel the heat radiating off his skin. Her stomach quickened. Poppa, still on display before the victors outside the tent, felt the weight of their constant scrutiny. She was aware of their interested stares as his hand came around her waist and made its way over the curve of her hip and onto her thigh, where he gently squeezed her muscle and whispered into her ear. His breath was hot and arousing on her neck.

“I once had a slave girl after a battle. She had teats the size of your head. She was wet and welcoming, as if she wanted it.”

“Despicable savage,” she yelled at him. He jumped back laughing as she spit at his feet. “And they say a priest baptized you as Robert the Christian!”

Rollo wickedly smiled and mimed a crude gesture with his hands and hips.

Poppa’s cheeks flamed.

Their Norse audience roared with laughter.

Infuriated by the feelings he aroused in her and embarrassed that the crowd was witnessing this further humiliation, Poppa’s anger boiled over. Her mouth spat an insult of its own accord: “You’d force yourself upon a woman, even when she’s tied up and defenseless. How very noble of you. Perhaps that’s the only way you can sate your lust.”

The laughter vanished from Rollo’s face.

“Remove these ropes and then try me. Let’s see how far you get!”

Laughter again ensued as she twisted in her bondage. The ropes cut painfully into her wrists. Warm blood flowed down her fingers, but her anger was so great she hardly took notice.

Rollo gave her an amused smile as he filled his cup with more ale. She scoffed and turned away. She dropped to her bottom and tried to sit as comfortably as she could, given that she was tied to a pole with her hands behind her back. She only had to endure this night. On the morrow, her people would ransom her back and she would lead the party to find Myra. Bayeux was lost to them, but perhaps they could go to Paris. They could become ladies-in-waiting to the queen or the princess. Or maybe they could travel and see the world they'd only learned about in books. She let her mind wander with all the possibilities that lay before them once freed. It wasn't until much later, when her eyes closed in sleep, her head resting against the pole, that Rollo came and sat beside her.

Outside the tent, the celebration wore on. Fires burned tall, twisting above the heads of the Norsemen and into the night sky. The music, drumming, chants, and wails of an ancient culture floated on the night's cool breeze. The number of Norsemen standing outside Rollo's tent had dwindled. Paired off with their females, many of them retired to their own tents or to the castle itself. Poppa's eyes started to open when she felt Rollo beside her, but she didn't speak.

Rollo observed his captive carefully. Beautiful and tempting, she wrapped herself in bravery and strength during what must be the scariest day of her life. She possessed a wildness he hadn't witnessed in the other noblewomen he'd come across in this country. She surprised him with her strength and resolve. Even now, she didn't fall into hysterics. In fact, he hadn't seen her shed a tear. "You don't weep for your people nor your lord father."

Myra would have wept. Poppa couldn't bring herself to cry. Even though the day had brought such horrors. Even though she could still hear the ax falling on flesh. Even though she now sat in the middle of those celebrating the destruction of her city . . . She still held on to the hope that Myra had escaped.

"Tell me of the woman you mean to trade me for," Poppa prompted.

He smiled. "Ragnhild is a fierce warrior who's known for her leadership on the battlefield. She has felled many men and women with her sword. Like you, she's a noblewoman. The gods blessed us when we captured you, for you will offer an equal trade. I had a mind to keep you for myself, but I would like Ragnhild returned. I'm sure your people hiding like old women in the woods will agree to the trade."

Poppa ignored the insult, "She sounds fearsome. I can see your admiration for her. Is she your wife?"

This made Rollo laugh. "She's no man's wife. Though Ingmar is fond of her and would like to have her."

"Ingmar? The warrior with the blue eyes?"

Rollo nodded.

Poppa studied his face. His face looked softer as the firelight and shadows danced across his features. She couldn't help herself, she found him handsome. His chestnut-brown hair fell in long, messy waves past his shoulders, with part of it pulled back from his face and plaited. He had a square nose and a thick beard, absent of gray, surrounding his lips. His deep brown eyes spoke of his intensity with their flecks of gold that shone every time the light hit them. She noted again the light curved scar slicing through his left eyebrow. It made him look more dangerous than the legend that preceded him.

When he spoke, his deep and soft voice moved like a slow river current over shallow stones. It came from deep within him as he explained, "I had a wife once. She was from nobility just like you. She was a princess in her own right."

"A princess?"

She wondered why she hadn't heard of this union before. He spoke her native tongue as well as a highborn lord, which surprised her. She wondered if his late wife had been the one to teach him.

"Don't look so surprised, my lady," he replied. "I was foolish then. The gods mended my error when they took her in the birthing bed along with the child she carried."

Poppa let out a sigh as she read the pain he tried to hide in his expression. "I lost my mother the same way," she spoke by mistake.

"The countess?"

"Uh," Poppa hesitated. The countess was indeed dead but had only died the year before of a sudden illness. "Yes," she lied, hoping he wouldn't call her bluff.

She could feel his gaze upon her. Her stomach betrayed her by rumbling loudly.

"You must be hungry."

She nodded rapidly. Despite her nerves and the stress of the day, she felt desperate for food. Since the castle had fallen under siege, she couldn't remember the last time she'd eaten a substantial meal.

He called out an order she couldn't understand, and a moment later a young man came running with a leg of meat. Burnt and crisp on the outside, the meat dripped grease and smelled holy.

He smiled at her as he bit into it and chewed. "Mmm." A satisfied sound escaped his lips.

Her mouth watered.

He bit into the meat again before taking a long pull of his ale. A mischievous grin played across his face.

She groaned and rolled her eyes. She took comfort that this would only last the night. On the morrow, she wouldn't have to beg for her food. She'd share a meal with Myra, and they'd celebrate how they'd remained unscathed. She humbled herself and whispered, "Please."

He raised an arched eyebrow, and she gave him a pleading look. The meat smelled so tempting she could hardly bear it.

"Please," she croaked in a hoarse voice. Her head spun with hunger and thirst.

"What would I receive in return?"

Poppa's eyes narrowed at him. The turkey leg dangled before her face, just out of reach.

"What will it be, my lady?"

"What do you mean?"

Rollo smiled sardonically. "I've not kissed a lady of noble birth for some time."

Her eyes widened with surprise. The smell of the turkey overpowered her. "Fine." She stood slowly and gingerly. Her bones ached from inactivity. She met his stare.

He grinned and leaned in closer.

Her heart beat faster, and her chest rose and fell with each shallow breath.

His face moved even closer. Defenseless with her hands still bound, she trembled before him. When his lips touched hers, their warmth and softness surprised her. His beard tickled her cheeks. She could taste the turkey and ale on his breath. It wasn't unpleasant. She lost herself in the kiss. Her mouth opened and his tongue invaded her. She moved hers to match his and then felt his hand behind her head, pushing her deeper into the kiss.

As suddenly as it had begun, he pulled away. He grinned as his eyes roamed over her. Poppa saw that, even when pleased, his eyebrows arched in a permanent ferocity.

Poppa balked under his stare. She breathed heavily, gasping for air, while he drained his horn and chuckled to himself.

"The meat," she finally spoke when she had regained her breath.

"For that kiss, you deserve some ale as well." He held the leg out for her as she clumsily ravished it with her hurried teeth. Grease dripped down her chin, but she didn't care. She tried to lick it away when he left the tent laughing to himself. He returned shortly, still laughing, with more ale.

"Drink." He placed the horn on her lips and tipped it deftly so she could take a long, satisfying pull before he took another for himself. "Where did a lady like you learn to fight the way you did today?" Rollo tipped the horn and allowed her to drink again.

"My father—"

"Your *lord* father, the count? The one who ran like a wee girl when we broke open the door to the hall? He was the one that taught you to fight?"

Poppa grimaced. "My lord father *hired* the best swordsman he could find to serve as his master-at-arms. He insisted that we all train for sport and exercise. I first held a sword when I was three."

He nodded in approval.

"I'm tired," she confessed dreamily. The effects of the ale were going to her brain.

Rollo, emboldened by the kiss, smiled devilishly. "Would you like to share my bed?"

She narrowed her eyes at him and spat, "On the morrow, I'll be returned to my people and your Ragnhild will be returned to you. The kiss was the payment you requested for food, and nothing else."

"That was more than payment, my lady, and you know it."

"I don't know what you mean."

He offered a sardonic smile. "So be it. Enjoy the ground."

She watched as he bowed and climbed into the comfortable bed with all its layers. He paused, took pity on her, and tossed a thick wolf pelt over her before snuggling back into the warmth of his bed.

Poppa huffed loudly, consciously aware of the coldness seeping up from the ground and into her skin. She tried to snuggle into the fur as best she could. Then she rested her head against the pole and let exhaustion and grief take over. That's when the snoring, as loud as a bear's roar, began.

BLESSED BY FRIGGA

THE NEXT MORNING CAME WITH MOVEMENT and excitement. Even before she was fully awake, Poppa noticed Norsemen rushing in every direction as they went about their morning duties. Many carried valuable loot from the castle in their arms and greedy smiles on their faces. A man chased a woman servant past the tent. The woman screamed in protest. The man laughed as he tied his breeches so he could continue to run after his prey without losing them. Another man crossed the path with an armful of silver candlesticks and reams of fine scarlet. The load looked heavy, too much for him to manage. It wobbled back and forth as he took careful steps. A woman leading stout pigs crossed his path and almost overset the man. Curses and then laughter from the two filled the morning air as they passed each other unscathed.

"Come," Poppa heard Rollo call.

Her eyes fluttered with sleep and then opened fully. The sky slowly brightened into the familiar hazy blue of the time just after dawn. A chill could be felt upon the air, but the fur he had given her the night before kept her warm. She couldn't feel any part of her body that touched the ground, and she shivered within the fur.

"Come."

She gave him a beseeching look and twisted in her bindings.

"Right," Rollo huffed as he moved to untie her.

She watched as Rollo took a gleaming knife from the belt at his side. He stood before her and wrapped his arms around her. He leaned into her as he sliced the rope tied to the pole in one fell swoop of his blade. She felt the rope slacken as she breathed in his scent of cedar and woodsmoke. He took hold of the end of the rope, her wrists still bound and tethered to the end of it. With his free hand, he gripped her upper arm roughly. Every fiber of her body screamed in protest as he helped her to her feet. Poppa gave out a small whimper but stifled it when her eyes met Rollo's. He wrapped another fur around his shoulder and then drew near to her and did the same for her. She could feel the heat from his body as he moved his arms around her. She searched his eyes. She thanked him for the small favor with the ghost of a smile.

"Come," he repeated for the third time as he pretended not to see.

"What's happening?"

"Your people have come to make the trade."

He pulled on the rope, signaling that she should follow, but she pulled her arms back. He gave her a look of impatience.

"Wait," she pleaded.

"What is it?"

"Cover my face."

"What did you say, woman?"

"Hurry," she replied and then added, "Please."

He pulled her rope in protest.

"No." She spoke more forcefully this time and, though painful, pulled back and dug her heels into the ground.

A crowd of onlookers gathered to regard the scene as it unfolded. She forced him to meet her pleading stare. She could only hope he would obey. She didn't want her people to realize she wasn't the lady they sought until after the Norsemen freed her.

Poppa ignored the onlookers and focused her intense, honeyed stare on Rollo's dark eyes. "Do you trust me?"

"No."

She stomped her foot in frustration.

His eyes narrowed and his eyebrows knit as his face twisted in consideration. "How will they know it is the Lady Myra we have under the hood and not some random maiden?"

"It is our custom in Francia. To protect the dignity of the highborn," Poppa lied.

"I have conducted several highborn trades in this country and have never heard of this custom before."

"Perhaps your other captives didn't care for your honor or how you look before our people."

"And you, my lady, care for my honor?"

His voice sounded surprised, with a hint of emotion that made Poppa's stomach quicken before she answered honestly, "I don't know."

A moment stretched between them before he finally replied, "I'll do as you ask."

She watched as he took a small rucksack out of a nearby chest. Dust fluttered in a cloud, and then her world went black. She coughed as the remaining dust filled her lungs.

"You're a strange woman."

Poppa smiled under the cover that concealed her identity as she felt the pull of the rope and followed. She stumbled several times as they walked. Then she felt his strong arm around her waist to help guide her. In a sudden jerk of the rope, they stopped. She could sense others around them. She gave a sigh of relief. She could almost taste her freedom. Her heart fluttered. Then she heard the one voice she'd dreaded.

Of course he'd survived. Cunning and self-serving men like him would always survive the worst situations. Unskilled with a sword, he didn't possess the ability to best any of these large Norsemen in swordplay. She wondered if he'd been the one to betray the castle. *What deal did he make with these men that allowed him to keep his life?*

"My Lady Myra, we're happy to see you alive. We had feared you'd perished." The voice of Bayeux's steward, Lord Peter, cut through the air with a sharp and shrill tone.

Poppa shivered instinctually and leaned back into the man who held her bonds. Her heart began to beat rapidly. Either Myra hadn't found the survivors, or she'd instructed them to play along with the ruse. Poppa hoped with all her life that the latter would prove true.

"Did they harm you?"

Poppa shook her head, still covered in the rucksack, confirming they hadn't. She tried to imagine what the scene around her looked like. She still leaned into Rollo, who held her bonds behind her. She sensed at least four others close by. She heard the sound of metal on leather, a repetitive sound as if someone was toying with a sword and preparing the weapon for the slightest provocation. She could hear horses pawing nervously in front of her, most likely where the steward sat on his gray palfrey. She could only guess at who else had survived the siege and sat at his side.

"You're free to go," the steward's voice screeched.

Cheers from the men beside Poppa rang out as the woman warrior joined her kin. Poppa could hear the woman's heavy footfalls on the dirt road as she passed by. All too suddenly, the sack was pulled from her head. A hand shoved her forward. She stumbled as a collective gasp went up from the men on horseback. Peter jumped off of his horse and flew to her side in a flurry of movement. "What's this? What are you playing at?"

His expression was wild as his eyes moved rapidly from her to the Norsemen behind her. Poppa could feel the tension thicken around her. Poppa, bound and defenseless, stood shaking between two foes.

Rollo swept his arm in a slow and stupid motion toward Poppa. "Your Lady Myra."

"This isn't the Lady Myra!" Peter said loudly and frantically. "This is her handmaiden. Where's the young noblewoman?"

Peter searched the wild men before him. His suspicious gaze turned back to the Norse camp, as if they'd kept the girl captive and hidden. Then he registered the confusion on all their faces and realized they didn't have the missing lady. He sneered at Poppa, and she recoiled from his wrath. His face reminded her of a weasel's, all points and sharp lines. His greasy hair fell over his eyes, and he wiped it away to reveal a sweaty brow. He'd asked for her hand in marriage only a short time ago. She'd refused. The steward hadn't received the slight well. Now it felt as if that life had belonged to someone else.

His rank breath assaulted her as he leaned in. "What mummer's farce have you concocted now, Poppa? Where's your lady?"

Poppa glimpsed Rollo's face over her shoulder. He looked confused. His brow furrowed, the scar above his left eye white in the morning light, his mouth slightly open. Involuntarily, she remembered kissing those lips the night before. Heat swelled deep inside her. She turned back to Peter's narrow, ugly face.

"Where is she?" he asked as spit flew into her face.

Poppa's voice rambled frantically. "She's safe. We switched places, and she fled into the forest using the escape door in her room that leads to the tunnels. I stayed and took her place. I fought them off and bought her time to flee. Alas, I was taken—but not before one of the enemy fell beneath my sword. You'll find Myra in the woods. I'll help you search for her."

Poppa stole another glance at Rollo. His expression was dark and foreboding, though she detected something else hidden beneath. Admiration, perhaps?

"The escape door! The forest!" The steward's face fell. His breathing became hurried, and his voice cracked as he yelled, "You fool! They blocked the forest road and killed everyone who fled! They knew about the secret tunnels."

Poppa sucked in a breath, and then it caught. Her lungs wouldn't take any more air. Tears filled her eyes. She looked around at her countrymen. Several crossed themselves and hung their heads, their faces grave. Again, she tried to suck in more air in rapid bursts.

The back of the steward's hand hit square on her cheek, and she crumpled to the ground, sobbing.

"You stupid, stupid girl!" he yelled at her.

"I'm so sorry," Poppa choked. "I thought she would be safe. I thought—"

"You thought wrong. And your assumptions led to her death. You'll face the consequences of your actions."

Poppa blinked as she tried to clear her eyes. She could see the sadistic hunger in his eyes and knew her fate in his hands led to danger and pain. Rollo also saw the twisted and hungry look in the steward's eye. He didn't like the thoughts that played out in his mind, but it was Poppa who would save herself.

Through her grief a thought emerged. She rose from the ground and rounded on the steward. "How much, Peter? How much did they pay you to reveal the castle's secrets? How did the Norsemen know about the tunnels?" Her voice rose in accusation. "Only our lord's family—and the two of us—knew of them. Not even the guards posted outside her room knew about the secret passages. Only one of us could have betrayed them, and it wasn't I."

Her loud accusation hung in the air between them. Her countrymen began to talk amongst themselves. Peter's eyes widened in shock, as if she'd slapped him back. For a moment he didn't speak as he deliberated his next move. He glanced to the knights who'd accompanied him and saw the knowing judgment in their eyes. Not one of them moved against him. His men remained loyal—at least the kind of loyal that can be purchased with coin. He couldn't be sure how long that would last. He had to be rid of her. He couldn't have her sowing seeds of doubt among his men. His expression transformed from shocked to sneering. "Don't weave false tales to get yourself out of trouble, girl." Peter turned his attention back to Rollo. "I don't care what happens to her. She's nothing to us. Have her."

"You can't be serious!" Poppa cried after him.

Events played out too quickly. This wasn't part of the plan. Her mind raced with options but then clouded over with emotion at the thought of Myra fleeing from danger right into the hands of the enemy. Poppa had sent her there. Poppa had sent her to her death.

The steward turned his back and walked to his horse. She looked around at the other men—familiar faces, all of them. She'd danced and flirted with them. One, Charles, had ridden at her side in more than a couple of hunts. They had even shared a kiss in the woods on a dare. Another, she'd caught staring at her often in the great hall, she could never remember his name. Would none of them speak for her now? They stared at her with pity in their eyes.

"The castle is yours, and, by right, so are the surrounding lands and any other *plunder*." Peter spoke to Rollo from atop his horse but sneered again at Poppa at the last word. "If it pleases you, my lord, we will serve at your command and keep the castle for you until you wish otherwise."

Rollo nodded but made no verbal promise. He would allow the weasel man to serve as steward of the city for the time being, but at first chance, Rollo would find a worthier man to take his place. Most likely a man of Norse birth.

Peter turned his horse and left the company first. The men, all of them, consigned Poppa to her fate and followed their steward's lead. They turned their backs on her, leaving her to the savages.

Poppa hung her head and fell to the ground once more. Fresh tears carved wet paths down her dirty face. She deserved this. Without warning, strong arms wrapped around her and lifted her to her feet. Rollo pulled her along through the crowd as they followed her with hungry looks. Rollo moved so fast she could barely feel her feet touching the ground.

"Stop. Wait," she tried, her feet scraping painfully on the earth below.

Rollo wouldn't stop. He wouldn't wait.

"The sword of yours. Who did it belong to?"

"It was my father's. But I don't—" She stopped talking when he smiled back at her wildly.

"The day today?" he called to a woman passing by.

"'Tis Friday, m'lord!"

Rollo laughed deeply. "It's as if Frigga planned this herself!"

They reached his tent. They stayed only long enough for him to retrieve her sword and cut the bonds that remained around her wrists. She sighed as they fell to the ground, but her relief was short-lived. Rollo grabbed her by the arm and pulled her out of the tent and along the path.

They stopped a few tents down. Darkness filled the small tent and a musty smell pervaded. Candles burned all around, giving the room a smoky haze. Purple smoke tendrils rose from an urn on a table in the middle of the tent. Strewn about the table were carved runes, along with a skull and a curved knife. Beautiful tapestries lined the walls of the tent, and herbs hung from the ceiling. Their scent made Poppa dizzy as she looked around.

A woman, hunched with age and covered with deep grooves of wrinkles, appeared from behind a curtain. She smiled at Rollo and then turned to Poppa with a look of curiosity. She nodded her head in understanding and went to her altar. She lifted the curved and menacing blade. She took Rollo's left hand and brought it to rest in hers above the wood carvings of men and women. Poppa recoiled with shock when the woman drew the blade across his skin. He didn't flinch as his blood fell in bright rivulets over the figurines. Poppa had no time to register what Rollo had brought her into before the woman had taken Poppa's hand in her own. She ran the blade over Poppa's palm. Poppa flinched at the cold sting as a dark red line followed in its wake.

"Ahh," Poppa cried out. "What is this? I don't understand."

Poppa looked down at the cut in her hand. Rollo took her hand in his. Together their blood mixed and dropped over the wooden statues. She focused on the droplets of crimson as they met and mixed on the statues below. Then the woman moved their hands to an altar made of carefully piled stones. Suddenly, the door to the tent lifted open. A hazy and dim light filtered inside the tent, and Poppa saw a crowd of curious faces peering inside.

"Blood of my blood," Rollo stated in a firm voice.

Blood ran down their hands and Poppa's palm stung. A drumming began to beat in her ears, and she could feel lightness in her head. The abbotess gathered their mixed blood with her forefinger and used it to draw a symbol on both of their foreheads. A voice spoke to Poppa in the back of her mind. She understood. This was a wedding of barbaric and pagan traditions. The abbotess, a holy woman of old, performed the rights to the pagan ceremony.

The aged woman began to speak to the crowd in a dialect Poppa didn't understand. Rollo still clasped her hand in his. His eyes bored into hers, willing her to understand. Her lightheadedness passed, and slowly she came back to her senses. Rollo thrust the hilt of a sword into her hand. The weight felt familiar. Instinctively she knew that she held her father's sword. Poppa saw that Rollo held a sword in his hand as well. With the other hand, he broke a chain around his neck and handed it to the abbotess. Poppa saw the old woman pull two rings from the chain and put each on the point of the blades they held.

Rollo leaned the blade toward her and offered her the sword, ring and all. He gestured toward her, and she understood that he meant for them to trade. That explained why Rollo had cheered when she confirmed that the sword had belonged to her father. The familiar exchange of property between a father and husband during a Christian wedding ceremony was mirrored using swords in this pagan tradition. Poppa's stomach twisted into knots of distress.

She noticed the crowd and became shy under their gaze. They wore expectant expressions. Poppa looked for a way out but could see no way through them. Even if she escaped, where would she go? Her people had forsaken her. Rollo had saved her from an unspeakable fate. She needed him and his protection. She had nowhere else to go. She was trapped in this place. Trapped in this tent and trapped in this ancient ceremony that meant to unite her to the savage man before her. Her heart raced when her eyes met Rollo's again. It hurt to look into his intense brown eyes too long. She had no choice but to receive the sword he offered, yielding her own to him. Then his mouth pressed upon hers. His lips muffled her cry of surprise. His kiss felt warm and gentle upon her lips. For a moment, she felt anchored to the earth, finally solid in a flurry of confusion, before the crowd's cheers brought her back to reality.

She saw as many happy faces in the crowd as those wearing solemn expressions. She even saw a few of them spit on the ground before they walked away. She turned back to Rollo, who smiled crookedly and whispered into her ear, "Ase has united us. Run. Now. Back to the tent as fast as you can."

She stared at him confusedly. Her head felt light and dizzy, as if she had drunk too much wine.

"Don't fear. It is the *bruð-hlaup*. We will race each other to the feast. Go now!"

With that last instruction, he pushed her gently. The crowd parted, and she ran for the tent that had served as her prison only the night before and now represented her goal of safety. Poppa, vaguely aware of the crowd running behind her, cheering and hollering as they went, ran as fast as she could on her stiff and sore legs. Her muscles burned. The late morning air felt cool on her face and welcoming after the stuffiness of the tent belonging to the abbotess. The wind whipped her hair all around her. As she neared the tent, a line of Norsemen stood and blocked her from running further. The line led right to the door of the tent, where Rollo already waited. An amused grin played across his lips.

Poppa stopped as she neared him and looked at him incredulously. She had run her fastest, and he had still beaten her back. She breathed heavily as she glanced over her shoulder. The crowd also slowed and closed in. "How did you do it? I left before you."

Rollo laughed in response, a deep and throaty sound she felt in her bones. He handed her a horn of mead. "Drink, wife. Come inside. We have much to discuss."

Poppa accepted the mead and drank it down fully without stopping. She felt parched after the run and nervous about what might come next. Rollo lifted the flap to the tent. She walked past him to enter. Her shoulder brushed his chest as she went. He let the flap close behind him as he followed her inside. The tent looked the same as it had when they left that morning—except for the addition of an ornate golden trunk sitting next to the familiar wooden pole. She instantly recognized it as Myra's. She let out a low moan and fell to her knees before it. She opened the trunk without delay and began to rummage through the items. Many of the finely made dresses were missing, taken by the conquering men for their wives at home. Nevertheless, she found the dress she sought. She pulled out the simple black wool-spun dress and hugged it to her body. On impulse, she brought it to her nose. She breathed in the comforting scent of lavender and frankincense. Myra had worn this dress in mourning after her lady mother had passed. The black dress had emphasized her long, pale neck and made her green eyes shine.

"Myra," she said, part whisper, part whimper. Her head lowered. Her eyes closed tight against her tears.

Rollo observed her and gave her a few moments before he spoke. "I recovered what I could." He paused. "It is my wish to clean the wound on your arm."

Poppa startled. She'd forgotten her surroundings and that Rollo lingered close by. She rose mechanically, the dress still clutched in her arms. Rollo stood by a gold basin of water and clean strips of linen to bind her wound. The golden light from dozens of candles flickered and danced around the tent as she went to stand beside him.

She let out a low hiss as he peeled a fragment of the rich silk dress back from the wound. It had stuck to the dried blood and came away with difficulty. He let the sponge drink in the warm water and then pressed it to the wound to help loosen the cloth and the blood. He held her arm gently in his hands. "It doesn't look as deep as I had thought, but you will need to keep it clean. When I'm done, I'll give you time to wash and dress, but you should hurry. They are eager to celebrate our union."

Poppa raised her eyes to his. "Why did you do it?"

Rollo continued to wash her wound as he spoke. The warm water felt soothing and seductive on her wound. "When your kinsmen surrendered you to us, you became a spoil of battle. Do you understand what that means?"

Poppa's eyes widened, and he affirmed her thoughts with a nod.

"But these men belong to you. They would have listened to your orders not to harm—"

"Some of these men fight for me, but they do not all belong to me. In their minds, by right, you're theirs. Earned in their victory. I couldn't guarantee your protection if I didn't claim you for myself. I didn't desire to enter into conflict with the men who fought for me."

Poppa nodded and then waited for him to meet her stare. "And why are you concerned for my protection? I lied, and I tricked you. I killed one of your men. And it was all for naught."

She hung her head to hide the tears that welled in her eyes. Rollo lifted her chin to look into her eyes. When he spoke, his voice expressed tenderness. "What you did was brave and in service of a friend. We don't always know what the fates hold for others. Nevertheless, you were willing to lay down your safety for the freedom of another. That's commendable."

Poppa shook at the intensity of his gaze, and words escaped her. Rollo smiled at her. "Besides, I wanted you for myself. Wash, and change your clothing."

Poppa watched him as he left the tent to join the merrymakers outside. A young serving girl silently brought in a fresh basin of warm water. For the first time, Poppa realized how filthy she had become. She doffed her dress, caked with dirt and splatters of blood, and threw it in the fire. It had belonged to Myra, but she had no desire to save the remembrance of her foolish plan. Poppa brought the wet rag to her skin, which had fared no better than her dress. The water felt warm and healing as she washed the dirt away. She found smallclothes in the chest, and a wave of gratitude came over her as she quickly changed. She had just pulled the dress over her last shoulder when Rollo returned.

Rollo stopped in the entryway. His mood was light from mead and celebration. He contemplated her for a moment and his breath caught in his throat. The black dress only made her smooth, sun-bronzed skin shine brighter in the firelight. She turned her back to him and moved her long brown hair to one shoulder. He saw the open dress, revealing her bare back, and felt a lightness in his chest. His eyes followed the delicate bones of her spine down the center of her back.

Rollo swallowed hard and moved closer so he could close the dress one clasp at a time.

His large hands deftly executed the fine movements. Poppa felt a shiver run down her back as he went about the task.

"Thank you."

She heard singing and cheering rising from outside, but inside the tent, the atmosphere felt charged with the quiet tension of the unknown. The silence and excitement one experiences on the precipice of a great storm filled the space between them.

"They won't wait much longer. Give me your hand," Poppa instructed as she reached for the hand that Ase had cut during the ceremony.

She took Rollo's hand in hers and washed the cut. His skin felt warm beneath her hands. Despite her rising heart rate, she moved steadily as she took a long piece of leftover white linen. Carefully, she began to wrap the wound. Rollo noticed a lock of her hair fall over one eye. He lifted his free hand to tuck it behind her ear.

"You're very beautiful, Poppa."

Color rose in her cheeks as she tied a knot in the linen.

Rollo remained silent as he helped her tie a piece of linen on her hand as well. When he finished, he lingered for a moment. Her hand in his. He leaned closer, crossing the threshold of tension between them. His nose inches from hers. Her wary eyes started to betray her as they slowly closed. He moved closer. She felt his breath brush her lips. She felt her lips part.

Suddenly, a commotion erupted at the entrance to the tent as three women entered. Poppa jumped backward. Her head turned to the noise and the fierce-looking women who shouted and laughed with one another. The three of them—a blonde, a redhead, and a brunette—were all young and beautiful. Surely, one of these would've made a better bride than her for Rollo.

"You've had enough time, you big oaf. Your bride has no family to represent her. We will do the job. It's our turn now. Out!"

The woman who spoke had long golden hair worn twisted about her head. The black kohl circling her eyes illuminated their crystal-blue color. She wore a tight leather bodice and trousers like a man. A sword hung fastened in a belt at her side. She stood a head taller than Poppa and moved with grace and strength in a wide gait.

Rollo smiled at the woman. He hugged her and kissed both of her cheeks before she pushed him out of the tent, the both of them laughing. Then the fearsome woman turned to Poppa.

"Well, here she stands. The girl blessed by Frigga. Ladies, get her another mead. She looks as scared as a young doe."

Poppa examined the woman carefully as she approached. Momentarily, the other two returned carrying multiple chalices full of mead. Poppa accepted one when offered and took a small sip. The drink tasted both sweet and sour on her tongue. She took another sip as the women assessed her.

"I heard you're a daring swordswoman. You killed Wagner with one blow." The woman's eyes narrowed, and she scanned Poppa with judgment.

Poppa stood tall and didn't cower under the woman's scrutiny when she spoke, "You must be Ragnhild. I believe we owe one another a debt. If you would've died in battle, they wouldn't have treated me kindly as a prisoner."

"And if you hadn't spun your tales, convincing everyone of your noble birth, I may have been killed."

"So it appears we're even."

"So it does, Blessed by Frigga."

"Why does everyone keep saying that? I know not what it means."

"Frigga is the wife of Odin, the most powerful leader of all our gods. She is the goddess of love, marriage, and destiny. Since circumstance demanded you to be married on her day, it appears she has chosen you. Your union destined. My people celebrate deeply on your account this night."

"I believe in the Lord Jesus Christ. He alone shapes our destinies."

"Of course you do," Ragnhild dismissed Poppa, rolling her eyes. "But your union was in accordance with the old customs, and Rollo's people will love you for it. A fact I'm sure wasn't lost on him."

"We've brought some gifts." The dark-haired woman changed the topic as she spoke for the first time. "I'm Sigrid, and this is Toriana. The tales of your youth and beauty are true, I see."

Poppa nodded to Sigrid and then to the orange-haired Toriana. Sigrid began to adorn Poppa with jewelry that she removed from a small ornate chest: silver cuffs inlaid with sparkling green emeralds, a heavy matching necklace, and fine earrings to complete the set. Ragnhild drank deeply from her horn of ale. She leaned against the table and watched the others work. As Sigrid fussed over jewelry placement, Toriana braided and twisted Poppa's hair. She placed parts on top of Poppa's head, swiftly pinning each plaited tendril in place. When she finished, she moved to put dark kohl around Poppa's eyes. Poppa waited patiently through it all as the women spoke around her.

"I've heard it said that Rollo is a generous lover," Ragnhild spoke into the silent lull of conversation. A wicked grin played devilishly across her face.

"A very generous lover." Sigrid made a crude gesture.

The Norsewomen laughed deeply. Poppa blushed.

"Oh dear, don't frighten her. I'm guessing she's yet a maid," Toriana spoke, not unkindly.

Poppa's blush deepened. "While I'm yet untouched, I do understand your jokes about lovemaking and the size of a man."

"Do you now?" Ragnhild scoffed incredulously. "Do you know what it's like to make love to a strong warrior of the North rather than a puny man of Francia?"

Behind her, the women snickered.

Poppa opened her mouth to respond, but Ragnhild interrupted her. "Now that Rollo has taken you, a lovely Frankish woman, for his wife, his men will want to do the same. Who then, my lady, do you think will be left for us?"

Ragnhild's icy and piercing eyes investigated Poppa's. Ragnhild took a long pull on her drink and threw the empty cup to the ground before she spat, "The men of Francia and their tiny members that are as big as their pinkies. That's who's left for us women of the North."

Poppa recoiled from the commanding woman before Ragnhild smiled. Poppa steeled herself. She wouldn't yield her pride so quickly. "I've heard that it's not the size that matters, but how a man uses it. I wish for you that you find a man skilled enough to please you."

The other two women laughed long and hard. Poppa watched as an amused smile played upon the lips of Ragnhild before she too couldn't help herself.

When the laughter died down, Ragnhild's face grew serious as she removed the sword from the belt at her side. "*Nei!* I don't care for a man or his member, big or small. This is my husband." She raised her sword, the blade gleaming in the light of the fire. "By his point I'll birth my children as I send them to Valhalla."

The other two women of the North laughed as if she had made a jest, but Poppa watched her carefully. Then Ragnhild made a mocking gesture with her sword and lightened the mood. Poppa couldn't help but to laugh along.

The sound of their laughter brought Rollo to the tent. He impatiently regarded the women in their jests as he appreciated the work they had done. Poppa stood shining amongst the other women. Easily the most beautiful, and now they belonged to each other. His heart lightened. She glanced his way. Her smile bright from laughter. The smile disappeared as her eyes caught his stare. The blush returned to her face, which only made her more beautiful.

"The people have waited long enough," Rollo called to her.

She came to him and placed her hand on his shoulder as he led her out of the tent and into a crowd of cheering and applause. Poppa smiled at the happy faces looking back at her, even as she noticed some weren't celebrating. She spied Ingmar and a man she didn't recognize huddled together and whispering. They didn't join in the cheers. Someone beside her handed her another horn filled with the familiar honey-sweet beverage; though her head felt light and dizzy from the day, she drank deeply alongside Rollo. The crowd had much to celebrate this night: a victory in battle, their fallen brethren's journey to Valhalla, and the wedding of their jarl.

Rollo and Poppa sat in seats of honor in the middle of those who celebrated their union. The area just outside the city walls, once so familiar to Poppa, now seemed foreign with its occupation of Norsemen and their pagan ways. She watched them carefully. Where her people would have dined in a richly adorned dining hall, the broader of shoulder and larger Norse folk feasted on pig and pheasant in the open air around the fire. The smell of roasting meat still lingered upon the air and made her mouth water. Where her people would wear silk garments, this wilder clan clad themselves in leather and fur. Layered upon their expansive frames, the hides only made them appear larger to the eye. They decorated their garments with feathers and bones from the birds of the air. She quickly realized that the jewelry bestowed upon her made her stand out amongst the others. They were an attractive race of people, if one could get beyond the fierce coldness they shared.

Poppa watched as a large red-headed man rolled another cask into the circle and cracked it open with a howl. The Norsemen had raided the castle's cellars for casks of ale and wine. What had taken four moon turns to brew and store, the Norsemen would use up in a night. Her head felt light with the drink she had imbibed along with them.

Women danced for the crowd in front of the fires. The light turned into shadow and back again as they moved. Men beside Poppa, their faces battle-worn and dirty, drank and hollered as they watched the women. The music the revelers danced to soared throughout the night air and hovered around them. The unfamiliar words and melodies intoxicated and seduced the revelers. The sound coupled with the mead made Poppa's head dance in time with the women as they swirled with the fire.

Rollo took notice of Poppa's yawn and sleepy eyes. The revelers stopped on an unspoken cue when he rose. He raised his bound hand to them, then placed it over his heart in an affectionate gesture. He held out his other hand to Poppa. She placed her hand in his and allowed him to lead her back into their tent. Outside, the celebration continued well into the night.

THE DAYS NUMBERED THREE TIMES THREE

Rollo and Poppa came in from the night's celebrations. For a time, Poppa forgot her grief. Her head felt weightless and her mood was light with drink. In the glow of dozens of candles, Rollo followed her as she clumsily removed her jewelry and placed the pieces on the table. He winced when he saw the deep grooves in her wrists where the rope had cut into flesh. He watched as she studied the marks carefully.

"Can you believe only last night I lay bound to this pole?" Poppa wrapped one arm around the pole and viewed him under her heavy-lidded eyes.

He began to undress under her gaze.

Her heart beat faster with nervous energy, but the mead had freed her inhibitions and made her bold. She walked over to him and began to trace the tattoo on his arm with her finger. He focused on her as a small smile grew upon her lips. The candlelight attached to her and illuminated the softness of her skin. Her honeyed eyes, darkened and hooded, conveyed her innocence. He felt his need grow. He swallowed hard as he looked down at her with narrowed eyes.

"You're in mourning," he replied gently as he pulled her hand away. He took a step back from her. "And you're besotted."

His reproach stung, but the mead had made her argumentative. "Isn't that what a man wants on his wedding night? A drunken maid too intoxicated to fight him off?"

She leaned forward again. He brushed her away.

"You've a poor view of the world, Poppa. That's not what most men want."

Poppa laughed nastily at the insult. "But it's what you wanted when I was your captive. You, the Norseman who raids villages and rapes their women—you would deny a willing and ready woman at the foot of your bed?"

The implication hung in the space between them. Perhaps her willingness was the problem. The drink made her brave and, coupled with his rejection, helped to bring the next words forth: "Or is it only when they are bound and defenseless that you are able to perform?"

Rollo's eyes darkened. His scar seemed to flicker as his eyes narrowed. Poppa watched as his hands clenched and unclenched. He took a deep breath before delivering a warning stare.

Fear crept up from her stomach.

"Get into bed and go to sleep," he said with an impatient huff. "In the morning, you'll be thankful I didn't touch you this night and we did nothing you wouldn't remember."

He crawled into the bed and covered himself with the many furs. Rejected, Poppa stood at the edge of the bed. Her head spun with confusion.

"I was unkind to my first wife. That's why her God took her from me. I mean to correct the foolish behavior of my past. Please, Poppa. Get into the bed."

She did as he asked but kept as far away from him as possible. Still, she could feel his heat radiate through the furs and her heartbeat increased. "I don't see what that has to do with anything—"

Rollo sighed heavily. "In our culture, there's a tale of the god Freyr. It started when Odin, ruler of the gods, asked Freyr to keep watch over the worlds for him. After looking upon the nine worlds from the great throne of Odin, his eyes fell upon a beautiful giantess. Her name was Gerd, and she was more stunning than all Freyr had looked upon before. He couldn't eat. He couldn't sleep because of his love and need for her."

Poppa rested her head against the pillow and closed her eyes. Her anger was melted by his smooth, deep voice as he spun his tale of foreign gods, other worlds, and encompassing love. Her heartbeat slowed as her body welcomed the needed rest.

"He resolved to marry her and sent a messenger with word of his proposal. Gerd didn't accept at first. It wasn't until he threatened her homeland that she sent word back to Freyr. She would come to him, but he would have to wait for nine days. This was her answer to the threats the messenger had delivered. Though tortured, Freyr waited for her, and the gods blessed them in numbers of descendants. From their union, a dynasty of kings was born."

"So you would have us wait nine days," Poppa said through a yawn.

"Our marriage was rushed, if not forced, by necessity. I'd have us wait until you, of sound mind, come to me willingly."

Poppa, her head still fuzzy and her eyes heavy, glanced at him with a small smile of understanding as she drifted off to sleep.

◇◇◇◇◇

She could feel the sting of salt water against her exposed skin. The droplets rode upon the wind, which tossed them around mercilessly. The waves hit the hull, the sails, the oars, and all the people who rocked inside the boat. No light shone in the sky above. The only light came when a strike from above would crack through the skies and illuminate the ships around them for only an instant.

The flash blurred her vision for moments afterward. Only Rollo's voice boomed above the noise of the sea and storm as he shouted instructions to the men and women. Poppa, however, found herself frozen to her spot, her eyes wide in fear as she rocked about on the waves. The boats, at the mercy of the sea, creaked and groaned as they moved over the water.

Suddenly, fire fell from the heavens to meet the sea. Poppa saw a large wave overcome the ship to her right. She barely heard the shouts of the men and women above the roar as they overturned and were lost to the depths of the sea. Poppa shook. The cold and fear bit into her flesh and took over the rest of her rational mind. The same imposing wave now threatened her ship. She watched the dark gray water swell and then fall. She screamed. Seawater filled her open mouth as the wave crashed over her.

Rollo sat before her. Shaking her. His lips moved but sound and meaning evaded her. His brown eyes were intent upon her, almost pleading. She shivered. She coughed and sputtered as she tried to get the water out of her lungs.

"Poppa, wake up!"

As quick as a whip snaps, her mind returned to her. She could breathe again. Her hand still clutched her throat, sore from coughing. Rollo's large hands cradled her shoulders as she sat. She shook her head and then scanned the tent, barely seeing the items before her as images from her dream mingled translucently with reality like a ghost.

"I—I—" Poppa stammered as she shook her head.

"You had a dream." He had risen and offered her a flagon of wine.

Poppa's head throbbed from the night before. "No, thank you."

Rollo smiled at her as he pushed the ale closer to her face. "It'll help with that too."

As the sour smell reached her nose and twisted into her gut, she flew off the bed and raced to the edge of the tent to vomit. Rollo shrugged and laughed as he gulped down the horn in one pull.

Poppa wiped her mouth on her sleeve, humiliated by his laughter.

"Come, wife. There's much to be done. Today we set sail for Rouen."

Poppa looked around the camp. In the early morning light, she watched as the Norsemen dismantled tents and packed trunks. Some lowered tarps and rolled them into tight cylinders while others lowered wooden poles and stacked them in piles with precision. Poppa turned her gaze back to Rollo. "Sail? We won't travel by land?"

Rollo smiled and chuckled, "I, sit a horse? *Nei*, wife. Besides, our loot will travel better over the seas than on land."

Poppa shook her head. "We can't sail. That wasn't a dream I had; it was a vision. A storm will overcome the boats. I saw men and women swallowed by the sea."

Rollo's eyes rolled and he looked at her in amusement. "A dream, from a frightened girl about to leave all she's ever known, won't delay us. We sail by midday."

"I won't go," she called out to him.

Rollo rushed to her in frustration. "For an orphaned handmaiden, you're sure acting the part of a spoiled princess. As if you had any choice in the matter. Ragnhild will come to escort you to the beach soon. Be ready."

His words stung as if he'd slapped her. She opened her mouth, but no words would follow. He didn't wait for her to argue any further. He pulled his furs around his shoulders and left her alone with her frustration. She waited for her head to stop throbbing before she rose from the bed again. A pretty serving girl came with hard bread and cold meat from the night before to break her fast. Poppa forced down the food and prayed it wouldn't come back up again. The thought of drifting upon the seas, paired with her sickness, made her shiver and rock in place. She waited for Rollo to return, and when he didn't, she knew she had no choice but to ready herself. She browsed the items in the tent. She had precious few items to pack. She picked up the jewelry from the night before and placed it in the trunk. Then she washed herself and donned a simple warm emerald dress. Her temper and frusteration grew as the time neared for their departure. She couldn't run, but she could refuse to go.

THOR'S PROTECTION

A wild gale blew up behind Poppa where the dark clouds began to build. The midmorning sky turned a leaden gray. Poppa stood with her feet rooted in the sand. The wind whipped her long brown hair before her and across her face. She contemplated the skies as the Norsemen loaded the holds of the carved wooden longships. Marvelous to behold, the expertly shaped boats bobbed lightly in the water. Long, smooth planks of wood fastened together and curved in a seductive way to hold fast and float. The wide belly in the middle of the ship narrowed to a point at each end. On the port and starboard sides, oar ports appeared every couple of feet, each holding an oar in place. A tall mast stood sentry in the center of each ship and would proudly hold the decorated sail that would carry them swiftly over the waters. Ropes slanted to meet the mast and the sail. They contained firm clamps that expert hands would use to tighten and adjust the strong woven fibers. Though the foreign boats were breathtaking, Poppa couldn't shake the foreboding sense left by her dream. With the memory of the dream still vivid in her mind, she couldn't bring herself to move.

She stood sentinel as she watched the men move the loot into the belly of the ships. Rollo, busy with the last-minute preparations, took little notice of her. Once they finished, people started to board the ships. Captured women and children climbed in first. The Norsemen treated the captives kindly, but Poppa could see the hollowness of surrender in their eyes. Poppa wondered what would become of them. Another gust of wind blew from behind her, and she turned to scan the clouds as they rolled in from the south and inched ever closer.

When she turned back, Rollo was walking quickly toward her. Sand kicked up around his heavy footfalls. His eyebrows were knit together and his mouth was set in a firm line, giving him a look of grim determination. His stare never wavered as he stomped easily upon the sand and approached his target. She wondered how many men before her had buckled under that expression alone. He managed to keep his impatience at bay when he instructed her through clenched teeth: "Get in."

She watched as the men boarded the longships and the crowd on shore dwindled.

"No." Poppa defiantly crossed her arms over her chest. She leaned her weight into her heels as if that would keep her rooted to the sand.

"Get in the boat, wife."

A couple of boats started pushing away from the shore. Rollo glanced at them and heaved a heavy sigh as Poppa raised a challenging brow.

"No."

The people in the remaining boats craned their heads to get a better view of the spectacle on the beach. Rollo would suffer her insolence no longer. Nor would he give his people cause to laugh at the challenge to his authority.

"Já!" he bellowed.

In an instant, the ground beneath Poppa's feet fell away. Her world turned upside down as Rollo scooped her up and flipped her over his shoulder to a chorus of raucous laughter.

She beat him with her fists and kicked her legs, but he held her fast. She made no gain. He carried her weight easily and laughed as she tried, fruitlessly, to fight him. He flung her none too gently on a seat covered with animal furs, leaving her bottom sore from the impact. She clenched her teeth and refused cry out. She wouldn't give him the satisfaction of showing him he'd caused her pain. The boat left the shore before the feel of the sand left her feet. It would be much longer before the indignation left her spirit.

She shivered as laughter and unintelligible words sounded around her. She pulled the furs Rollo had given her closer around her shoulders. She watched as her land, her home, and all she'd ever known swiftly shrank into the horizon as the boat glided away. A flock of white gulls circled above them. One dropped down to the water, searching for fish to eat. The rest waited in midair before the gull returned to them and, together, they flew back to the shore. Poppa longed to share their freedom.

As the wind blew from the shore, the sail billowed. Beneath the pregnant canvas, Poppa rested her back against the mast. She wondered at the great speed of the boat as the oarsmen rowed in perfect unison beneath her. The gray clouds diminished into the distance with each stroke of oar on water and every gust pushing the sail. Perhaps the storm wouldn't reach them. They could outrun it at this speed. Her heart began to lighten. Her fears subsided. She found it difficult not to feel a little excitement as they set out into the unknown. Her stomach began to flutter.

The thrill didn't last long. Suddenly vivid images from the previous night's dream replayed in her mind. She could all but hear the screams of the Norsemen from the overturned ship. She turned to her right. The Norsemen on the ship laughed with delight as they passed around horns of ale and flagons of wine. Some tightened the ropes. Even the oarsmen, who had the most laborious of jobs, seemed light of heart as they rowed lazily, letting the wind do most of the work. A pit formed in her throat and she swallowed hard, only for the fear to land in her belly, heavy and steadfast. She closed her eyes and hid her face. The sweet and salty smell of the sea still penetrated the furs. Above the smell of the sea, she could smell Rollo. Though she'd known him only a couple of days, his smell had become familiar and strangely welcoming.

She could feel a pull toward her right. She looked up and saw that the boat was listing slightly into the ocean on the starboard side. Poppa gasped and then swallowed hard. She wrapped her arms around the mast and held fast for fear of falling overboard.

"Don't worry." Ragnhild squeezed in beside her. "The ship is just turning. We'll stay within sight of land the whole time."

"Yes, but the dark clouds that rolled over Bayeux are following us. It'll be a race to Rouen."

Poppa observed Ragnhild as she looked off into the distance. Her blue eyes narrowed as they keenly judged the sky. The shield-maiden smiled and said, "The storm that follows us is a good omen. Thor protects our rear and sends winds to glide us swiftly upon the water."

"Or the Lord God is sending his wrath for the destruction of my city," Poppa spoke matter-of-factly.

To Poppa's surprise, Ragnhild laughed sardonically, "Well, then it's a good thing we have you aboard, my lady. Perhaps your innocence will cover us all in safety when the storm hits."

Poppa shrunk from the sting of her words. Ragnhild rose and used the ropes above her to walk confidently across the benches toward Rollo. Poppa watched her move with feline grace as the boat rocked. Ragnhild joined Rollo and another man in conversation. Rollo cast his eyes over Poppa, but she wouldn't hold his gaze. She could still feel his stare on her as she turned to the sea.

They had a couple hours of calm sea and gentle rocking before the storm blew up behind them. The fleet of longships could no longer outrun Thor. The skies darkened and the day looked like night. Poppa looked around at the faces of the sailors. They were calm. Not one mirrored the fear she felt knotting within her. She realized the Norsemen, brave and eager for excitement of any kind, saw this as another kind of battle. Not all of them would survive, but at least those who perished would fall from Thor's mighty blow. An honor to them, madness to Poppa. The wind picked up and sent her hair dancing on the sky. She could feel the energy and anticipation flow around her. She felt helpless as the men moved quickly to brace for the storm.

The oarsmen worked harder in their rowing as the tillerman maneuvered and guided the ship over the swells. Standing beside Rollo, a man called rhythmically to them with directions and encouragement. He wore his hair shaved and tattooed on one side; on the other, braided black hair laid over his shoulder. He held on to the rope to steady himself as he scanned the seas. Poppa's heart calmed upon seeing his steady expression.

A large swell of water grew before her. She felt sure her heart stopped once before it began a rapid beat. Poppa closed her eyes and wrapped her arms tighter around the mast. The longship rose on the swell and tipped at a frightening angle. Last night's vision crashed into her mind. She pictured the ships around her capsizing.

Lightning cracked and Poppa flinched. Then the ship traveled over the swell. Poppa let out a sigh of relief, only to open her eyes and see another before her. She turned to her right and could no longer find the comforting sight of land. A knot churned in her stomach. She could feel bile in the back of her throat. Water whipped all around them and stung her exposed skin. It lashed at her eyes, making it difficult to see. Rollo came to her side as another impossible wave started to swell before them.

"I told you this would happen! I said I didn't want to go!" Poppa yelled at him. Her voice was a whisper beneath the storm.

Rollo laughed and spoke loudly. His voice boomed along with the thunder. "You were right, wife. I'll do better to listen to your visions in the future. For now, prepare yourself. If we flip, hold on to the crossbar or make your way under the boat to find it. The boat will create an air pocket. Hold yourself up. I'll search for you there first."

Poppa, wide-eyed, nodded. "Will you not stay by my side?"

Rollo smiled again. "I've seen much worse than this. It's the men who need my encouragement now. Be brave, Poppa. We'll be through the worst of it soon."

The wind bellowed and the rain pelted them as he leaned in to kiss her. She needed the comfort and she pressed back hard, willing him to stay. Rain and seawater splashed against them. The water had soaked her through, but his kiss sent a warmth down her spine and, for a moment, drowned out the storm.

He pulled away. He looked at her, stunned, before he shook his head and turned to help the others with the oars. She watched as he moved with the rocking of the ship, bellowing orders and encouragement. A boyish grin covered his face, and she could find no traces of fear. She tried to draw off his courage, but just then a loud crack sounded from above. Light flooded around them and a wave overcame the longship traveling on their starboard side.

◇◇◇◇◇

By morning, only three ships had overturned. The other ships had rescued many of those thrown overboard before they drowned. A young girl of about six, recovered from the ship that had overturned, clung tenderly to Poppa's side. Her mother, among the missing, was feared dead. At least the young girl had ceased her whimpering. The morning sun rose to warm them. All around Poppa, people stripped off their wet clothes and laid them over ropes and benches to dry.

Poppa helped the young girl change into dry clothes that hung loosely on her frame. The Norsemen passed around salted and dried fish along with ale and fresh water to break their fast. All around they echoed praises to Thor, who had protected them through the storm. Poppa, still feeling queasy from the night before, couldn't stomach food. With the danger over, she drifted in and out of sleep. The girl by her side nestled into her, and they kept each other warm as the longship bobbed incessantly over the waves.

Seine's Embrace

By early afternoon on the third day since they were wed, the longships started to turn toward the shoreline. To protect against further Norse raids, King Charles had given Rollo the river and the surrounding area to protect and rule. Tall towers rose up on each side of the river so watchmen could see far out to sea and scan for enemy ships. On the right side lay a vast sandy beach that backed into the woods beyond. Poppa imagined the first time Rollo's Norse ships landed on the beach, unopposed by the surprised citizens of Francia. Or would a battle have ensued, dyeing the beach red as it soaked in the blood of its countrymen? It would have been a battle the ill-prepared and doomed Franks couldn't have won even if they'd seen it coming.

The raids on these lands and those further up the river had decimated the buildings and farms, but Rollo had then convinced the Franks to work with his men to rebuild the area. They made it more beautiful and spectacular than before. Both the Norsemen and the Franks took pride in this accomplishment, and Rollo's celebrity grew. Gossip and legend said he had endless wealth and resources at his disposal—and that he possessed an undeniable charm to convince once-reluctant men to bend to his will. His steadfast character appeared to inspire loyalty in all who swore their oath to him.

These last few days, Poppa had observed the men and women who served him. She could see the joy upon their faces. They found pleasure and purpose in the care of his affairs. She didn't question their respect and loyalty. Poppa pondered upon this as the river neared.

Rollo appeared at her side. "The mouth of the Seine," he whispered into her ear. "The river will take us all the way up to Rouen. We will stop for the night when we reach the area of Vexin. On the morrow, I'll ride out to survey local farms to gain insight on the expected harvest."

Poppa looked ahead as the river's mouth grew closer. "This river has been good to you, has it not?"

She could feel his smile beside her as he leaned into her and said, "It's another reason I enjoy sailing over moving on land. This river, her arms you see on either side, she welcomes me in a maternal embrace. Já, she has been kind. This is where I entered with fifteen ships and overtook Rouen."

"I heard you walked in unopposed."

"Já, but that was after we set traps and feigned running for our ships. When I held Rouen, the lower valley became mine. I've settled the area with my men, and they have cultivated it. It's very prosperous for us and for Francia. We protect this gateway to Paris from other Norse attacks. No other Norseman would dare oppose me here."

"Can you be sure?"

Rollo contemplated her out of the corner of his eyes. "It hasn't happened yet."

As they made their way through the mouth, the oarsmen worked hard against the current. Poppa felt comforted by the land that closed in on both sides of the wide river. The boats rowed two by two as they started the winding path.

"You would fight your own people? Does the word *turncloak* translate to your Norse language?"

Rollo's face darkened and Poppa feared she'd said too much.

"It's always been my nature to conquer and to rule. I couldn't do that in my home country, so I left. My loyalties are to the chieftains working for me and to the king. My vassals manage the land I've given them and keep order with their laborers. I'm concerned only with protecting my people and the land granted to me. These are my people now, Poppa. They'll be your people too."

Poppa listened intently. Rollo hadn't yet discussed these things with her.

"Though we wed in haste and to ultimately protect you from the horde, our marriage has other advantages. It's a union between my Norse past and my Frank future. I'm hoping my chieftains will follow my lead and take Frankish brides. We could create a new culture of people to populate the realm. I'm sure you noticed the Norsemen are comfortable speaking your Frankish tongue. I commanded my people from the North to learn the native language should they choose to stay."

Poppa breathed deeply before asking, "And would your men force their brides to endure a ceremony that I experienced, or would they honor their wives with a Christian marriage? One blessed by God."

Rollo grimaced.

"You want a union of people with different backgrounds and different beliefs. They'll look to you to show them what's true. I don't think you have an answer. You were baptized in the name of God, and yet you hold to pagan rituals and legends. You answer to the name of Rollo rather than your baptized name of Robert. You saw nothing wrong with bringing me, a Christian, into a union performed by a . . . a—"

"A *gyðja*, abbotess, of the old custom."

"Yes, but what I experienced . . . Rollo, do you understand why it's difficult for me to see how this union can be blessed by God?"

"I was married once before the eyes of the Lord, and my wife died in a bed of blood. My newborn daughter followed not long after. Do not lecture me about the blessings your God bestows upon those who follow the rules of the Church. I've seen the hoards of gold and jewels your men of faith hide in their houses of worship. I've been made rich by raiding them. Tell me, lady wife, is it these men whom you wish would speak a godly blessing over our union?"

The conviction in his voice resonated in her being. Perhaps she had pushed too hard. Myra always told her she should stay silent at times when her tongue would get the best of her. His palpable anger felt embittered by time and not directed toward her. He'd accepted the faith of the Church, and God had let him down. His disappointment had turned to resentment, heavy like a burden carried over many miles. She cast her eyes down as she pondered what he'd revealed and said nothing more.

Later that evening, they reached a small village in the river valley. Poppa regarded a crowd of captives who stood clustered on the beach. A tall Norseman with dark matted hair sauntered around them, assessing. He then ordered them to form two lines as he chose who would go where. She felt Rollo pull her arm away from the scene. Happy to feel her feet on dry land, she didn't protest, but she did look over her shoulder when she heard terrible wails. Behind them, a mother cried with outstretched hands as she desperately pleaded with the dark warrior. He ignored her as he roughly held a boy and pushed him into the other line. The boy, no older than five and terrified of the threatening presence of the Norseman, cried silently to himself but he did not move.

"No," Poppa argued as she tried to pull her arm from Rollo's grasp.

"Keep walking, Poppa."

Poppa put all her weight into her feet and planted them firmly. Rollo, exasperated, sighed heavily as he explained, "It's the way of things."

Tears filled her eyes as the cries of the mother filled her ears. A loud slap came as skin met flesh and the woman fell to the ground. Poppa pleaded, "Do something, please."

Rollo scrutinized her as he assessed his next steps. Then he thrust his pointer finger in her face and ordered, "Stay here and say nothing."

She nodded, looking on with hopeful pride as he made his way back to the beach. He whispered words with the cruel-looking man before returning to Poppa with his face set in a hard line. She followed the scene on the beach with satisfaction as the man reluctantly grabbed the young boy and placed him in the other line, next to his mother. The mother's sobs grew muffled as she flung her arms around her son and held him fast to her body.

At the time, Poppa didn't understand the pain in her heart as she examined Rollo on his return. He walked toward her with determined steps. His face was set in its seemingly permanent state of annoyance mixed with amusement. Her heart hurt, yet at the same time, in contrast, it felt light. Her head was dizzy. She wanted to run toward him, and she wanted to run away. A smile of thankfulness formed of its own accord and she couldn't hide it from him. Rollo noticed the confused emotions play across her face. She smiled, but it took time to reach her eyes as she studied him. He felt naked under her gaze and gave her a shy grin of affirmation. Later she would look back upon this moment with a realization of all she'd felt—admiration, gratefulness, and quite possibly something deeper.

VEXIN

THE FOLLOWING MORNING, POPPA AROSE before her husband opened his eyes. Married for four days now, she felt oddly comforted by Rollo snoring throughout the night. The memory of his warm body against hers made her cheeks flush red. Had she really wrapped an arm around him or had that been a dream? Rollo's comforting presence, coupled with the lavish accommodations offered them, left her feeling refreshed. She dressed in a simple dark-green dress embroidered with gold trim. The lady of the house had gifted her the dress when they arrived last night. Rollo explained she should expect many more gifts in the coming days. People would want to celebrate their union while paying homage to their jarl.

Rollo woke while she was still pinning her hair up in a small looking glass. She felt his eyes on her as she went about her work.

He sighed deeply before he spoke. "We have one more day in this area before we travel the rest of the way to Rouen. Today I plan to travel the countryside to visit some of the chieftains and their farms. I hear the yield has been high this season. I long to see the land myself. There's also a market today. I'm sure you could busy yourself there while I'm away."

"Or I could come with you?"

Rollo's mouth twitched. "The riding will be fast and hard."

"I ride well. Grant me the use of a good horse and I'll keep pace with you."

Rollo chuckled as he nodded to her dress. "Though I admire your choice of clothing this morning, you'll need to change into something more practical. I'll send in Ragnhild." Before Rollo left to make water and wash, he surprised them both by kissing Poppa on the forehead. His lips were warm and remained imprinted on her skin long after he left the room.

Poppa sat atop a white palfrey in the garments Ragnhild brought her. Tight brown leather pants allowed her to place one leg on each side of the horse. A long-sleeved tunic in the same color was belted at her waist to keep the clothes tight to her and block the wind. She kept her long hair pinned back and twisted on her head so it wouldn't whip around her face as she rode. Rollo let his eyes roam freely over her before giving her a nod of approval.

He clicked his tongue several times as he kicked the side of his horse. Those accompanying them followed suit and closed in behind. As they fanned out into the countryside, the party changed formation into a protective semicircle around the newlyweds riding side by side in the lead.

Poppa rode hard. The strong wind whipped through her hair and cleverly pulled out the less secure pins. Tendrils danced on the air, but she barely took notice. The thrill of riding fast over the green countryside made her feel as light and free as the gulls she'd observed from the ship only a couple days before. Laughter escaped her lips, and she couldn't restrain the smile that formed there. She turned to share her amusement with Rollo.

After less than an hour, they arrived at a large farm. Poppa dismounted and led her horse to the drinking trough. A bin of hay lay close by so the horses could feast before they were needed again.

When she arrived at Rollo's side, his strong hand laid affectionately on an elderly man's shoulder. They spoke closely together. Rollo laughed heartily and shook the man gently.

"Come, Poppa. We'll walk the short distance to Lothar's fields."

Poppa followed behind the men as they walked closely together, discussing the soil and weather. Lothar gestured wildly as he regaled Rollo with stories of the planting and harvest. Poppa smiled as she listened. His tales certainly sounded embellished for the jarl's approval. The scent of manure became stronger the closer they got to the edge of the fields.

Lothar was still explaining the rows of tilled earth and the seeds he had planted when Rollo crouched down and grabbed a handful of rich, dark earth. The soil tumbled out of his hand in clumps. Rollo nodded to himself and picked up another handful, bringing it to his nose. He inhaled deeply and—shocking Poppa—tasted a small sample. He looked up at Lothar with a satisfied grin. Lothar nodded his head and gestured with both hands, encompassing the whole of the property. Rollo rose and placed his hand again on Lothar's shoulder approvingly.

He noticed Poppa's perplexed expression and smiled at her confusion. "My people were farmers before we were warriors. I take great pleasure in the bounty of the harvest. The rich soil of your country suits me well."

They visited several more farms, where Rollo performed the same soil ritual, before they returned to the village. Along the way, Poppa humbly received gifts from the farmers: dried lavender, handmade jewelry, even a pink-and-brown-spotted pig she had to politely refuse because there was nowhere to stow the creature for the journey back. She noted that most of the farmers in this area were Franks, meaning they must have been allowed to keep their lands after Rollo had ended the raids and taken control of the area.

She enjoyed watching Rollo connect with the people who served him and his lands.

On their way back, Rollo surprised her once again by leading her to the top of a bluff overlooking the Seine. He dismounted, and she followed suit. The sun shone brightly upon them as they stood at the edge of the bluff. The air was crisp and carried a whiff of salt from the sea. The river below twisted back on itself. Its blue water, disturbed by the wind, crested white in the sunlight. The wind did the same to Poppa's hair, now almost fully out of its bindings. It danced freely in all directions around her face as she looked around. Nature's gift of serenity invaded her being. She sighed in contentment and closed her eyes. Whatever came next, she would remember this day as a time Rollo gave her a taste of freedom.

"Did you enjoy your day?" Rollo asked.

"Very much."

"We should return to the village soon. Tonight we'll feast before heading home on the morrow."

Home. The word caught in her heart for a moment, but she couldn't let anything disturb the peace of this day. She smiled and followed him back to the horses. Hours later, when she rested beside him, her belly full, her head a little dizzy from drink, she closed her eyes and could still feel the wind on her cheeks.

JARL OF NORMANDY

On the fifth day of their marriage they reached Rouen in the early afternoon, as Rollo had said. Poppa heard the cheering before the ships even docked in the harbor. A large crowd of common folk who loved their ruler gathered in excitement to see him return. Rollo smiled and waved at them. He threw coins upon coins as they reached the dock. Poppa watched the coins arch into the air, catching the light of the sun, and fall to the ground in satisfying clinks. The common folk dove competitively for the gifts. Poppa smiled despite her weariness, thankful she no longer had to suffer the rocking of the ship.

On the dock, a tall, well-built Norseman waited for them. He appeared intimidating, in black leather and furs and carrying a sword at his side. His white hair, long and frizzy with traces of red illuminated by the light, fell in a braid over his shoulder. He had kind blue eyes that focused on Rollo as they shared a smile of homecoming. Rollo turned to help Poppa onto the dock. She swayed on her feet, the sea still moving beneath her, though her feet were planted on steady land. The night before, she had felt the motion of the boat and rocked in her sleep despite laying in a warm bed beside Rollo, on land. Rollo kept his arm around her waist to steady her as he embraced the man with the other arm.

"We're happy to see you finally home, jarl," the man said before turning to Poppa. "And you're the beautiful captive Rollo took as his wife. Welcome, my lady. If you don't mind my saying, you seem indisposed—green, even."

Poppa tried to smile and nod. "It was a long way across the water. I only hope I don't embarrass myself in front of all these people."

The man smiled at her kindly before giving Rollo a questioning look. For them the trip represented a small journey in comparison to others they had taken in their life.

"We must get you through the crowd first," Rollo stated. "Herleif, your help please, my wife has not gained her sea legs yet."

Herleif nodded and turned to the common folk, shouting, "Citizens of Rouen and beyond. Our jarl has brought home not only a victory and the acquisition of new lands but also a wife of fine Frankish stock. She's the daughter of Count Berengar and Gunhilde de Vermandois. I'd like to introduce you to the lady, Poppa de Bayeux!"

The common folk smiled and clapped in welcome.

Poppa looked at Rollo questioningly with wide eyes.

"I thought it best to serve the ruse to these people. You're now the highborn daughter of a count and not just a favorite of his family," he whispered in her ear.

"But if someone knows that I'm not—if someone here knows my father—" she argued through a smile as she acknowledged the common folk assessing her.

"Poppa, these lands belong to me. You said the people will look to me to tell them what the truth is. This is the truth now."

Rollo turned back to the crowd and waved again, throwing more coins as he did so. He passed a bag to Poppa. "Hand these to your people and they will love you for it."

"The newlyweds rode over the waters for days and would like time to rest and to enjoy each other the way newlyweds do."

Poppa blushed as the crowd laughed at Herleif's jest.

"Please don't disturb them as they seek the refuge of their home."

"Thank you," Rollo whispered to Herleif. "See that what's left of the loot is split evenly between you and the other chieftains. I've taken my portion already. If there's some leftover, spread it amongst the common folk. When you're ready, come to the house. We'll discuss the list of newly acquired lands and who will settle them."

"You're most generous, Rollo. They will sing your praises over mead this night. Will you join us?"

Rollo smiled as he replied, "The festivities will go on for many nights, I'm sure. Once we've chosen which men will settle the lands around Bayeux, we'll celebrate on the eve of their departure.

Herleif winked at him. "I'll come see you on the morrow so we can finish the work. Then the celebrations can begin."

All around them, Norsemen worked to unload the ships of their bounty. Hands worked together to pass along the looted items. Poppa recognized a chair from the dining hall. She remembered sitting on its finely embroidered cushion once for Myra's birthday feast. The girls had laughed as the tiny men from the Far East had tumbled and contorted before them. Poppa's vision clouded over, and for the moment she forgot her seasickness. A twinkle of light caught her eye and she turned. She bristled when she spotted two young ladies in the crowd admiring a golden mirror. They turned it over in the sun and then pushed each other out of the way, each fighting to see only their own face framed in the ornate device. Poppa remembered Myra's delicate hands as she'd lifted the same mirror to look upon herself. She'd looked at Poppa through the mirror and mimed kiss faces as she'd divulged how she had feelings for her lord father's friend. Her green eyes had sparkled with hopefulness in her play.

The two girls shoved and pushed. In Poppa's mind, she saw the mirror fall to the ground and shatter.

"No," Poppa said under her breath. She broke away from Rollo and snatched the mirror from the surprised girls' hands.

"Poppa," Rollo scolded.

She held it up before him, "This was Myra's. I won't part with it or any of her things."

Rollo smiled at the ladies who stood in shock. He gave them each a couple of gold coins, and they bowed in thanks. He looked hard at Poppa and frowned in disappointment. She glared at him in a challenge. He glanced around them and noticed some had stopped to stare. He swallowed hard and nodded once before he turned and wove her through the crowd.

The crowds graciously cleared a path for them as they walked through. Some bowed their heads in respect. Poppa, eager for something familiar, clutched the mirror to her chest. She studied the buildings surrounding her. Work had stalled so the common folk could welcome the return of the longships and their plunder. Now workers slowly made their way back to their respective tasks. Poppa marveled at the sights of the town. A city at the center of it all. A great hub of energy as items moved in trade upon land and water. When Rollo first laid siege upon the town, he and his men nearly destroyed it. Buildings were burned and torn down to the ground. Little evidence remained from that dark period of destruction.

In the years that followed, Rollo and his people rebuilt the city from its ashes. The buildings, made from new material, stood sturdy on their stone foundations. Shops overflowed with an abundance of items on the ground floors while the living quarters of the shop's owners jettied outward on the upper stories. The buildings were built on top of one another with narrow and dark alleyways breaking them apart every few blocks.

Similar in size to Bayeux, Rouen bustled with new life in its restoration. Poppa wondered to herself if Rollo would rebuild Bayeux in the same way. She paused to watch builders as they fit a long plank of wood into place. The piece completed the frame for the second story of the building below. Rollo gave her a satisfied grin. He liked the wonder on her face as she admired the rebuilding of the city, plans for which he had orchestrated and overseen.

Rollo put his hand in hers and led her steadily up the path as it turned from stone to dirt. The crowd thinned at the base of a steep incline. Poppa felt him pull her upward; her legs followed of their own accord. They walked steadily upward on a path that wound and doubled back on itself. In the distance, she noted workers gathering hay with their pitchforks and throwing it into the belly of a wagon. The sun shone brightly and warmly upon them. Guided by a soft breeze that blew in from the sea, the clouds moved slowly across the sky and cast shadows upon the land. She could see the contrast of light and dark for miles.

At the top of the hill stood a fine home with a rich and abundant garden. The house, built of stone and wood, looked five times the size of the homes they'd passed in town. Two stories high, with large windows that would let in the morning sun, the house had a stately feel that mirrored its owner. A massive oak door hung large and foreboding as the main entryway to the house. Bushes with small white flowers lined the base of the home and covered the stone of the foundation. Parts of the structure seemed older than others. Poppa wondered if Rollo had allowed this place alone to remain while the city burned in the valley below . . . For this was the place that the man beside her had made his seat. From this place, he would rule his people and build the numbers of Norsemen and Franks devoted to him.

To her left stood a large stable. Chestnut horses grazed the rolling hill beyond. A servant carried hay into the barn while another balanced two pails. Water sloshed over the edges of the pails and splattered on his feet and the ground. Poppa could smell the calming fragrance of lavender. She turned her gaze to the right and saw the purple bushes blowing gently in the breeze as they sat in tidy rows in the garden. She walked toward them slowly, stopping to lift a white rose to her nose on the way. She noticed a bumblebee buzzing close by. It took no notice of her as it went about its task of feeding on one plant and then the next, pollinating as it went. She felt Rollo's eyes following her as she watched the small insect.

Rollo contemplated her eagerly. "Does it please you?"

She looked around and smiled. "It's beautiful." Then her expression darkened. Her lips pouted into a frown as her eyes glazed over. She could feel tears well up behind her eyes.

"What is it?"

"All of this. It shouldn't belong to me. Myra. Myra was the bride you should have had. I don't belong here. I should have been left for dead. I—" In that moment all sense left Poppa. Her head spun. Her ears began to ring. Black spots appeared at the edges of her vision. Panic set in, and she couldn't catch her breath. The motion of the sea came back to her, and she started to sway on her feet. She felt her grasp on Myra's mirror loosen as she fell, and the ground rose up to embrace her.

When she woke, a thin blue light filtered in from the window. It fell across the unfamiliar bed she rested on. The bedding felt soft, as if she lay on clouds. Everything around her looked white and warm. For a moment she thought perhaps she'd died. Perhaps she drifted slowly through the sky as the earth moved and bustled beneath her. However, she didn't feel the sensation of movement, and she soon became aware of the strong walls that surrounded her in the vast room. She was alone. A fire crackled in the hearth across from the bed. Lavender and tansy hung from the bedpost. Instantly she could smell the sweet scent that would ward off insects from taking up residence in the bed. She slowly rose but instantly felt dizzy once again.

"Oh, you're awake! I must alert the master at once," a stout woman in a plain light-blue dress spoke as she entered the room, carrying fresh linens.

"Who are you? Where am I? What happened?" Poppa felt disorientated as she slowly sat up in the bed.

The woman smiled at her sympathetically. She sat on the edge of her bed and placed a motherly hand upon Poppa's knee. "To be sure, the siege of your home, your new marriage, and the travel to this place has put you into bit of a shock."

Memories came back to her all at once and she knew she rested inside the house she'd seen only from the outside.

"How long have I been asleep?"

"You've been sleeping for more than a day. It's early evening, the day after your arrival." She paused and smiled warmly. "My dear, you must be hungry. I'll go and fix you some dinner and let the master know you're awake."

Poppa smiled at the lady. "And you are?

"I go by Mrs. Laurent around here. My husband's family have worked this property since the Roman occupation. We're happy to serve Rollo. A woman hasn't roamed these halls for many a year. The master is lonely to be sure. Well, I probably shouldn't have said that, but it's the truth. The Lord says it's not good for a man to be alone, and I'd agree with that. The jarl is a fine man, but he needs grounding and—"

"Ahem."

"Oh, m'lord, you startled us—I was just—well, the lady is awake. As you can see now. I was, I—"

Poppa smiled and then smiled sheepishly over the woman's shoulder.

"I'll just leave you two alone. I see you've brought her food. That pleases me."

Mrs. Laurent left in a haste. Poppa sat up in bed, only to realize she wore only a thin shift. She blushed and pulled the blanket up to cover her chest and let the waves of her brown hair fall neatly around her. Rollo observed her carefully before he gave a slight frown and placed her food on the bedside table.

"You're still pale. Eat. Please."

He spooned some of the stew, blew on it, and brought it to her mouth.

"Really, I'm not a child. I can feed myself. I simply had a bit of a fright."

"The bowl is hot. Let it cool down before you hold it. Here's some bread instead."

Poppa inhaled the welcoming scent of sweet, warm bread and her mouth watered. "I didn't realize how hungry I was."

She ate greedily for a moment, relishing the taste of the warm bread as it melted in her mouth and filled her stomach.

"Was I really asleep for a day?"

"Já. The household waits. They've been eager to meet you. They were worried when you didn't wake."

"I'm sorry I embarrassed you. I hope I didn't cause too much trouble. I don't remember why—"

"The household is happy to have someone to fuss over. Especially Mrs. Laurent. Rest this night. On the morrow, I'll show you the house and surrounding land." Rollo paused before continuing, a hint of shame in his eyes. "Forgive me. I didn't consider that only six days ago you were a girl hiding behind walls as your home was besieged and destroyed around you. Then only to be captured and hastily married to your enemy. I'm sorry for the shock these events have caused you."

Poppa smiled slightly at his apology. It was a small sweetness. She considered him silently for a moment. He had bathed. His hair hung loose and long past his shoulders, part of it pulled back from his face. He wore a rich but simple tunic of white and gray. The shadows of the early evening hours played upon his face and made him look younger. He looked handsome, more pleasing than any other man she'd seen, with his strong and wide shoulders. His arms and legs rippled with muscles under his tanned caramel skin. She wondered what it would feel like to make love to him. Would he crush her? She blushed again at her own thoughts and quickly shook her head as a tingle grew inside her belly.

"I need to . . . um, I need to use . . . I'd like to relieve myself."

"Of course. Let me help you."

He helped her gently rise out of bed and waited for her equilibrium to stabilize. His touch was gentle and sure.

"I'm not sore from the fall."

"No, you wouldn't be. I caught you."

He gave her privacy as she made water. Poppa still felt lightheaded and fatigued. She was thankful to climb back into the bed. She let the covers envelop her again. She fell back asleep before Rollo returned to check on her.

HOUSE AND HEARTH

ON THE MORNING OF THE SEVENTH DAY since they were wed, Poppa donned a simple gray dress trimmed with dark gray thread that swirled and pointed in an appealing design. She had washed from the bowl of water that sat on the cabinet but still longed for a deep cleanse. In Bayeux, Myra's family owned a large basin that servants would fill with scorching water. When it had cooled, Poppa would sink her whole body inside. She would drift under the water and soak to her heart's content. She and Myra would take turns seeing who could submerge themselves in the heat for the longest. They would pour rich oils into the water, let the steam turn them to vapor, and fill the air with exotic scents.

That life was gone. She must stop dwelling on the past, for fear of suffering shock again.

Thankfully, a distraction waited by the door. "Your color has returned," Rollo said.

She gave him a small smile. "I feel much better."

"Come, I'm eager to show you the house."

She followed as he moved along the hallway. He showed her the master bedroom first. The room was double the size of the room she'd rested in. It looked richly decorated, similar in fashion to his tent. On the wall, tapestries hung next to the horns of various animals slain on the hunt. A bed with large posts at the four corners rested to her left. Dressed in white linen and embroidered with gold thread, it held countless matching pillows of various sizes. Someone had propped them up against the carved headboard. It didn't look like the bed of a fierce Norse berserker. She smiled to herself as she pictured him lying in such a bed.

A small chamber pot sat off to the left of the bed behind a divider. Animal furs, in shades of varying browns and whites, covered the floor. Poppa wondered if they belonged to the animal heads that hung on the wall. She could see wide planks of stained wood between the gaps of the rugs. A fire danced straight ahead in a large hearth. Above it sat an intricately carved mural in patterns that matched the bed's headboard: a large tree connected in a square by both its roots and its limbs. Poppa walked to the fire and traced the pattern on the mantle with her fingers.

She felt Rollo come up close behind her as he spoke softly, "Yggdrasil, the World Tree."

"It's beautiful."

"It shows that the nine worlds are connected."

"The nine worlds? You spoke of them briefly in your story of Freyr."

Rollo gently covered her hand in his and traced the carved line to a point that had blended in when she had stood at a distance. Now, up close, she noted the point harbored its own square area in the tree's upper branches. She also noted that several other similar square areas took up residence throughout the carved tree.

"Asgard, home to the gods. Odin, Thor, Freya, Frigga, and many more rule and reside here."

Rollo moved her hand along to another small square in the middle of the tree.

"Midgard, home to the humans created by Odin and his two brothers. Loki had three monstrous children born to him by his giantess wife Angrboða. One of them, Jörmungandr, the serpent, circled himself around the lands of Midgard after Odin threw him into the sea."

Rollo moved her hand along again to the right upper branches. His touch was gentle, his hands rough as he held onto her own.

"Vanaheim, home to the Vanir. Old gods skilled at sorcery."

Their hands moved again to the upper left branches.

"Alfheim, home to the elves of light. Freyr rules here."

Their hands moved downward in unison to an area where both roots and branches blended.

"Muspelheim, the land of fire, is home to the flame giants and demons."

He moved her hand across again to another square that mirrored the last.

"Niflheim, the land of mist, is the coldest of all the worlds. This is where Odin cast Hel, daughter of Loki and the giantess. Here she would create a home to receive those who die of sickness and old age."

He moved to the center again and down to the left half of the roots.

"Jotunheim, home to the giants—"

"Where Gerd dwelt," Poppa interrupted. She felt captivated by his stories, though she hadn't understood the depth and complexity of the legends.

Rollo smiled at her and confirmed her observation before he moved her hand to the opposite end of the roots.

"Svartalfheim, home to the dwarfs, fine craftsmen. This is where Thor's hammer was forged."

Finally, he moved her hand to a dark place in the tree's roots. Originally, she thought the wood had a knot in it, but up close she could see charred marks where Rollo had intentionally burnt the wood to carve out a blackness.

She noted the changes on his face as a more serious and somber mood came over him. His eyes grew darker and lines appeared on his forehead as he spoke. "Helheim, the home of the dishonored dead. Where all go who aren't taken to Valhalla, hall of Odin . . . or Sessrumnir, hall of Freya."

A cold chill spread over her and she pulled her hand back abruptly. She quickly tried to change the subject. "You said Loki had three children by the giantess, but you only mentioned two. What of the third?"

Rollo gave her a small smile. "Ah, the third is known as the wolf Fenrir. The largest and most dangerous wolf. He was tied with magical silken bonds that grew tighter the more he fought to escape. He's kept in bondage in Asgard, where the gods themselves dwell. Until Ragnarök, when he will break free."

"Ragnarök?"

Rollo's smile grew. "One question leads to another in our legends. Ragnarök is the end of all things. It's not a happy story, so I'll save it for another time."

Poppa's eyes widened with fascination as she said, "I had no idea your culture had so much depth."

Rollo smiled at her, "I've only just scratched the surface. I'll share more. You may find that the stories of the Bible have some similarities. Odin once hung himself from Yggdrasil, sacrificing himself in the pursuit of gaining the wisdom to lead and rule the worlds. He stayed there for nine days and forbid anyone from helping him. Christ, too, hung from a tree as a sacrifice in the atonement of man's sin, so God could once again dwell with his creation."

Rollo viewed these legends as true and real in the same way she viewed her faith, Poppa realized. Finding harmony between the two would most likely prove to be her biggest challenge. She let him lead her out of the room and to the kitchens and stable areas. Next, he showed her the terrace outside and the rolling hill that led back to the path to town. Housed on the lower level of the home, to her astonishment, was a bathhouse. Rollo explained that the Romans had constructed the bathhouse when they occupied the area hundreds of years ago. Throughout the centuries many others had contributed to the building of the house around it. As she'd suspected, Rollo intentionally saved this house from the destruction of Rouen.

"A tepidarium," Poppa spoke in amazement.

"You've seen one before?"

"No, but I've heard of them. I've always wanted to bathe in one." She smiled as she tested the water. Translucent steam rose up from the water and curled as it disappeared into the air. "It's kept warm by its own heating system, is it not?"

Rollo, impressed, smiled at her. "Já, we had to restore it, but eventually, with some toil, we were able to get it to run smoothly."

"Amazing," Poppa exclaimed.

"Rouen has a much bigger one known as the thermae. It's open to the public at all times of the day. I'm convinced it aids in the general health of the people."

"If not health, at least morale."

Rollo smiled in agreement.

The room they entered last, which was four times the size of the master bedroom, served as a large living area. The oak doors she'd seen from the outside opened into a small hall off this room. Dark smoke blotches stained the stone of the massive hearth that sat against the eastern wall. Billowing lounge cushions rested around the base of the fire. They begged for Poppa to rest upon them. Richly embroidered tapestries hung from the walls with scenes of the hunt and past battles. Rollo had collected them from many raids over his lifetime. Colored light filtered down to the floor from stained glass windows set high in the walls. Poppa wondered if they were salvaged from felled churches. Large dark beams crossed from one end to the other, making the ceiling appear lower and the room feel cozier. The room spanned from the front of the house, where the morning sun would shine through the windows, to the back of the house, where a wide window would show the evening sun's face.

"Look here," Rollo said excitedly as he pulled her to the back window. "It looks down on the terrace below and over the whole valley."

Poppa watched the mist settle over the small city below. The river, glistening as it reflected the fading sun, flowed on her left. Down in the valley, she could see the streets winding through buildings of varying sizes. Common folk milled about on these streets, finishing their daily tasks and making their way home to start the evening's meal. She could mark the training grounds by the men dancing with swords as they sparred with one another. She longed to join them, to practice again and hear metal clanking against metal. She could still hear her father's calls of correction or admiration as she moved about the practice circle.

"It's wonderful," Poppa smiled.

Rollo's smile grew satisfied and proud as she observed his land. "Here we stand on a small hill above a flat piece of land. It's different than where I come from. In my homeland, the mountains tower like sleeping giants. They reach into the sky, and there's snow on their peaks even in the summer. You could climb for hours and still not reach the top. We built our homes in the valleys and farmed the fertile land at the mountains' bases. The town began at the river and ended pressed against the mountains."

"Do you miss it? Your homeland?"

Poppa noted carefully that the smile on his face had faded and turned into a frown. His gaze turned inward. Poppa quickly realized she'd asked the wrong question.

Rollo walked to the hearth, where a fire burned hot. He stoked the fire further and spoke over his shoulder. "As I said before, there was never anything there for me. My future is here."

"Then we're the same," Poppa spoke as she slowly came up behind him. "I, too, have nothing to return to."

She sank into a warm cushion by the fire and focused on the dancing flames while working up enough courage to ask her next question. "Why did you really do it? Why did you marry me and bring me here? Why did you save a simple handmaiden from the fate of your men?"

He glanced at her, assessing whether or not she would believe him. "I've seen what happens to many ladies of your stature; you're right in assuming so. Ladies-in-waiting, handmaidens, women close to nobility but not born high enough to afford an acceptable ransom. It has never bothered me before. Until you. You moved me, Poppa, in the worst way and then there was . . ."

"Was what?" Her heart beat rapidly.

"I fear you won't believe me if I tell it."

Poppa watched his face change when he looked to her. His eyebrows knit and his eyes took on a boyishly pleading look. He looked humbled. Almost fearful. She'd never seen him look this vulnerable before.

"Please."

Light from the flames danced across his handsome face. He watched the fire, but his dark eyes had a distant cast, as if he looked inward while trying to remember.

"I know you're bothered by the nature of our marriage. It was the quickest solution I could find, and I was . . ." Rollo paused. "Well, I was instructed to."

"What do you mean? Instructed by whom?"

"I'm not sure. I heard a voice—as clear as you hear me now—say, 'Save her. Go now. Take her to Ase.' You'd fallen to the ground, so I lifted you up and ran."

She let out a heavy sigh at the memory. Silence hung between them for a long time before she spoke again.

"Tell me of your first wife," Poppa spoke to the silence. "You've only said that you were unkind to her and that she died in childbirth."

Rollo rubbed his hand over his face and resigned himself. "Já, but first, we must have food. I'm starving."

He clapped his hands and the two young servants waiting at the edge of the room left only to reappear a few moments later with cheese, fruit, and bread. Rollo smiled, placed a piece of cheese on his bread, and took a large bite. He chewed a bit before speaking around the mouthful. "I'll go hunting on the morrow. Steady game roams this area and I have received word that a herd is close by."

"I'd like to go with you sometime. My father used to take me when I was a young girl. I admired the chase and stealth. Myra and I enjoyed the competition of the hunt, whether we went for the prey or the attention of the other hunters." Poppa smiled to herself and then paused and looked down upon her hands, which sat folded in her lap. She paused before returning to the subject of her curiosity. "You were going to tell me of your wife."

Poppa gave him time to gather his thoughts. After a while Rollo shared, "Her name was Gisela. She was of noble birth. She was wise in the affairs of state and very beautiful. Her beauty was tempting enough to lead a man to accept a new religion and a Christian baptism. I should mention, too, that it was not only her beauty that tempted me; her hand in marriage also came with a large portion of West Francia." He winked before his face darkened.

"She wasn't a willing participant. She thought me a savage and, in those days, she was right. She called out the truth in my conversion. She accused me of renouncing my gods and accepting the faith only for her lord father's favor and the lands I'd receive. She said God would know my sin and know I wasn't righteous. The truth of her words wounded my pride and made me angry. I allowed that anger to grow and fester within me. I left Paris to view my new lands without her and took comfort in other arms. I built new churches and restored old ones that had been leveled by previous Norseman raids. I thought this would make my new wife happy. When I was ready, I sent for her. She arrived here in Rouen in the company of two young men. I was furious she'd traveled all that distance with only two men. Also, my people gossiped and spread rumors, as smallfolk do, that tarnished my wife's reputation and mine. Word that she entertained these men in private began to circulate among the common folk. I had no choice. I had the men arrested. In the morning, I walked my wife to the town's center and had them executed in front of her and all the people who had gossiped so freely."

Poppa's eyes widened and her hand covered her mouth.

"She claimed they were only her bodyguards. Perhaps she wasn't false, but I wasn't sorry for my decision to have them killed. No amount of new or restored churches could make up for what I'd done. Despite her loathing, she stayed obedient after that. It didn't take long for her to be with child. While she resigned herself to her fate, her mood grew helpless and weary. Nothing would make her smile. It caused me to fear what kind of mother she'd become. I wasn't as attentive as I should've been in those days. Perhaps I'd have noticed sooner the signs of the darkness that overcame her in the end. She took to bed early and was uncomfortable. She stayed in bed when she should've enjoyed the fresh, bright weather outside. Often she refused to eat more than a little bread and water. We all feared for her and the child. When the labor finally came, it was long, lasting the course of two days. She screamed in terror and begged to die. She lost too much blood. I was in the room when the baby was born. Gisela sighed and took a shaky breath before she closed her eyes and breathed no more. I held my daughter in my arms. Her breath and pulse were weak from the start. She took a few short breaths and then followed her mother in death." Rollo paused in his grief before he continued in a raspy voice, "I can't describe the weight of my grief and shame. I—"

Poppa's tears flowed softly down her face as she listened to his heartbreak. She rose from her cushion and enveloped him in her arms. Pressing his head into her chest, she held him. She held him to help him forgive himself, and she held him to absolve her own sin in sending Myra to her death. She held him for all the lives lost, and she held him for the new beginning. She held him. Then she lifted his face to hers and kissed him through her tears. She kissed him for all the reasons she had held him. He returned her kisses and hopefully received her message.

"Pardon us, jarl."

Surprised, Poppa jumped back and they both turned their attention to the voice from the doorway.

Herleif and Ragnhild stood there, amused expressions playing across their faces.

"What brings you here?" Rollo's thick voice sounded breathless and annoyed.

"I'm sorry to bother you, jarl, but you said you wanted to go over the distribution of lands. With the hunt on the morrow and the celebrations set for that evening, it's best we get started."

Rollo gave an annoyed, but resigned, sigh. Herleif moved to sit at the table. It wasn't long before he was ready with parchment and quill. Rollo inspected Poppa with longing. The intensity of it made her knees collapse, and she sat gracefully in the cushions. She was grateful that the heat of the fire hid the blush on her face. Reluctantly, Rollo turned away. He gave an exasperated sigh, but then he clasped both Ragnhild and Herleif on a shoulder and shook them gently in a familiar, friendly gesture.

"As always," Rollo began, "my expectation for all who are granted land is that they rebuild what we have destroyed. They will uphold my laws against robbery and violence. They will serve me when I call and am in need of warriors."

"What of the Frank survivors?" Ragnhild wondered.

Rollo glanced at Poppa. "Encourage the men to take the widows who willingly accept their offers of marriage—widows still of child-bearing age before maidens. The same goes for our women who will inherit lands, though I'm guessing there will be fewer widowers."

Ragnhild scoffed and gave a knowing look to Poppa before moving the conversation along. "And the orphans?"

"Offer the true orphans, those who have no one to claim them, as apprentices or squires. The rest are to be sold."

Poppa gasped loudly.

"It's our way, Poppa. We can't have them running wild or forming a rebellion in the future."

"Surely the Church would take them into service or find good Christian homes for them."

"Then the Church can pay for them as anyone else would," Rollo resolved. "I don't doubt they have the funds."

Poppa closed her mouth in a thin line but didn't press him further. Rollo moved on with his orders.

"If any resist our rule, they shall be killed. We have no time for people who harbor prejudice or those who won't accept a Norseman as their ruler. If this makes more widows and orphans, then so be it. If it's found that the families had a part in the rebellion, then they will share in the fate. They must bend the knee to me as their authority as I bend the knee to their king. I'm tired of fighting against their distrust of foreigners. It's time to make a statement."

Ragnhild smiled as Rollo continued.

"If anyone is found hoarding valuable items, I want them fined and punished. They're essentially keeping wealth from their liege lord and from their king. I want justice served swiftly and publicly."

"If I may interrupt my lord . . ." Poppa spoke quietly but in a strong voice.

Rollo motioned for her to continue.

"What if people come forward in good faith and return items after they have seen the consequences?"

"The consequences of stealing from the crown are well known," Ragnhild informed her.

"Yes, I know, but perhaps a show of mercy for those who have made mistakes would be wiser in this matter," Poppa argued.

Rollo nodded in agreement. "Let an order go out that if any Frank, in good faith, surrenders items they have hidden prior to the siege or looted afterward, their crime is forgiven, though a tax of one-fourth the value will be imposed on all items they surrender. As Ragnhild has said, the consequences of stealing are known to all. They will accept the small tax. They have seven days from when the notice is posted to surrender items. If items are found after that, my chieftains will enact the punishment law dictates. Anyone found trying to trade items or slaves without the consent of their chieftain or myself and without proper documentation will be dealt with swiftly and punished by death. I won't tolerate robbery or uncontrolled markets of any sort."

"I don't think the small changes to our usual policy that you've suggested today will pose a problem amongst your chieftains. If I may move the conversation along, jarl, now is the time to discuss the division of the land of Bayeux." Herleif spoke with confidence as he rolled out a map with suggested lines drawn around the area Poppa had called her home.

"The city itself is under the stewardship of its previous steward Lord Peter. However, I believe this man has proven himself disloyal." Rollo paused and winked at Poppa. "The people must see him investigated and found guilty of treason. He sold out his own people, and although we benefited, I don't trust him. I fear, if offered enough, he will turn his cloak again. No, it'll go to Brynjar. He fought bravely and has proven himself a good leader. He lost a brother and two sons in the battle. It's a small consolation."

Poppa thought of Peter's fate as Rollo suggested various others to take ownership of the surrounding land. Rollo confirmed the assumption she'd made when the Norse and Franks had attempted her trade. Peter had sold the castle's secrets for a price and his own life. Rollo would serve justice on her behalf. She couldn't help but respect him for that.

"What of Ingmar?" Ragnhild asked, a bold question. It was well known among all that Rollo and Ingmar hadn't parted on good terms when the ships sailed for Rouen.

Rollo winced. Poppa wondered what had come between the two men after her capture. "What would you suggest I do?"

"Ingmar is forever loyal, jarl—though he disagrees with your hasty decision to marry. I don't need to explain to you that she would have been his, as your second-in-command, to do with as he pleased after her people surrendered her."

Poppa winced at the new information and pictured Ingmar in all his savage glory. His piercing blue eyes had cut to her soul. She had an inkling he wouldn't have treated her as kindly as Rollo had. Rollo glanced briefly at Poppa.

"My second, já, but not my equal. He has no right to be upset. How deep does his disagreement run?"

Ragnhild sighed, "As I said, he's loyal. But I think he expects recompense appropriate to the scale of the slight he believes he received."

Rollo's fist slammed onto the oak table, disturbing all the items on it. The inkwell tipped over and spilled on the map. Poppa startled, but Ragnhild and Herleif reacted with neither surprise nor fear.

"What's your suggestion?" Rollo asked through clenched teeth.

"If the management of Bayeux is spoken for, give him the vast lands that touch the sea." Ragnhild pointed on the map. "Task him with building a bigger port and protecting it from invasion. It will honor him to serve you in this way. Also, arrange his marriage to Sigrid so he can populate his new home. It'll keep him far enough from here while covering all his needs."

"Sigrid?" An amused grin played upon Rollo's features. "For so long now I've thought him interested in you."

Ragnhild, her blue eyes shining through their kohl rings, smiled. "I didn't say he wasn't. This union will serve me as well. I won't take a husband, and he won't settle until he has a bride. Besides, Sigrid speaks often about how bravely he fought in the battle. It's time she's wed."

Rollo returned her smile. "See that it's done."

A happy and attractive solution to a possible threat. Rollo would make many of his men happy and rich. They would become lords over Poppa's people by obtaining the lands around Bayeux, and they would gain a future of further riches from all the land would offer. She left them to their planning as she took her seat by the fire.

Her gaze went back to the flames as she listened. Remotely, she wondered who would get her father's old property. He'd sold his land when he went to work as the master-at-arms. Her mother had died giving birth to her on that land, and her father had buried her there. The fire licked and danced in the darkness of the room. It lulled her into sleep. She didn't remember when she finally closed her eyes. However, she did remember the strong arms that lifted her up and carried her to bed.

SEER

THE NEXT MORNING, ROLLO LEFT for the hunt early. Poppa didn't see him for the whole of the day. She used her time to become more familiar with the house and the land. She would walk aimlessly around the grounds, get lost, then try to discover her way back. When Rollo sent word that he'd go straight to the celebrations from the hunt, she'd been disappointed. Their marriage was eight days old, and they hadn't yet consummated it. Over the course of those days, she'd grown closer to him. She hoped he felt the same. It weighed heavy over them both. He'd said that she should come to him, but what would she say? What would she do? He'd asked her to join the night's celebrations at her leisure because they'd continue into the morning hours. She'd take the time to consider her next course of action.

After a dinner of roasted grouse and steamed vegetables, she went down to the tepidarium, where she could soak and rest alone with her thoughts. The floor felt warm beneath her bare feet as she doffed her clothing. She dipped her toe into the smooth surface of the water, testing its warmth. Satisfied, she slowly lowered herself in and gave a relaxed sigh as the water cocooned her and the steam curled through her nostrils. She leaned her head against the side of the pool and let her eyes close.

She'd experienced much change these last eight days. In all that confusion, only one thing remained true: her feelings toward Rollo were growing with each passing day. He'd become more than the stranger she'd married. More than the man who'd captured and ransomed her. More than the terrifying berserker who'd slammed through the doors of Myra's bedroom. They'd opened themselves to each other, passing into a new level of intimacy. He'd confessed his brutal judgment, and she her guilt, over Myra's death. Their hands had been equally dirty as they'd kissed by the fire the night before.

That kiss had replayed in her mind many times throughout the day. She could still feel his mouth, warm and eager against hers. As they'd kissed, he'd moved his hand right below her waist. He'd held her hip firmly and pressed her to him. She hadn't objected. She felt a fluttering. The need she'd experience during the kiss grew again within her. Yet she struggled with the origins of their union. Would God bless their marriage? Was she truly his wife even if it wasn't recognized by the Church? Would it be a sin to consummate a marriage not performed by an abbot?

The uncertainty flooded her with anxiety, and she opened her eyes. She moved about the pool slowly, her arms pushing the water aside as she kicked her feet slightly to keep her head above the water. She thought again of the kiss and the feelings it arose within her. She'd felt reckless, the kind of abandon that felt sinful yet natural. The contrast of the two feelings made her head dizzy. Her thoughts, fueled by questions she didn't feel qualified to answer, warred with each other. If God is omnipresent, does that mean He was present in the tent, in all of its pagan unholiness, as a witness to her marriage? Was that enough for His blessing? And if not, would not having God's blessing be enough to stop her when he kissed her again?

She sank into the water to muffle a frustrated cry. She watched as bubbles escaped from her mouth and floated up. When she surfaced, she knew what she needed more than anything. She needed a sign—a confirmation that their union wasn't cursed, that God had a hand in it, despite all else. She swam back to the edge of the pool and rested her head against the rim. She closed her eyes as a wave of heavy tiredness swept over her.

The water still felt warm when she woke with a gasp. She took a minute to reorient herself with her surroundings, thankful she hadn't gone under in her sleep. The sky outside had darkened from when she had entered the pool, so she could tell some time had passed. Her heart raced in pace with the images dancing through her mind. She'd seen so much in her dream. She knew what she needed to do.

With renewed purpose she flew out of the water and almost slipped on the floor. She caught herself with a hand on the wall and exhaled heavily. "Steady, Poppa, steady."

She chided herself for talking to herself before she let out an excited laugh. She felt giddy. The burden was lifted. God had delivered the sign she'd requested. She dried herself in haste and donned her white nightdress. It clung to the water that still remained on her skin. Her wet hair hung in tangles around her shoulders. She had no time to make herself more presentable. Her message was too important.

She left the house in a flurry, telling no one where she planned to go. The night air felt brisk and cold on her bare skin, yet she barely felt it as she ran toward town. She didn't have time to follow the path. Instead, she bounded down the hill, passing the path a few times as it circled back on itself. She flew, a streak of white against the night sky, distantly aware of the sharpness of the pebbles on her bare feet. She stumbled once or twice, but she took little notice as dirt and grass stained her dress and hands. Her mind only focused on the images of her vision and how she would put them into words that he could understand. She had to make it real.

Despite the falls, going down the hill took much less time than it had going up. In truth, it felt liberating to run and fly the way the gulls had when they had left Bayeux. Her heart felt light. She couldn't stop a smile from forming on her lips. The smile died, though, as she neared the great hall at the center of town. The revelers had made their way into the streets, and she could hear their shouts and laughter.

It was evident by the crowd that the night watchmen had not rang the bells to sound curfew this night. They roamed amongst the people as they patrolled the streets. She passed one, light flickering from the lantern he carried to illuminate his surroundings. To her right, in the wake of the watchman's lantern's glow, she saw men naked from the waist up and covered in blue tattoos. They wrestled each other in the middle of the street. Onlookers cheered them on and exchanged coins with one another. Before her, a man pulled a giggling and voluptuous woman into a small passageway between two buildings. On her other side, a crowd stood drinking from horns of ale and speaking to one another. They followed her with startled and questioning looks as she pushed through them. Some even shouted ribald jokes, not knowing who she was. She became more self-aware as she, barely clothed and barefoot, passed through them.

The door to the great hall stood open. Golden light shone from inside and illuminated the entrance. Seductive pipe music played loudly over the voices of hundreds of celebrators. She paused at the door, her hand upon the wooden frame. Finally, she became keenly aware of her appearance. Her fine silk nightgown clung to her damp skin, leaving little to the imagination. Her hair hung in half-dried tangles all around her, knotted and wild from her run. She looked down at her bare feet and saw several cuts, curious that she couldn't feel them at the moment.

She steeled herself. She'd made it this far; she couldn't go back. Though her heart beat fast, she entered slowly, floating upon the ground like a ghost. All around her common folk drank, danced, and laughed. She became dizzy as she watched them. She allowed them to blur into the background as she looked for Rollo. Sensing her desperation, the crowd at the door parted for her. She had no time to dwell on their stares as she drew nearer to the middle of the hall. She walked cautiously but purposefully to the middle of the hall, where a large fire burned.

Then she saw him a small distance away, sitting on a faldstool atop a wide platform. He faced the crowd and the fire. The wood of the chair was intricately carved, with the arms flowing into the heads of open-mouthed lions on each side. One of Rollo's large hands covered a lion's head as he leaned to his right, his thumb caressing the carving. An amused grin played upon his lips as a beautiful young girl with blonde hair, loose and long, massaged his neck. Another, wearing only a thin shift, danced before him slowly, keeping time with the music that played. He casually regarded her as he spoke to Herleif, who sat on his right. On his left, Ragnhild stood sentry and scanned the crowd. Occasionally her gaze drifted to the two young girls on the dais.

Hidden by the crowd, Poppa considered the players on the stage. The dancer moved with grace between Herleif and Rollo. She had long reddish hair and teased them as she slowly lifted up her thin slip. A sting of jealousy overcame Poppa. She almost forgot why she'd come and now considered going back. Only the strength of her vision and her confidence in its truth gave her the courage to go on.

Poppa carefully raised herself above the crowd as she stood on a chair, the fire at her back, so that she too had a sort of platform. She felt the attention of the room turn toward her, but she only cared about the attention of one. Ragnhild spotted Poppa first and watched with an amused grin as she waited for Rollo to notice his wife. Poppa ignored the other woman's stare as her gaze fell back to her husband. He laughed heartily and pulled the dancer to his lap. The girl giggled as he held her there, and he turned to Herleif. In that moment, he noticed Poppa standing in the middle of the room. Wearing white and lit by the fire, she glowed like a beacon in the dark hall. The firelight cast shadows that darkened her eyes as she stared intently upon him. He stopped midsentence and stared in wonderment. Poppa noticed that he didn't move the girl from his lap. He held her there, shameless.

"Wife, what is it? Are you unwell?"

His eyes were wary as they roved over her appearance. Fire and shadow framed her and seemed to flow through her.

"I'm well, my lord. I had to speak with you and couldn't wait for morning."

Rollo raised a hand and the music stopped. Poppa could feel the eyes of the curious people around her as they fixated on the two figures. Only now the thought crossed her mind that she might have embarrassed him or wounded his pride. She thought of the bodyguards he had executed all because they had traveled alone with his last wife, causing the common folk to gossip. Now, here she stood, disheveled and clothed in her nightwear in front of them all. Perhaps she'd risked too much. *Would he punish her?* She fretted that they could see the pumping of her heart through her clothes. She swallowed nervously, but bravely she kept her determined eyes upon him.

His expression looked tense. His mind was probably traveling the same path as hers as he considered what to do next. His brown eyes, lit by the fire at her back, almost looked blue. She could clearly see the scar above his left eye twist as he knit his arched brows. She thought of all those who'd endured that stare while they awaited judgment. Her breathing hastened. She could see her chest rise and fall and hear the beating of her heart in her ears.

Finally, he nodded his head once and leaned forward in his chair. He released the girl from his lap. With one flick of his wrist, they both left him and disappeared into the crowd. The redheaded one gave Poppa a smirk of annoyance as she left. Poppa pretended not to notice, keeping her attention only on Rollo.

"Come forth," Rollo beckoned her.

Poppa took in the crowd's inquisitive stares. She took a deep breath and summoned all her bravery. In order for the people to respect her, she needed them to hear her as well. It was not only a promise for her and Rollo but a promise for them all.

"No." Poppa paused. "Jarl," she added at the end to soften the disrespect—a term of reverence that she hadn't used with him before. She hoped he would understand the humility in her choice of words. "I want everyone to hear."

She noted the twitch of his hand. He felt annoyed and struggled with his patience. She could feel it coming off of him in waves. Not only had she presented herself in the most untoward fashion, but she also challenged his authority in public. He tilted his head incredulously.

She gulped back her fear and spoke in a strong voice, "Please forgive me, my lord husband. I've been rude and untoward. I've news that's most urgent." She paused. "A vision came to me this night."

Rollo rubbed his finger on his lips and shifted in his seat. She could feel his anger rising, but he read the urgency of her demeanor. She prayed he'd allow her to continue. He leaned again to his right. His thumb traced the lines of the carved lion's jaw. With his other hand he made a motion for her to continue. Though the message was meant for everyone, she only spoke to him, gripping him with her eyes as she did.

"As I was bathing, I descended into a deep sleep. I found myself standing with you on the top of a large hill. The grass was green with the lush foliage of spring. Below us, a valley opened up, the ground littered with the bodies of our foes. Both men and women lay upon the grass for as far as the eye could see, dead or dying. We held swords in our hands. They dripped with blood. The victory was ours. But it belonged mostly to the tall man who stood between us. Pride and thankfulness swelled in my heart as I turned to look at his handsome face. However, when our eyes met, the brown of his irises pooled into a starry blackness that spun before me and held me. I fell into his gaze and watched from above as a map of the whole world unrolled upon a long table. A stain of red ink blotted Francia. I understood it to represent the man who still stood beside me.

"Together we surveyed the map as the red stain grew darker and wider. It spread over the seas and over the lands to far and distant places I didn't recognize. Many would fall before it. Victory was not always certain, though, for there were times when the stain would spread backward as if hindered. Nevertheless, it persisted to rule across the map. In this red ink, I saw the descendants of the man beside me. I saw them multiply to a number greater than the stars. I saw kingdoms rise and kingdoms fall. Around me, the sun moved across the sky and day became night over and over again as the stain spread about the map. Until it spread so far that the sun would never set on the empire that was built. The bloodline was so strong and so victorious that the sun continued to shine on it always. Thousands of years must have passed and still the color grew darker and stronger. A dynasty that had no end."

Water filled her eyes and she shook with the vivid memories of her dream. The room stood still and quiet as they listened. Standing above them, she could speak softly and still be heard by all.

"Then I was back on the hill. With you by my side. The victorious man stood before us with his longsword in hand. He offered it to us as he kneeled."

Poppa glanced down. She needed a break from his gaze.

"This man," Rollo asked, his voice cracking with emotion, "who was he?"

Poppa's eyes found him. She held him with the urgency of her stare. She said nothing as a tear traced down her cheek. She took a deep breath. In the exhale, she spoke each word clearly: "He is our son."

She saw the shock play over his face as a mighty roar went up all around them. A celebration of the promise of fruitfulness in their union. Fruitfulness and victory over centuries. The noise became an unimportant buzz in her ear as Rollo received the promise of the blessing he'd waited for all his life. Poppa couldn't stop the tears from flowing, nor could she stop a smile from forming on her lips. The clear vision of her son would be etched on her heart forever. She watched as Rollo's mouth twitched into what looked like a small smile.

He'd left his seat and scooped her off the chair and into his arms before she could process his expression. She felt light in his arms as his feet swiftly crossed the room. His mouth closed on hers as he held her and pressed her to the wall of the great hall. She kissed him and matched him in his need. He tasted of sweet mead, and his hair smelled like the oak smoke in the room. She placed her hand at the back of his head to hold him in place as he kissed her. His hand crept under her nightdress and pushed it up past her thigh. Cheers from all around them rang out. Poppa became fearful he would take her right there in front of all those people.

She pulled away reluctantly, and he began to kiss her neck as she whispered in his ear, "Rollo, not here. Take me home."

Rollo pulled back, his eyes roaming her face, and then carried her out the door and into the night, a chorus of voices shouting their blessings on the way. She buried her head in the crook of his neck and breathed him in. She allowed his warmth to envelop her in the coolness of the early morning air.

"I can walk," Poppa insisted as they made their way up the hill to the house.

"You've hurt your feet."

"I had to see you. To tell you what I saw."

"That was a foolish thing to do."

"Yes, I know, but I don't regret it."

She kissed his neck, then his ear, which caused him to let out a low growl before she kissed his lips.

He put her down carefully on her feet. She tried to hide the wince from him as her bloodied feet hit the earth. She put her hand in his and pulled him up the rest of the path. They entered the house quietly and made their way upstairs to the bedroom.

Rollo saw that she left bloodied footprints behind and gave a heavy sigh. He left her in the bedroom, sitting on the bed, and returned with strips of white linen and a bowl of warm water. He kneeled at her feet. Slowly he cleaned one foot and then the next. His large hands were gentle as they skimmed the small cuts and gashes. Poppa gazed at him from above as he held her feet in his hands. He washed and dressed them with deft movements that made her wonder how often those strong hands had bandaged wounds before. She pictured how gentle he would hold his own babe in his arms. Her stomach quickened and fluttered.

When he'd finished and removed the dirty water, she stood gingerly on her feet before him.

"Thank you," she whispered as her fingers trailed the lightness of his linen shirt.

Bravely, she lifted it over his head to reveal the muscles of his chest and the ink of his many tattoos. She traced the lines gently with her fingertips as he stood still before her. She kissed his chest softly and kept her hands pressed against his chest. She felt his hand in her tangled hair as she rose to bring her lips to his in a soft, warm whisper of a kiss.

Rollo pulled away from the kiss first and looked to the window. Outside, the sky was still black, twilight a few hours off. Inside, the only light came from the fireplace. He smiled down at her. "Poppa, the vision that came to you arrived on the ninth day after our marriage. We're blessed once again by the gods. Freyr and Gerd, they bless us in the early hours of this morn."

Poppa shook her head. "Perhaps, but my vision came to me as I prayed to God for a sign of His approval upon us. You say we're blessed by your gods, and I say we're blessed by mine. Neither of us will win this battle tonight. However, there is one thing we can find unity in. Come, husband, we have a marriage to consummate."

She walked over to the edge of the bed and waited for him. He kissed her lips slowly as he slid the strap of her nightdress down from one shoulder and then the next. It fell to the floor in a hush. She fondled the laces on his breeches as she stepped out of the fabric that pooled at her feet. She didn't feel shy before him. She had a deep sense of confidence, as though the world had aligned perfectly for this moment. She was grateful to offer herself to him. Rollo traced the scar on her arm that she'd received the day of the siege. Light purple and blue bruises had formed around the opening, and it itched with its healing. He moved to kiss it tenderly. An act of apology. This body meant so much more to him now than it did on that fateful day.

As he kissed her, the laces on his breeches came undone. She allowed him to lift her onto the bed and position her on her back. He propped himself up with one arm and looked down upon her once before kissing her again. His hands roamed over the newly exposed territory of her breasts. He thumbed her nipples and then smiled against her mouth as they hardened. She felt his length grow and press against her thigh. His kisses moved to her neck and then down to her chest. She sighed as lips and tongue caressed each nipple. She barely noticed that his hand moved down around the crease of her underclothes. As he kissed her breasts, his hand slid underneath and one finger deftly entered her. She gasped as the need built within her. She put her hands in his hair and pulled his mouth back to hers. Her kisses moved as urgently as his finger at work between her legs. She didn't think she could contain the feeling much longer.

"Now," she whispered in his ear.

Her breath came out ragged, but her hands worked deftly to free him from his underclothes. He slowly guided himself inside her. A sharp pain came from deep within her. For a moment, she feared he'd break her in half from the inside. He gave a small grunt as he pushed harder and through her. She felt instant relief. A pleasurable sensation moved upward so quickly it overcame the whole of her body. He smiled down at her and kissed her again as he began to move his hips and thrust in and out again.

She cried out loudly and placed her hands on his buttocks, pulling him closer and deeper inside herself. Instinctively, she wrapped her legs around him, her thighs tight against his side. His stamina matched her need, and when he climaxed, she had already matched him, but she rose to meet him again. He let out a primal shout as he spilled his seed. She silently prayed for it to accomplish the task set by God and nature so she would be with child soon.

He collapsed on top of her, staying inside her as she wrapped her arms around him. She listened to his labored breathing until it slowed in time with the shaking of her legs. He kissed the inside groove of her neck as she slowly moved her hands up and down his back. Then she pulled his face back to her and kissed him, hard and needing.

"Careful, wife, or I won't be able to give you rest and I'll have to mount you again."

Poppa laughed, "Why on earth would you think I'd need a rest?"

She pushed him off of her and to one side. Then she positioned herself on top of him, straddling his chest. She glanced down and saw that his need for her grew.

"It'll be I who mounts you this time, my lord husband," she said with a wicked grin.

She carefully held on to him as she moved her hips and guided him inside her. She sat for a moment with her head back, her gaze unfocused. Her body opened beautifully before him. He placed his hand around her neck and carefully but firmly held her for a moment, wanting to take into memory all that he saw before him. Then his hands went to her hips and encouraged her to move. She swayed forward and back in a rhythm only she could hear, her eyes open only a slit while soft moans escaped her lips.

As the pleasure built, her movements became more frenzied. He rose to meet her, and she gasped as he positioned her to sit in his lap, entering even deeper. He could kiss her now, slowly and deftly as they moved. He pulled only a breath away from the kiss, her lips still brushing his as she rose and fell. For a moment, only the hush of their labored breathing was heard between them. Tendrils of hair fell before her eyes and mouth, and he moved a hand to tuck them behind her ear. Her moans grew louder as she reached her climax. Rollo gave his last good thrust and she screamed. Her legs went loose as she crumpled around him. She wrapped her arms around his neck and rested her head on his shoulder as she waited to catch her breath.

"Now, I think I need a rest," she whispered as her breathing restored itself.

He laughed against her hair and kissed her forehead.

"You've done well, my love," he spoke in her ear.

Poppa, still sitting in his lap, brought her face level with his. Her eyes danced as they gazed into his. The first word of love uttered between them. She searched for the truth as he wiped the sweat from her brow and pulled slightly on her hair. He smiled at her and placed his forehead upon hers.

"Those were not meaningless words spoken in passion, Poppa. You're my wife in every way. I'll love you until my dying breath. If I go before you, I'll wait for you and love you again in Odin's hall."

Poppa smiled and kissed him deeply and passionately. She shivered in the cold and he helped tuck her into the warm bed before he wrapped his arms around her and pulled her tightly against him. He kissed the back of her head and the hollow of her neck. Then, for the first time in a very long time, he prayed to the Lord of his baptism, thanking him for the blessing of a second chance.

CONFESSION

The morning light filtered softly through the east windows as Poppa awoke in the late morning. Between her legs, she noticed an unfamiliar soreness, a dull ache that spread to her thighs and hips. She rolled over in the bed and let her vision fall on her sleeping husband. He looked peaceful and serene. The whiteness of the sheets softened the caramel of his skin and the darkness of his hair. His thick lips pouted sweetly across a relaxed face. She thought she caught a glimpse of what he would've looked like in his boyhood. Certainly this wasn't the Norseman who pillaged and raided the countryside, killing as he went and spreading terror among her countrymen. In the light of this new morning, he seemed different.

Poppa propped her elbow on the soft down mattress and rested her head on her palm. She let her hair, tangled and messy, fall softly around her face. She was blissfully aware of her nakedness beneath the sheets. With their legs touching, she was aware of his nakedness as well. She allowed his warmth to flow into her as she studied his face. His skin felt warm to the touch. In the corners of his eyes, small wrinkles suggested many smiles. His facial hair, chocolate brown in color with traces of lighter hair over the upper lip, bristled her fingers when she touched him. She followed the thick hair down as it traveled in stiff lines to inches below his chin. With her free hand, she lightly touched the soft hair on the side of his cheek that traced between hairline and face all the way to his ear. The soft skin around her own mouth still prickled from the touch of his facial hair. She smiled to herself and bit her lower lip with the memory of the night before. Her heart felt light and giddy as it beat in her chest. Her eyes traveled over his mouth. His upper lip thinner than the bottom. She remembered how it had felt between her teeth when she had softly bitten it. She studied his square and proud nose and then the scar that curved through his left eyebrow. She wondered how he had received it, this scar so fierce. She traced the shape lightly with her fingertips and longed to kiss it gently.

Rollo, his eyes still shut, smiled at her touch as he answered her unspoken question. "The point of a *krókspjót*, a hooked spear, from boyhood. I was training. I was never as skilled with a spear as my peers. I ducked too slowly. My brother Ivar scraped my brow in a curved swipe before I could put him down. It bled incessantly and blinded my vision until my lady mother cleaned and dressed it."

Rollo slowly opened his eyes to see her large brown ones, honeyed and softened by the light of morning, looking back at him. She leaned in and kissed the scar softly before placing her lips on his. A familiar need grew inside her despite the present ache of her muscles. She kissed him harder, her hands roaming under the sheets. Rollo laughed at her persistence.

"I don't understand why you laugh," Poppa protested between kisses. She moved to kiss his neck and his chest.

Rollo rolled onto his back with a smile still on his face. "Just yesterday you were a shy maid, and now you're like a she-wolf in heat."

He laughed loudly at his own jest, his head light with the knowledge that he'd gladly received the fruits of her endeavors.

Poppa scoffed and then paused. She grabbed a pillow and smacked him hard in the face. "You dare compare me to a dog!"

The small act of violence only made him laugh harder and louder. "If I remember correctly, lady wife, you once compared me to a dog."

Poppa looked at him incredulously.

Rollo mimicked her voice in jest: "'Why do you guard me like a dog, Rollo?'"

Poppa blushed as her words came back to her. She bit her lip and pleaded an apology with her eyes. He smiled widely at her. He gently laid her down on her back and climbed over her. He noticed her wince as he did.

"I didn't say it was unbecoming," Rollo spoke as he kissed her gently upon the lips. She could feel his length against her, and she craved it despite her pain. "You're sore."

It wasn't a question.

"I'll manage," she replied as she grabbed hold of him and guided him inside her.

He moved gently with his weight above her, and she felt grateful to him for it. When the release came, she kissed him softly, breathing in his scent. Burning cedar and sweat. He rested his head on her chest and closed his eyes to sleep a little more of the day away. Poppa rested her hand in his hair and joined him in his slumber.

Mrs. Laurent woke them later with a delivery of food. "I was going to bring you food to break your fast . . . but at that moment, you were occupied. You will need to sustain yourselves if you plan on continuing as you've been, to be sure."

She gave them an amused grin as she set the food down before them.

Rollo let out a satisfied grunt as he sat up in bed and dug in. "I'm famished."

Poppa came up behind him, pressing her naked body to his back, and reached over his shoulder, grabbing a few pieces of cold meat.

"The food tastes amazing this morning." Poppa licked her fingers and moved to take another piece of meat.

"You will find that many things look and feel better." Rollo smiled at her as he split a piece of hard bread between them.

"I'm sure I will, but for now I've no desire to leave this bed."

Poppa spread out over the covers, stretched her arms above her head, and gave a little squeal. Rollo considered her with delight.

"I told you the day we married that I thought you very beautiful," Rollo spoke. "Only now that I know the depths of you do I fully understand that beauty."

He kissed her belly and smiled against it.

She placed her hands in his hair again and twisted it around her fingers.

His kisses moved lower.

Poppa hummed, surprised that such pleasures existed. Her hand stayed in his hair, but she gripped it as if it tethered her to the earth. Her back rose off the bed of its own accord. She squirmed as he moved, not knowing how much more she could bear. The intensity of the pleasure built until she cried out loudly.

Rollo smiled devilishly up at her as she panted and tried to reclaim her breath.

He rose from the bed. For the first time, she saw him in his full nakedness. She admired him as he walked across the room and poured two horns of water. Muscles rippled even in his buttocks as he walked.

"That was," Poppa started, "I didn't know . . ."

She couldn't find the word she searched for. Her head and mind still reeled with pleasure.

Rollo faced the fire, but he watched her out of the corner of his eye before downing the contents of the horn.

"There's much I'd like to teach you in time."

She sat up in bed. The sheets wrapped around her. Her hair scattered around her naked shoulders.

"Well, I'm forever your willing pupil."

Rollo smiled and kissed her lips before lying on his back. She put her head on his chest and traced the lines of his tattoos with her finger, trying to commit them to memory.

Poppa remembered how he'd responded on the boat, as they'd neared the mouth of the Seine, when she'd asked him about his homeland. His mood had turned inward and sad. She trod carefully as she inquired, "Tell me of your family. You've said hardly anything on the topic. What were they like? Why did you leave them?"

Rollo didn't answer right away, so Poppa propped her elbow next to his chest and rested her head in her hand. She noted that his eyes grew sad and, though he tried to hide it, she recognized traces of pain in his expression. He picked up a tendril of her hair and smoothed it between his fingers as he talked. "Your hair is a rich dark brown. My lady mother's hair was the opposite. It was as bright and as golden as the sun. It fell like yours, in long waves over her shoulders. The ends touched her waist. Most days she kept it braided. I remember when I was young, she kept it down and flowing. I enjoyed sitting upon her lap and playing with it while she sang to me. She was always singing. She made the songs up as she went about her duties. I can still remember one about the night bird. It was a haunting tale of a woman leaving all behind in the night to venture out on her own."

Poppa gave him a crooked smile as he hummed the haunting tune in his deep baritone. The song's sad melody thrummed inside her and filled her being. He looked past her and far into memory. His eyebrows were knit together as he continued, "Her name was Hildr, and I can still hear her song in my ear. I can still see her hair. I cannot remember her face, but I know she was very beautiful."

Poppa smiled, showing him her white teeth. His hand moved to trace her high cheekbones before his thumb rested on the small dimple in her chin. "Like I know your smile is beautiful." He pulled her into a kiss before he continued, "My lord father never smiled. At least not toward me. His name was Rögnvald Eysteinsson. He was given the title Jarl of Møre after he helped the King of Norway fight off enemy Norsemen, chasing them to surrounding islands to finish them off. He had three children off of his various mistresses before he married my lady mother in his later years. That's when the last of his three sons were born. First Ivar, then myself—born Hròlfr. Thorir was the last of us."

Poppa smiled as he spoke. She enjoyed how his tongue rolled in his mouth when he spoke the names of his kin.

"My lord father favored the latter. My brother Thorir was a quiet boy, malleable, and he never argued. When it became clear our father meant to pass his inheritance on to the youngest of us all, I knew it was time to plan my departure. I deserved more, and I couldn't endure living under my younger brother's rule. Men would come back from voyages with tales of rich lands abroad and the weak people defending them. I saw the greatness I believed was due to me in the realms that they spoke of. So I left."

"Do you miss them? Your family?"

"After the siege of Paris, Ragnhild joined me. From her I received the news that the king's son had murdered my father. They trapped him and his men in his house and set the place on fire. Not one of them made it out alive."

Poppa's eyes widened.

"I was told that the king was angered and heavily grieved by the news of my lord father's death. He followed his wishes and made Thorir heir to all of my lord father's lands. Thankfully, my lady mother was spared the fire, for she had died a few years before."

Rollo sighed as he sat up. "But to answer your question—no, I don't miss them. My family are the men and women who fight with me. Although, I'd have liked to see my mother again so I could remember her face."

Poppa regarded him carefully as his hand returned to her hair. She placed her hand over his, pressed his palm to her cheek, and rested her head in it.

"Now I see the wisdom of what's written, that a man shall leave his family and go to the arms of his wife." He smiled at her tenderly, satisfied, then rose from the bed. "But I must leave you for some time as I attend to matters."

Poppa watched in dismay as he put on a fresh pair of small-clothes and breeches. She pouted prettily.

He gave her a crooked smile before he crawled to her from the bottom edge of the bed. He leaned in and kissed her pouty lip.

"Most likely I've missed the ships that have set out for Bayeux, but I'll visit the men leaving on foot. Then I have a few more items to see to, but later tonight I wish to take you in the tepidarium."

Poppa's eyebrow raised. "A thought that no doubt will play over and over in your mind until you return to me."

Rollo smiled brightly at her in agreement.

"If I could ask for a favor," she tried. She had waited for the right time to ask. "You may not like it."

"As if I could refuse you anything. Whatever you ask for, you will have it."

Poppa gave him a small smile. "I'd like to visit the church. I need to confess and receive forgiveness for my part in Myra's death."

Rollo's features screwed up into an expression of concentration, but only for a moment before they softened and he nodded. "You humble me, lady wife. I'll accompany you. I've many things I need to atone for as well. I don't remember the time of my last confession."

The cathedral, still under construction from the first of Rollo's raids, stood proudly, though battered and bruised, overlooking the city. Poppa noticed bricklayers working high up on scaffolds. Rollo explained his expansive plans for the building. Though he painted a beautiful vision of what the cathedral would look like, they both knew neither of them would live to see it completed. They entered through a side door, where a young man in a brown robe greeted them. He had a humble and nervous face. Conscious of his lazy eye, he kept his eyes downcast. From that angle, Poppa could see his tonsure, the purposefully shaved bald patch that rounded the crown of his head.

"Jarl Rollo!" The monk couldn't keep his surprise from his voice.

"We come for confession. Is there an abbot available?" Poppa spoke.

"Both of you?"

Poppa could feel the frustration building in Rollo. Afraid he might change his mind out of annoyance, she placed her arm through his and pulled him close to her.

"Yes, please."

The monk bowed respectfully. "Wait here."

He left them in the atrium. The silence that fills all holy places overtook them as they waited. To the right, a door creaked open and then closed. The relief Poppa felt when she saw the archbishop walking toward them echoed the relief one feels from the first drink of water after coming out of the desert. She bowed her head respectfully as he approached.

"My children, welcome." The archbishop spoke with open arms. Wearing a humble black tunic, he had a comely elderly face, and his brown hair shone with flecks of gray. "Brother Thomas tells me you come seeking absolution."

Rollo shifted from one foot to the other. Poppa eyed him sideways.

"We would be most grateful, Père," Poppa spoke for the both of them.

"Père Guillaume," he introduced himself. "And you're Poppa de Bayeux. I've wondered when you would visit here."

"Ladies first," Rollo spoke.

She turned to him, her eyes searching his. She gave him a small encouraging smile. "I can't tell you what this means to me."

She kissed him and then turned to walk away with the abbot.

He led her into the nave and down a long hall with polished wooden pews on each side. A sacred stillness hung lightly in the cavernous room. Colored light pooled from the stained glass windows and cast rainbows of light upon the surfaces. Poppa stood still for a moment and closed her eyes, letting the holiness of the place wash over her. The abbot observed her and smiled knowingly when she opened them again.

"It has been some time since you've entered in a church?"

"Not so long, but much has happened since I last stepped inside and felt His presence. I feel like a new person."

"We would be overjoyed to have you attend mass," Père Guillaume spoke. He had a pleasant and soothing voice.

"I'd like that very much," Poppa spoke as her vision traveled down to her hands.

"But today you're burdened."

Poppa felt the tears build behind her eyes.

"Tell me what troubles you."

Poppa told him the whole story of what had happened in the moments leading up to the end of the siege on Bayeux. She didn't hide anything from him. She told him of Lord Peter's order to kill Myra before allowing her to be captured. She spoke of the hopeless moments they'd spent waiting. Then, finally, she admitted her decision to switch places—how she'd encouraged Myra to flee to her death. She hadn't known the fate that awaited her friend at the time, but still. She described the battle that had ensued when the

Norsemen broke into the room, and the man who'd fallen at her feet after a blow from her sword. He listened intently to all she said without interrupting and motioned for her to continue when the telling became too difficult. When she finished, tears streamed down her face. "Do you think I can find forgiveness?"

Père Guillaume smiled warmly at her before he began, "The gospel of Saint John writes that there is no greater love than to lay down one's life for another. I believe you intended to do this when you took the place of your friend. You sent her out to what you believed to be her freedom and a second chance. You saved her from a fate possibly worse than death, while you yourself took that fate upon yourself. For that, I don't think you're at fault for anything that happened to her after she left your presence."

Poppa let out a heavy sigh as relief flooded through her. The weight of Myra's death lifted off her shoulders almost instantly.

"Now," Père Guillaume continued, "about the life you took after that. Though in self-defense, I do believe we should pray together for forgiveness and for the soul of the man who fell by your sword."

Poppa nodded obediently and prayed with him. When they finished, she rose and turned to go. Then she noticed he wasn't following her.

"The unspoken burden, my child," he called after her.

She turned slowly and stared into his kind and knowing eyes. She sat down again and waited.

"You're still worried about God's blessing on your marriage, and you question the truth of your husband's conversion."

Poppa turned her gaze away from his wise blue stare and into the hands in her lap. She gave a small nod.

"I baptized Robert myself," Père Guillaume confessed. "In honesty, I too questioned his devotion. But over time, I've come to a much different conclusion. The Word of God speaks to patience thirty-three times. It's my belief that we must exercise patience with those who have converted. Especially these pagans who rule our lands. We must look at conversion not only as a singular event but as a process that inevitably takes time to complete. Robert still clings to many of his pagan customs and will most likely struggle with that alongside his faith his entire life."

Poppa nodded in understanding and agreement.

With a twinkle in his eye, the abbot asked, "Can you be patient with him?"

"Love is patient, Père."

He smiled warmly and took her hands in his, kissing them both. "As for your marriage, I was instructed by Robert prior to your arrival to send a letter to both King Charles and the Pope requesting the designation *more danico*. Meaning 'in the Danish manner.' I find this appropriate, considering the nature of the union and Jarl Rollo's previous marriage—even though he was widowered. It is an affirmation that the Church, though not involved, recognizes the marriage in a sense. However, I must mention that under *more danico*, there is an allowance for him to take more than one wife, as that is allowed in Dane and Norse law."

"I was unaware he had done so," Poppa replied. "I thank you for your hand in this matter. I'm grateful the Church has granted us the title, though I may not favor that last part. It will have to do. I've had a great burden lifted off my soul today, Père."

She wrapped her arms around him and hugged him before leaving. She found Rollo waiting for her in the atrium.

"I don't think that I've seen you smile this wide in these short days that I've known you, lady wife."

"I hope you feel as light of heart as I do when you're finished. He's waiting for you."

Rollo gave her a nervous smile that seemed to make him grow younger as his hand clenched and unclenched at his side. Then he turned and walked into the nave, his footfalls heavy on the stone floor.

She waited a long while for him to return. When he did, he walked taller than before, as if lighter. She wondered if she'd looked similar coming out of the nave. He didn't wear the smile of relief, but his brown eyes sparkled in the light of the atrium. His face seemed younger, smoother. He didn't turn away from her as he walked toward her. With a crooked smile, he mused, "I do like that man."

Poppa returned his smile. "It shouldn't surprise you, then, when I tell you that in my vision, I knew our son as Guillaume."

Rollo shot her an astonished look and then put his head back for a deep, throaty laugh. The sound echoed off the walls of the atrium as he guided her to the door, his arm around her waist. Poppa paused for a moment and looked at him seriously. "Rollo . . ." She hesitated. "I have to know you believe what I told you and everyone in the hall last night. I need you to understand that it was as real for me as you standing before me now."

Rollo's face darkened for a moment as he paused and looked around the room. "Come outside with me."

Poppa followed him out into the bright light of the morning in the busy town square. Rollo led her to a large tree and grassy knoll, where it was less populated. He waited a moment before explaining, "The Norse believe all of our days are planned out before us. When we will be born, when we will marry, and when we will die. All life's events are known to the gods; therefore, the future can only be known if the gods choose to reveal it. So the initial answer is yes, I do believe your vision. But there's so much more you must understand."

Rollo paused. His expression was serious, his eyes narrowed, but his voice sounded rushed and excited. "Ragnhild is my family. Her grandmother was my grandfather's youngest sister. She was named after our great-grandmother, a famous queen of Norway who once had a vision similar to yours. A great tree grew from a brooch in her hand. The branches and roots spread all over Norway and to lands beyond. Colors were present in her vision as well . . . most notably red, for bloodshed. As in yours.

"She didn't understand the full meaning, and many wrote it off as *draumskrok*, the nonsense of dreams. But as time went on, our people prospered and multiplied rapidly. It became necessary for us to travel and raid for our resources. We found prosperous lands with weak defenses while we experienced overpopulation in our own homeland. The choice to conquer became clear. That's when my great-grandmother fully understood her vision. The tree was her bloodline."

Poppa let out a surprised sigh and lowered herself to a small bench. Her knees felt weak as Rollo continued.

"So you see, Poppa, your vision was an extension of an already promised and known future. Queen Ragnhild's vision is well understood among my people. Most often it's shared around the night fires before battle. It reminds our people that the lands we seek already belong to us. The blood we shed isn't only justified but fated. Though at first, I wasn't happy about your demands and assumptions before my people. Your untoward presentation was reckless and challenged my authority. Lesser men have died for such a thing. Nevertheless, you made the right decision to bring the message before the hall. Through your vision, you've confirmed not only my supremacy as their leader but also the might of our legacy to come. I and my people rejoice to know that the promises given to my great-grandmother will be carried through my blood. Her future, now ours."

Rollo stood before her, serene and at peace.

Poppa remarked, "I don't know how I can encourage you to abandon the traditions and customs of your youth. It seems we're blessed by both your gods and the Lord God."

"I'm trying," Rollo confessed.

"I know, and I'll be content. I don't want this to become a thorn between us. I'm thankful you came to confession with me today. I do want our children to know the Lord."

Rollo smiled at her. "And they surely will. As well as the promises given to them by the generations who came before them."

THE HUNT

THEY ASSEMBLED AT DAWN in front of the stables. Servants moved quickly through the crowd, checking provisions and securing harnesses on the horses. Though the day would feel warm once the sun rose fully, the night's chill still lingered upon the air. Poppa wrapped her furs around herself and held them tight as she watched a serving boy lead a golden chestnut palfrey in her direction. She stroked the fine beast and removed a tiny amount of sugar from a leather satchel on her waist. She offered the sugar to the horse and giggled at the feel of its rough tongue upon her hand.

Rollo bellowed orders and servants scrambled to do his bidding. Several of his men had joined them for the hunt. Sigrid, an older shield-maiden (not to be confused with her daughter and namesake, whom Rollo had married to Ingmar), stood beside Ragnhild as they shared a horn of ale and laughter. Eager for the hunt to begin, Herleif stayed close to his horse. He bounced uncharacteristically from foot to foot, and Poppa noticed that all assembled shared the same excitement. She imagined they behaved similarly on the precipice of battle. Rollo took the lead as he announced the assigned roles each of the gathered would fill.

Poppa lifted herself up onto the horse and swung her left leg around to straddle it. The saddle felt unfamiliar under her. She knew she'd be sore by the day's end. She carried a crossbow as her weapon. Rollo had reviewed its functions with her the night before as they stood on the terrace and took aim at a target several yards away. He'd even given her a tool to help span the thick string back behind the slot to ease the pull. Still, this would take time to accomplish. In anticipation, she had loaded one bolt before they left. She would have to make sure that she aimed her shot well. The loaded crossbow hung from a leather strap that she wore crosswise over her shoulder. The wooden quarrels, crudely formed, had a metal tip shaped like a crescent so as not to go completely through the prey. Rollo and many others would arm themselves with long spears they could throw from horseback to wound the prey and slow it down before they overtook it.

Poppa considered the commotion around her and felt nostalgic as she noticed the wolfhounds prance and bark. They too felt the excitement of the day's activities, for they would run down the prey to tire it out before anyone threw a spear. Poppa found Ragnhild, who wore kohl in a line across her eyes and symbols painted on her forehead and cheeks. Clad in her black leathers, she looked ready for battle. Her arm was extended out before her, a brown and white-feathered hawk perched and tethered atop. Ragnhild held fast to a small leather string dangling from its right claw. She would release the raptor if the wounded prey became lost to them. The party would follow its flight until it circled the air several times and dove at an amazing speed. Then the hunting party would ride to the spot directly below in hopes of finding the wounded animal.

Rollo conversed with the huntsman who'd gone out the week before to study the area and find the trails of the herd. Poppa moved her horse closer so she could hear the plans as they unfolded. When she arrived at Rollo's side, a serving boy greeted her with a plate of fruit and dried meat to break her fast.

Rollo ordered his hound keepers to start along the path he and the huntsman had agreed upon. The limer, a scent hound, stayed with the party. He would help lead them on the correct course. He glanced up at Poppa, clearly sharing her excitement.

She watched as Rollo mounted his large brown horse. It was the largest horse she'd ever seen, and it held Rollo's vast frame deftly. He looked striking in the early morning light as he swung one large leg around his ornate saddle. He had pulled his hair back from his face and plaited it down his back. Strands escaped and rippled upon the morning's breeze. As he surveyed Poppa, his intense eyes lightened with a smile. A smile framed by facial hair she had groomed and shaped as they'd bathed in the warm waters of the tepidarium the night before. He looked even larger in the tan hunting furs that were wrapped tightly around him. A large hunting horn made from the curved horn of a bull hung about his neck and fastened to a clip on his leathers. When blown, its sound would resonate deeply and signal to the rest of the party that a kill was imminent. He leaned down toward a serving boy to receive a spear that he tied carefully to his back. Two other young men would follow Rollo closely throughout the hunt to carry his spare spears.

Poppa again felt a now-familiar lightness of heart and pride as she observed her husband. Then she recalled his explanation for why they'd sailed from Bayeux to Rouen. She slanted a quizzical look at him.

He caught her studying him and said sardonically, "As you saw in Vexin, the rumors are a jest. I can sit a horse. Slei and I have seen many hunts together."

She returned his crooked smile with laughter as she watched him lovingly stroke the neck of the horse and whisper something into her ear.

"Slei?"

Rollo smiled. "Named after Sleipnir. Odin's faithful steed."

Poppa nodded knowingly. She should've known he'd choose a name tied to the legends of his people. Secretly, she wondered if he'd insist their children take names from the legends as well.

Rollo winked at her before turning in his saddle toward the assembly. He bellowed in his deep voice, "Let the chase begin!"

Cheers of excitement rose in answer as Rollo led the charge down the hill and away from the town. The shrill, excited battle cry that left Poppa's lips surprised her. She gave a meaningful light kick to her horse and felt it pull beneath her as they set off. Her horse kept pace with Rollo's. She looked over at him and smiled as her plaited hair flew in the wind behind her. She could hear the other horses gain ground behind her, but they left a gap to let Rollo stay in the lead.

They rode until the sun climbed to midmorning. The sky lightened to bright blue before they came upon their first group of hounds, in tall wheat that shone golden in the rising sun's reflection. The party slowed and let the limer sniff. The scent hound put his nose to the ground for a moment. Then suddenly his ears perked up, and he set off toward the left, where the open field turned into a wooded area. The assembly followed for some time until the limer led them to a small tributary of the Seine. The dogs lost the scent at the river's edge.

Rollo cursed in a language Poppa didn't understand. He dismounted and paced at the edge of the water. If the herd had gone in the water, the party could waste hours trying to search for it again. The guide took the limer, who moved willingly through the water, to the opposite bank. The river came up to meet the man just above his calf; they could cross easily. On the other side, the limer again put his nose to the ground. He darted back and forth on the opposite bank. The assembly watched with bated breath before the hound's ears perked up and his nose pointed to the right, where they could see a clearing in the woods.

Rollo smiled wide and white as he let out a hoot of joy and raised a fist in the air. The assembly followed his celebration. They quickly guided their horses through the stream. The slow-moving water felt cool on Poppa's leather boots and quickly soaked them through. This concerned her little. She knew they'd dry in the heat of the day's sun. The party followed the trail until they spotted the herd feeding on alfalfa in a large clearing several yards off. Does and stags mingled freely together, innocent of the chaos that would soon befall them. Rollo ordered his men to release the hounds. The assembly watched from afar as the canines caught the scent and went running. They scattered the herd, chasing the deer in every direction. The hounds, kept from their morning meal, ran hungrily toward the promise of food. Poppa watched three hounds as they banded together and gave chase to a large hart, a male red deer, into the woods before them.

Rollo signaled for everyone to disband and chase after their chosen prey before turning to Poppa and telling her to stay close to him. All in the party allowed Rollo to take the hart, the prize prey of this hunt. Their horses ran together into the woods where they'd seen the hart retreat. They flew over the fields of wheat and into the shadows of the ancient trees at the edge of the meadow. The footfalls of their horses rhythmically clomped as they galloped. The spearmen had followed in pursuit. Rollo and Poppa turned their path to the sound of barking dogs. Suddenly, to their right they heard the low sound of a horn. Poppa looked toward the sound and saw a dark shape circle in the sky. Ragnhild's hawk flew effortlessly upon the sky. Someone had wounded a deer.

A grim determination fell over Rollo. He was hungry for his own kill.

They moved stealthily through the woods, careful to make little noise as they drew closer to the hounds and their barking. It grew darker and colder as the trees filtered the light from above. Poppa glanced at her surroundings and saw moss growing on the deadfall beneath the dense tree cover. Thick brown leaves covered the floor of the forest, and the flora smelled sweet and intoxicating. She wanted to close her eyes and let the thick smell wrap around her, but Rollo had stopped up ahead. He signaled for her to do the same. She slowly came up behind him, careful to leave enough space should he need to throw his spear. As she neared, she saw what had caught his attention. A few yards ahead, the hart stood facing them. It's great rack of antlers slanted down, ready to attack the approaching hounds. Three hounds slowly crouched before their quarry, their teeth bared yet cautious about approaching any further.

Rollo blew his horn and then whistled to the dogs to keep them at heel. They obeyed, knowing it wasn't their job to attack. Poppa's heart beat faster as she focused on the scene. With small, careful movements, she unlatched the bow behind her, brought it to her shoulder, and aimed. At the same time, Rollo released his spear from its hold. Then he gripped the spear strongly around its middle and raised it in the air, preparing to throw. The hart had taken no notice of them until that moment. When it looked at Rollo, he threw with precision. The spear soared through the air before planting itself in the hide of the stag with a thunk. The beast stumbled and slowly tried to move through the woods to take cover.

With pity, Poppa lifted her bow and followed the slow-but-frenzied movements of the wounded animal. Her hand steady on the trigger lever, she narrowed her eyes but found no clear shot. She dismounted and slowly moved over the ground of the forest. The beast watched her warily. She lifted her bow again, steadied it against her shoulder, and then aimed. When she felt sure of her mark, she squeezed the lever. A bolt shot out at an amazing speed and hit the deer in the neck. Its lifeblood flowed swiftly from its carotid artery as the beast fell to the earth and died. Poppa was thankful for that.

A great cheer went up throughout the forest. Poppa turned to see the assembly gathered, coming from varying directions, between trees. She hadn't even known the others had joined them. Rollo came to her side and wrapped an arm around her approvingly. He pulled her close and kissed the top of her head.

Rollo retrieved his knife, as did the young men who carried his spears. It was time for the unmaking. They carved into the carcass with swift and calculated movements. Rollo retrieved the heart. It steamed when it hit the chill of the forest air. He motioned for Poppa to come to him. She could smell the stag's death as she neared, but she held her stomach and kept her eyes averted from the gruesome scene. What Rollo did next felt primal. He took two fingers and bloodied them on the heart; then he used those stained fingers to trace lines on her cheeks and forehead. Poppa could smell the metallic scent of blood, but she held still, allowing him to finish. When he finished, he made matching marks on his own face.

"A kill we made together," Rollo said solemnly to all gathered. "We honor this stag by wearing its lifeblood this day. Tonight we'll feast on its meat, and we'll use its hide to make our clothing."

Then he placed the heart in a small leather satchel at his waist and wiped his hands on the furs he wore. When they removed the choice parts, Rollo allowed for the curèe, rewarding the hounds for their part by allowing them to eat what remained. Poppa had to turn from the scene as they ravaged the beast who had stood so regal minutes before.

That night they feasted in the great hall of their home with all who had participated in the hunt. Rollo retold the tale of the chase and the final moments of the hunt often enough so that all who sat within earshot could pass it on in full for years to come. He sent a large portion of both meat and ale to the servants and allowed them to enjoy a celebration of their own. Rollo joked to all who would listen that he would place the stag's large rack above their bed. Poppa answered with a roll of her eyes as she poured herself another horn of ale. She felt light of heart and light of mind when they fell into bed later that night. Rollo wrapped his arms around her. He pulled her close in need and in celebration of their hunt.

Shield-Maiden

AFTER THE HUNT, A YEARNING RETURNED to Poppa's heart—the same kind of yearning for activity and excitement she'd often felt in swordplay. For days afterward, she allowed it to grow within her as her boredom fanned its flame.

◇◇◇◇◇

One evening, in the early hours, their bedroom darkened from the absence of the sun, they waited together for their dinner to arrive. A large fire provided enough light for Rollo to read from a leather-bound book. A journal, made of bound parchment, and a quill rested on an upholstered chair near him. He felt peaceful and content after their recent lovemaking. On the other side of the room, Poppa wasn't as calm. She paced back and forth from one wall to the other. She twisted around a thin piece of scarlet in her hands. Her head shook back and forth as she paced, arguing with herself. Rollo attempted to ignore her, but her anxiety grated on his nerves until he could bear it no longer.

"By the gods of heaven and Asgard, what's bothering you, woman?" Rollo rested his book in his lap. He turned his full attention to his wife, who had stopped her pacing. She returned his stare, eyes shining with an anxious gleam.

She nodded her head once and walked over to where he sat.

"No," she told herself and walked back to the bed.

"Poppa," Rollo said impatiently, his tone low with warning. "I'm getting nothing done with your incessant pacing. Tell me what's bothering you and what I can do to ease your burden—or be done so I can go back to my studies."

Poppa gave a resigned sigh. "I want to ask something of you, but I'm afraid you'll say no. I also know that if it's an answer that's not acceptable to me . . . I don't long to quarrel, but—"

"Well, stewing over it obviously isn't doing anybody any good. Have a seat and warm yourself by the fire."

Rollo rose to pour them both a horn of spiced wine, but instead of following his instructions, Poppa waited for him to rest in his chair again. When he looked comfortable, she kneeled humbly before him. A smile twitched on his lips, but he resolved to keep himself stone-faced and unaffected, already knowing he would give her whatever she desired. His gaze fell to the glow of the fire attached to her. Her head bowed, she cast her eyes down to look at the hands that still fretted and twisted a piece of cloth.

Finally, she shared, "For days on end I'm confined to the grounds of this house. It's beautiful, it really is, but Rollo, I've nothing to occupy my time. I wander around all day while you see to the management of your land and your people. When in Bayeux, Myra and I were always busy from one task to the next. We hunted. We danced. While she had her lessons, I had my own . . . on the training grounds with my sword—"

"You're bored and have need of a friend. We can find you—"

"I don't want a friend to stay with me. I want to do something useful! I long to train again. For the exercise and the challenge. I've already talked to Ragnhild, and she said she would train with me as long as you agreed. Then she said, 'May the luck of Loki be with you.' I don't really understand that. Wasn't he the bad one?"

Rollo laughed in his deep baritone and then dismissed her words with a wave of the hand. "Loki is neither bad nor good. He's reliable only in the sense that he'll always do what's right for him. He's a master manipulator. Perhaps that's what she meant. As for the question itself, I was there the day Ragnhild was born. I was a boy of eight. Our mothers were close for as long as I can remember. Ragnhild came out of her lady mother's womb with a spear in hand. She was combative her whole life and has bested men twice her size. No, we will find another occupation for you."

Poppa rose from her humbled position and towered over him as he sat relaxed in the chair. "Another occupation? Rollo, I'm not asking to go to war. I'm only asking for a couple of hours a day to hone my skills with someone who's well matched. Someone I could learn from. Are you only objecting because you fear for my safety?"

Rollo rubbed his temples and shrugged. "That, yes. And I'm not convinced of its necessity. As you said—you aren't going to war, and you aren't in need of protection. We have guards, and those guards have guards."

Poppa stared at him more calmly. She knew she'd won as she concluded, "Guards and the guards of those guards failed me the last time."

Rollo examined her for a moment in awe. She had beaten him with her argument. Inwardly, he fought with his pride. Outwardly, he rose and turned his back to her so she couldn't see the conflict warring on his face. Poppa waited patiently; perhaps she'd pushed too far. She hadn't quite learned how to balance on this tightrope of Rollo's power that conflicted with her will.

Finally, he called over his shoulder, "I'll speak with Ragnhild. That's the best answer you'll get this night. Be content with it."

Poppa wanted to run to him. She wanted to wrap her arms around him and thank him by bringing him back to bed, but his next words came out in a growl. "Now leave me. I long for peace as I finish my reading."

He'd never cast her from his presence before. When he turned back to her, his tall frame seemed to take up more space in the room. He looked striking in his loose linen shirt and breeches. His long hair was pulled away from his face and tied up in a bun behind his head. Less than an hour earlier he'd held her in his arms, her legs wrapped around his back as they entered into shared bliss, kissing and holding each other. Now her desire for him felt blocked by his haunted eyes and shuttered expression. She'd won but at the cost of his temper. She'd asked him to go against his judgment and his wishes.

She left the room quietly, relieved of her anxiety but shaken by his change in mood.

◆◆◆◆◆

Poppa sensed Ragnhild's presence in the house, but Rollo and Ragnhild hadn't invited her to sit with them as they discussed her request. Desperate to hear their conversation, she positioned herself on the stairs, out of sight but within earshot. Moments before, she'd made a point of announcing that she planned to pick apples from the orchard and take her lunch with her. Most likely, she wouldn't return for some time, so they shouldn't worry. Of course, roaming marauders might take her off guard and kidnap her, which Rollo could prevent by allowing her to keep a frequent training schedule. He had dismissed her impatiently but with a crooked grin, assuring her they'd pay the hefty ransom. Then, under the watchful eye of the amused Mrs. Laurent, she'd doubled back, entering the house through the servant's quarters and using their staircase to ascend to the second floor. Finally, she descended the main staircase and quietly took her perch on the stairs. She couldn't see them, but their voices echoed clearly up the staircase.

"You must admire her courage for even asking," Ragnhild spoke first.

Poppa could hear Ragnhild move a chair across the floor, and then a soft bang resounded up the stairs as she brought her leg down upon the table. A feminine sigh of comfort shortly followed.

"From the first day she came into my life, I knew not to question her bravery."

"How charming."

"You don't like her."

"I never said that, nor do I think my behavior suggests it. But she's not one of us. And you've changed since becoming her husband. She perplexes me with her contradictions."

"How so?"

"She's highborn, yet she's not proud. She professes her devotion to her faith in the Lord Jesus Christ, and yet she's fascinated by our gods and tolerates your indifference to Christianity. She challenges your authority but has come to respect your decisions. When I think I know how she's going to react, she surprises me and does the opposite, like when she came to me and asked me to train with her."

Rollo smiled as he listened to Ragnhild's observations.

"You're reluctant," Ragnhild observed further. "You're afraid she'll get hurt."

"If I do agree, that's one of the stipulations that should go without saying: you must not harm her. At all."

Poppa heard Ragnhild let out a snort. "You really do love her, don't you?"

"I'll confess, I didn't think it was possible. Perhaps that's what will make our seed strong."

"About that," Ragnhild queried, "any word?"

"Not yet."

Poppa sensed the darkness in her husband's voice and felt an uncomfortable knot in her stomach. She was embarrassed that the two were discussing her womb without her. Disappointment was her constant and unwanted friend these days. She'd bled two weeks ago, dashing their hopes. During the days of her bleeding, Rollo had come home late in the early morning hours, distant as he collapsed into bed and fell fast asleep. He hadn't acted unkindly to her, but disappointment radiated off of him. She couldn't help but feel she'd let him down.

"Don't worry," Ragnhild cheered. "There are many more chances before the moon turns again. Give her this distraction, Rollo."

"But if she's carrying and the baby is harmed . . ."

To this Ragnhild laughed sardonically. "Your own lady mother raised both shield and sword while she carried you in her belly. I remember my lady mother telling me stories of her fierceness and prowess despite the heavy weight of her womb. Perhaps that's why you're the warrior you are, and perhaps that's what your son will need to start his own training. What could be more our custom?"

"I see I'm not going to win. You females need not practice with swords at all, for your tongues are the blades by which men fall."

Ragnhild laughed, "I only beseech you to remember where you come from. Women were at liberty in our homeland—more than they are here."

"Two hours a day, and if you get any inkling that she's with child—"

"I'll ease up, but it's healthy for her to remain active."

"You think she can handle it?"

"Rollo, she bested Wagner after wounding two of our men. Some of our best. Elof still brags about the burns he received from her torch, and Ivar had the slash that brought him to his knees tattooed so he can forever remember. They're proud of her strength."

Rollo laughed, thinking of his men. "She'll start on the morrow. If it's to be a success, you must treat her like you would the other *skjaldmær*. Do not award her special privileges because of her station. Maybe then she'll give up and find a new hobby."

Ragnhild laughed delightedly, "Be careful what you wish for. I'll train her hard, and you cannot blame me if she's not able to take you to bed when she returns."

Ragnhild still laughed as she dismissed herself and opened the large oak doors to go. "One last thing," she instructed. "I don't want you present on the grounds. I don't need her distracted with thoughts of pleasing you. When she has made appropriate progress, we will dance with our swords for you."

Rollo smiled and nodded his head in agreement.

Poppa sat on the stairs, her heart beating loudly in anticipation. In the excitement, she forgot that she wasn't supposed to be there. She had no time to disappear. His heavy footfalls reached the base of the stairs and came closer every second.

Rollo didn't startle when he stumbled upon her several stairs up. An empty basket sat by her side. He gave her an amused grin and walked past her on his way upstairs, calling back over his shoulder, "It looks as though apple picking was quite fruitful for you, lady wife."

Poppa said nothing about the discovery of her deception. Instead she followed him.

"Did you think I didn't know your plan? We could have spoken in our mothers' tongues if we didn't want you listening." Rollo tried to hide a smirk at her shocked look before continuing, "I'm tired, Poppa, and I desire a nap. Come and warm my bed. I shall like to enjoy your body once more before it's too sore to move freely."

In the morning, Poppa donned the clothes Ragnhild had sent over. The two women were a similar size, but Poppa's muscles had room to grow in the concaves of cloth that fit a more trained woman. In time, Poppa would have her own clothes made. Mrs. Laurent had come to pull back her hair in plaits. Currently, she showed Poppa how to tighten the brown leather bodice over her linen shirt. The leather matched the belt across her waist. She pulled to tighten it. She had a more difficult time reaching the buckles over her shoulder. Then she placed the two leather wrist cuffs on her arms, and Mrs. Laurent pulled the laces tight and tied to hold them fast. Poppa buckled the leather boots that reached right below her knees over her leather pants as Rollo came in.

He whistled at the sight and then quietly assessed her. It wasn't the first time Poppa felt naked under his glance, but she yearned to please him more than before, and her heartbeat increased under his heavy-eyed scrutiny. He began to check the fastenings and adjusted them to his liking. Though his fingers sent chills throughout her body as they grazed her, he meant nothing sensual as he pulled and stretched the leather tighter.

"It's too tight." Poppa fussed with her fingers as she tried to loosen the leather bindings.

"It'll loosen as you move. It will fit you better this way." Rollo placed his hands over her fidgeting fingers. He brought them to his lips where he whispered a kiss upon them.

He turned and retrieved a long blue sheath from the table in the bedroom.

"My father's sword." Poppa smiled with gratitude as he handed her the familiar blade.

Poppa pulled the sword out, freeing it from its sheath. She savored the familiar swoosh of metal against the inside of the case. She held the blade before her to admire its shine. A swordsmith had paid close attention to the sword. It had been cleaned, polished, and sharpened. She ran her thumb over the blade lightly.

She turned it over and followed the light that danced upon the ripples where the smiths had folded the metal and beat it in the forging process. She had memorized those ripples as well as she had memorized her father's thin frame as he'd danced upon the ground, holding the sword in his hand and besting men two at a time.

Poppa smiled at Rollo through her tears. "This means very much to me. Thank you."

"Someday you'll tell me more about your father. For now, you must hurry. Ragnhild is most punctual and doesn't favor pupils who arrive late."

Poppa kissed him and stepped back to let him admire her garments. He smiled then and kissed her forehead tenderly. "There's one more thing."

He pulled a small silver object, barely smaller than her pinky finger, from his pocket. His large fingers fumbled clumsily with it as he turned it around and showed her the small figure of a woman. She had long hair, a tiny sword in a belt at her side, and a shield in her left hand. Poppa scanned him with questioning eyes as he pinned it to the leather bodice above her right breast.

"It belonged to my lady mother," he explained. "It was the only item I took from her before I left. My lord father searched for it everywhere, but I didn't confess. I hid it, knowing I'd keep it forever."

Poppa placed her left hand over the pin and covered it protectively. Rollo smiled down on her. Poppa thought she saw his eyes glisten, but he moved quickly past her and into the room. "Thank you," she called after him before she left.

The late spring sun kissed her skin warmly as she entered the training grounds. Word had traveled through the city that she would start training. Ragnhild had cleared out the eager onlookers, much to their dismay. When Ragnhild returned to stand before her, Poppa couldn't help but admire her fierceness. She clad herself in a similar dress, but she wore it more naturally, as if it was her skin itself. Following her custom, Ragnhild had ringed her bright blue eyes with black kohl. However, today they seemed more menacing than Poppa remembered. She had her long blond hair twisted, knotted, and gathered behind her head, battle ready.

"We'll warm our muscles first," Ragnhild instructed. Poppa followed her in a series of stretches. As Rollo had said, she could feel the leather hug and adjust to her body as she moved. When they finished with their stretches, Ragnhild asked, "Are you as familiar with a shield as you are with a sword?"

Poppa confessed she wasn't. She'd practiced with a shield before, but the majority of her previous training had focused on swordplay alone.

Ragnhild nodded knowingly. "We'll begin with the shield, then."

Ragnhild pulled a round oaken shield from the wall. About a meter in diameter and painted forest green with a white rune spanning from top to bottom, the shield looked cumbersome. A metal cone protruded outward from the center. Its intent was to assist in the push of rushing soldiers. It felt heavy in Poppa's arm as Ragnhild passed it to her. She gripped the leather backing tightly, though, and felt the muscles of her left arm strain.

"The shield is a weapon as much as a means of defense," Ragnhild started. "As the sword is an extension of your arm, the shield is an extension of your entire body. You will learn to move your sword around your shield, and how to use your shield to bludgeon and move objects out of your way. But first you need to get used to its weight."

Ragnhild grabbed her own shield from the ground and lifted it above her head in one swift motion, over and over. Poppa followed suit, straining a bit under the weight.

"You will do ten of these with each arm in the morning, afternoon, evening, and before bed. We won't waste time with this during practice. In a week or so, we will double the number."

Poppa reluctantly agreed. She hadn't expected that the training would extend outside the training grounds.

Ragnhild left and came back with a blunted training sword. Poppa received it and spun it in her arm to test its weight and balance. When she felt satisfied, she made a routine of upper and lower slashes. Ragnhild considered her before striking her sword against Poppa's sword. Poppa felt the blow reverberate into her hand and down her shoulder. She sustained the shock and strengthened her grip on the sword. She swung the steel extension of her arm in a wide arc and returned the blow. They parried like this back and forth for some time as they tested each other's strengths and weaknesses.

Poppa had a sheen of sweat upon her forehead and breathed heavily when they broke for water. She wore a satisfied grin on her face as she confessed, "I'd forgotten how much I missed this."

"There's no doubt you're very gifted," Ragnhild complimented. "Much better than others I've trained. Don't let that go to your head though. You've much to learn. Your feet need firmer grounding or you won't succeed in holding the weight of an oncoming charge. You favor your right side, leaving your left side open for attack. If I remember correctly, that's where Wagner left his mark. The shield will help with that, though. Come—let's see how long you can hold onto both."

In a short time, Poppa found herself on the ground, coughing on soft dirt. Ragnhild circled her like a hawk as she rose to her hands and knees. That's when the kick came. It wasn't hard, but it was enough to topple her over and flip her onto her back. Poppa looked up, the bright sun shining into her eyes—until Ragnhild eclipsed it. The young woman stared down upon her, blunted sword pointed inches from Poppa's face. Exhausted, Poppa breathed heavily and raised her palms in surrender.

"Third time's the charm?" Ragnhild laughed at her. "You're allowing me too much ground. You—ah!"

Ragnhild stopped midsentence as Poppa clamped the sword pointing in her face with both hands. She held it in place as she kicked her legs hard in a twist, wrapping them around Ragnhild's legs and forcing her to the ground.

Ragnhild fell on her back, the wind knocked from her lungs. Then she turned her head and looked over at Poppa. Both of them laid on their backs and breathed hard. Poppa thought she would see anger, but instead she found pride in Ragnhild's eyes. Then she laughed, deeply and heartily. "Never give up," Ragnhild instructed between her laughs. "I see the fight in you. I won't be so kind in the next lesson."

Poppa rose to her feet first and offered her hand to Ragnhild, who accepted and allowed Poppa to pull her up from the ground. At that moment, Poppa noticed small droplets of red drop into the sand at her feet. When she removed her hand from her nose, she saw her fingers covered in red. Ragnhild produced a rag from inside her sleeve and handed it to her. Poppa wiped her bleeding nose before putting pressure on the bridge to stem the flow.

"Remember the shield. Carry it all the way home for good measure. The common folk will like it."

Rollo wasn't home when Poppa returned in the late afternoon. She could already feel the soreness creeping into her muscles. She didn't know how she would move, let alone raise a sword on the morrow. She employed the help of Mrs. Laurent to undress in the tepidarium. The thought of the warm water enveloping her muscles almost made her want to cry.

She closed her eyes and let the relaxing water do its work on her muscles. She awoke to the sound of water splashing. She could feel the ripples against her skin as the water displaced. Rollo, naked, entered the bath gingerly. Poppa smiled tiredly at him as she admired the tattoos that twisted in angles across his chest. He didn't break eye contact with her as he stepped in and let the water cover his nakedness. His long hair was loose and soon wet at the tips. He swam over to her.

"Keep your distance," Poppa teased as she splashed water into his face.

"I can be gentle," Rollo teased as he, unhindered by her splashing water, moved toward her.

"Everything hurts," Poppa whined.

"This is what you wanted," Rollo reminded her unsympathetically as he kissed her neck and behind her ear.

"Yes, but I had forgotten how much it hurt," Poppa said defensively as she haphazardly pushed his chest away from her.

Rollo growled with need, and his kisses became more urgent.

"You're a beast."

"Tell me no, Poppa, and I'll stop," Rollo breathed against her lips as he kissed her.

Poppa felt her need grow, and despite her sore muscles, she kissed him back. She took the lead by pushing him against the wall of the bath. "I pray that this time we make our son," she whispered in his ear before she took him.

LEGACY AWAITS

Two weeks later, Poppa woke in the early morning hours with wetness between her legs. She gingerly crawled out of bed to make water and saw the stain of blood in her smallclothes. Behind the divider, Rollo snored noisily. Her mind left her at the sight of the blood. She quickly grabbed a new nightgown and clean smallclothes. She ran down the stairs, through the halls, and into the kitchen, where she grabbed a large scrubbing brush and some lye. Then she made her way quickly to the tepidarium. She could think of no other place that contained a large bin of water readily available. If she could move quickly enough, no one needed to know.

She doffed her clothing at the side of the pool. She took a moment to swim and clean herself. Then she dried quickly and donned the clean smallclothes and fresh nightdress. She kneeled beside the pool as she rubbed the lye into the rich red stains on her soiled smallclothes and nightdress. She pushed the lye into the stains until her palms ached. Then she took the brush, wet it in the water, and scrubbed the spots. She scrubbed and scrubbed, watching as the red faded to a rusty brown, but it didn't disappear. Her hands ached with the effort, her abdominals cramping and then releasing a fresh batch of blood.

She let out a primal wail of frustration as she removed her nightdress before the blood could soak through. She hurriedly bent back to her work. Mrs. Laurent found her in this frenzied and wild state.

"My dear lady. What are you—? Oh my!"

Poppa, tears running down her cheeks, ignored Mrs. Laurent. She barely noticed the older woman scuttle out and swiftly return with her master. Rollo found her still scrubbing at the stain with the brush. She hadn't noticed that she had torn a hole in the cloth during her frantic brushing. "Poppa, what is this?"

She startled and her face snapped upward. Her eyes widened and darkened in the thin light of the room. Her hair hung messily around her. She shook with cold and fear. He observed her as she instinctively cradled her body over the heap of white clothing, hiding it and her nakedness. Her voice was manic as she spoke. "It's all right. It's all right. I can fix this. Everything's fine."

"Fix what?" Rollo asked, perplexed. He moved to go near her, but she jumped and shook all the more. She cradled her body to protect what she guarded. Rollo raised both palms up in surrender. "Poppa, I'm not going to hurt you. You need to tell me what has happened. Are you hurt?"

"I'm fine. I—I'm fixing it. Everything's all right. I'm not hurt. It's going to be fine," she reassured him as she attempted a smile. It came off lopsided and unsure.

Rollo lost his patience. He grabbed a towel and moved toward her.

"No! *No!* Stay back!" she yelled at him, but he didn't listen.

Rollo wrapped the towel around her as she pushed the clothing further into her stomach to hide it from him. Fresh, warm tears of disappointment began to fall. She knew all was lost. She rocked back and forth. Rollo watched for a moment, then glanced at Mrs. Laurent, who stood helplessly by the door. He picked Poppa up and cradled her to him. The move only made her sobbing increase. He carried her upstairs and helped her into new, warm clothes. Then he tucked her back into bed and kissed her forehead. Though warm, she couldn't stop shaking and her muscles began to ache from it.

Rollo waited for her to drift off to sleep before he went back downstairs to retrieve her soiled clothes. He walked up to the main room and threw them into the fire. A disheartened frown formed upon his face, and the fire danced in his sad eyes as he watched until the garments burned completely.

"Be kind to her, m'lord," Mrs. Laurent advised as she placed a tray with warm milk and bread into his hands. "A disappointment for all of us, to be sure, but I don't believe it was a miscarriage—though she may think so. There wasn't enough blood, and it's time for her moon cycle."

Rollo nodded in understanding and then left to bring his wife the tray of food and drink.

Poppa lay awake on her side, cradled in the fetal position, when he entered the room. She didn't move or make a sound. He placed the tray on the bedside table and sat at the edge of the bed with his back to her. Neither of them said a word for a long time. The morning sun slowly lit the room, and its inviting light warmed the room around them.

"Can you explain to me what happened?"

"I woke to blood, and then I think . . . I went a little mad."

"But why? It wasn't enough blood to signify losing a child. It's your moon's blood."

"Yes, and with it came the failure of another moon's turn. You said your first wife was with child right away. Have we not matched or even doubled the number of times you and she tried to make a child? Why is it taking so long? What's wrong with me? The promise of the vision—"

Poppa whimpered, and she could feel the bitter tears bite her face as they fell silently. Rollo found himself at a loss for words. He had the same questions. They had more than doubled the times he'd coupled with Gisele. It had taken less than a moon's turn for him to get her with child. Though, he'd been younger then.

"I don't know what to say. Sometimes these things take time. We'll try again."

Poppa curled around herself, and Rollo laid a warm hand over her midsection while she cried.

The week of her bleeding, Rollo left each night and did not return until the early morning hours, when he would come in drunk and stumbling. He bumped into the furniture and once overturned a pitcher of water. Poppa thought back to her previous moon's blood, when he had done the same. Feelings of shame and disappointment flooded through her and fueled her resignation. She thought of the scene in the great hall that she had witnessed so long ago. The half-clad young women dancing before him. Laughing as they touched and caressed him. All sorts of scenes unfolded before her mind, and the more she thought of them, the more depressed her mood became. In the morning, Poppa felt the distance between them grow as she rose from the bed. Quietly and carefully, as not to wake him, she donned herself in her new practice clothes and did her own hair before leaving.

Poppa had tried to talk about her concerns with Ragnhild, but the woman kept a distance of confidence between the two of them that Poppa couldn't figure out how to breach. When she tried to talk about her feelings, Ragnhild quickly changed the subject and pushed Poppa back into training. Poppa grew in strength. She recognized the training as a gift and an outlet for her anger and frustration. On the day after her moon's blood ended, Ragnhild broke form and finally spoke to the matter. "You've weathered these days well."

"What you do mean?"

"He's not easy to love, nor is he easy to live with. I cannot say he made the right decision here, but he's coping as well as he can."

"Coping in what way?" Poppa felt her heart plummeting at the insinuation.

"As I told him last night, I'll not enter into whatever this void is between you both. I'll tell you the same that I told the jarl: you must talk to each other."

"If he's around and not clumsy with drink, I might actually get a chance to do so," Poppa spat back in frustration.

Ragnhild gave her a small smile and then moved to pack their things. Poppa took her leave and walked slowly back home as her anger with Rollo began to fester. Her head spun with all the frustration she had felt over this past week. When she walked into the living area, Rollo sat with Herleif and a couple of other men. They studied maps, their fingers moving and pointing at the parchment as they spoke of their plans. Rollo glanced up as she walked in and then motioned for her to wait a moment.

To convey her annoyance, she let her shield and sword fall to the floor with a loud thud and clank. Rollo winced but finished listening to Herleif speak about the developments around Bayeux.

"I look forward to seeing them myself soon," Rollo exclaimed as he ushered out his men and then slowly turned around to meet Poppa. She stood in the middle of the room, her arms crossed over her chest as she watched him walk toward her.

"That's far enough," she spat before he could get too close.

"Poppa," Rollo's voice came out in a hushed tone meant to soothe. His eyes were soft, as if he pitied her.

"Don't. Don't make me out to be crazy."

Rollo sighed and wiped his forehead with his hand.

"You're leaving?" Poppa asked.

"Já, in a fortnight. I'd like to go and check on the reconstruction of the area around Bayeux."

"I'll come with you." Poppa could not help the desperation creeping into her voice. Her face blushed with vulnerable embarrassment.

Rollo gave her an impatient sigh as he again regarded her with a pitying look. Her anger melted as rejection crept in with that single look. She turned toward the stairs.

"Poppa, wait," Rollo called after her.

"Don't," Poppa pleaded. "Don't give me an excuse to explain your behavior. I'm not a foolish girl. I know of a man's need and what happens when his wife fails him, but I won't hear your excuses. I can't bear it. I can't bear to hear about you sharing with someone else what we've shared."

"Poppa, what are you saying?"

Poppa scoffed, "You've been gone every night this week while I suffered through my moon's blood. You couldn't touch me, so you found your pleasure elsewhere. Do you think I'm a fool? Every night, you came to bed in the early morning hours! Would you deny it to my face?"

"Já! I do deny it, and I do think you're acting a fool." Rollo's accusatory voice was harsh, but his eyes remained soft as he watched her.

Poppa felt as though he'd slapped her. At the same time, she noticed a confusing lightness of heart. He came nearer to her, and she didn't stop him as he placed his large, warm palms on her shoulders.

"I won't lie to you and say I've not been tempted. With my rank, Poppa, you must understand that there will always be women, either by their choice or their families' urging, parading in front of me. I'm faithful to you, but you must also know there are limitations to that."

"Limitations?"

"I'm a man with a man's needs, as you said. I also have people that I rule over. I allow some of these young ladies to think they have my favor. In truth, some of them do. It makes their families easier to control. I won't lie and say I mind the distraction either. The dancing, the flirting, and the teasing in the hall—this is what I ask you to bear."

Poppa searched the ground as she thought over his request. He waited quietly until she gave a gentle nod before meeting his gaze. The flames behind him were mirrored in her eyes. As he watched the reflection dance, he knew she had more to say. He waited patiently while she searched for words.

After some time, she took a deep breath and said in an authoritative tone, "Never within my sight. I don't want to see such things. It does damage to my pride as well as my heart. If you don't put a stop to it in my presence, note that I'll have the freedom to do so myself."

Rollo chuckled, "I'd expect nothing less." He kissed her forehead. "Come, wife, I haven't had you in a week's time and I ache."

When they finished, they basked in the glow of the early evening light that flooded in from the windows and the relaxed excitement that rushed over their bodies. They laid above the sheets, Rollo trailing fingers lazily over the curve of her body as she rested on her stomach. "You're so beautiful, Poppa." He kissed the curve of her back above her buttocks and she shivered.

"Do you have to go? Couldn't you send someone?" The words came out in a yawn of sleepiness.

"I'd like to see it for myself."

"How long will you be gone?"

"A moon's turn or two, no longer."

"Two months!" Poppa sat up quickly and turned on him, her face a flood of emotion. "I don't understand why I can't go with you."

"The rebuilding isn't yet finished," Rollo explained. "I'll bring you when the restoration is complete. When there are crops where the fires once burned and when the buildings are rebuilt into something even more beautiful than your memory can conjure."

Poppa smiled at him slyly. "You speak with honeyed words, husband."

"Are they working?" He smiled as he brought his face just inches from hers.

"The words may work better if you put a baby in my belly before you leave."

He gave her a crooked smile and kissed her eyebrow, her nose, and then her lips before taking her again.

The time for his departure came more swiftly than either of them wished. They spent the night before in bed together saying goodbye. In the morning, Poppa waited dockside with the other women seeing their husbands off. A crowd of citizens from Rouen joined them. Poppa, wearing a fine purple gown trimmed and stitched with golden thread, stood regal among the common folk. She wore her hair drawn up in a pretty crown of braids, leaving her shoulders and neckline bare. The new summer sun felt warm as it beat down on them from clear skies above.

"This is different than the departures of old. I can still see my lord father's last goodbye to my lady mother. How he became smaller and smaller as the longship sailed farther away. Those left behind bore the cost of their absence. Especially when they went off to face unknown battles. We didn't know if we would ever see them again—or, if so, when," Ragnhild explained as she appeared on Poppa's right side. "You must bear your burden well for the common folk. They will judge your strength upon it."

Poppa arched her back and stood tall for her people. She was a beacon of courage as her eyes followed Rollo, who talked with Herleif and the crowd of men staying behind.

Then Rollo stood before her. She longed to return to the hours they'd spent in bed together the previous night. Her eyes danced over his face, seeking to remember every inch. She wouldn't cry, and she wouldn't beg. She stood tall and clasped her hands in front of her to keep them from shaking. He kissed her forehead, and then he kissed her long and deep as the crowd looked on. He boarded the ship with the same boyish, excited grin she remembered from their last voyage. The ships quickly steered away from shore. She stayed dockside with the crowd until the ships sailed out of view, then turned toward her empty home.

The sickness had started before Rollo's departure. Poppa woke each morning dizzy and out of sorts. At night, she felt tired and weary, which she attributed to her training. She'd tried a lighter routine, but the symptoms had only worsened. She'd neglected to mention this to Rollo. She hadn't wanted to burden him while he busied himself with trip preparations. She'd feared he'd tell her to quit training altogether. So she'd kept quiet and hidden her symptoms from her husband.

On the way home from the docks, a wave of the now-familiar sickness overcame her. She scanned her surroundings but only noted servants working in a distant field. She breathed heavily and quickly as she walked to the edge of the road, where she emptied her stomach. The day had grown warmer. She felt parched. Her head swam. She barely made it up the path and to the doorstep.

When Poppa entered, flushed and pale, Mrs. Laurent flew onto her like a mother hen, lecturing Poppa as she retrieved a horn of water for her. Poppa blamed it on the heat of the day and the emotion of Rollo leaving. Mrs. Laurent said little but didn't let Poppa leave the couch until she ate something and the color returned to her. Poppa felt much better later but still acquiesced to Mrs. Laurent's requests to rest for the day.

Despite her feelings of sickness, she threw herself into training in the weeks following Rollo's departure. It kept her mind off his absence and helped her work through her longing and need. She could lift and maneuver her shield with ease and moved on to work with groups of other trainees as they studied the shield wall formation and learned how to fight with comrades close at hand. Though she knew she may never use this training on the battlefield, she learned to train her muscles to move differently and her mind to problem-solve more quickly.

Poppa entered the training grounds one morning distracted and dizzy. Twice that morning, she had lost her stomach. Perhaps it was bad water or spoiled food. But she couldn't remember any foul-tasting food or water, and no one else in the household showed similar symptoms. She always felt better by midafternoon, so she tried to pay it little mind.

"You look wretched," Ragnhild came up beside Poppa and lifted her preferred practice sword and shield. "Are you feeling all right?"

Poppa swallowed back bile. "I'm fine."

She picked out her sword and shield and went to the center of the pit under the careful scrutiny of Ragnhild.

"Perhaps you should drink some water before we start." Ragnhild waved her hand at a serving boy in request.

"I've had enough water."

Poppa lifted her shield and stumbled. She slashed her sword and then brought it behind her shield, waiting for the charge. When it came, she pushed with the shield. As quick as a viper, she slashed the sword over her shield. Ragnhild smiled at Poppa's swiftness but anticipated the move and spun to miss the blade. Poppa moved to meet her, but the churning in her stomach reached a crescendo. She dropped her things and ran to the side of the ring. She propped one hand against the wall and vomited for the third time that morning.

Ragnhild, an amused smile on her face, went to Poppa's side. Ragnhild held Poppa's hair back as another wave overcame her. "I'm so sorry," Poppa apologized between gasps. Her body trembled. "I don't know . . . I must have eaten something that disagreed with me."

"Food? Is that where you're casting blame?" Ragnhild laughed heartily before her look became serious. "Sit down."

Ragnhild made Poppa sit on the ground with her back against the wall and her knees pulled up to her chest, then sat beside her in like fashion.

"What else could it be?"

"How long has this been going on?"

"How long has it been since the men left?"

"Six weeks."

"That long? Time has passed so quickly." Poppa thought over her sickness before she answered, "Then about eight weeks."

"Eight weeks! Gods have mercy, Poppa. Did your mother never tell you the signs to watch for?"

"I didn't have a mother," Poppa explained. "Well, I did, of course—everyone has a mother. But she died giving birth to me. What do you think is wrong with me?"

Poppa felt confused as to why Ragnhild grinned so broadly at her. "Poppa, when did you last have your moon's blood?"

Poppa's eyes searched the ground as she tried to remember. She had little need to track her moon's cycle in Rollo's absence. Besides, she had felt unwell and distracted.

"Wait . . ." Poppa placed one hand over her mouth and the other on her belly.

Ragnhild's smile grew. "You're with child, Poppa!"

"Can we be sure?"

"I've seen the signs countless times. If you're not with child, then you're surely dying and would already be on your deathbed."

Poppa laughed giddily as tears filled her eyes. "I have to send word to Rollo right away."

Ragnhild shook her head. "No. Wait until he returns. Otherwise, he will make rash decisions and rush home. Tell him in person. It will be sweeter. Congratulations, Poppa. You will have a baby in about six turns of the moon."

The two women, who practiced sparring daily and spoke only words of weaponry and battle, shared an embrace of celebration. Poppa felt light on her feet when she returned home.

One afternoon, the horns began to blow. Poppa could hear the haunting sound reverberate in the valley below. The ships had returned. She abandoned her book and prepared to flee out the door in hopes of watching the ships come in. Mrs. Laurent stopped her and reminded her that the ships would take some time to arrive. She should take that time to dress and prepare herself to receive her husband.

Mrs. Laurent combed Poppa's hair and let it flow, long and wavy, past her breasts. She wove a small part of the front into a crown around Poppa's forehead and then placed small white flowers in the folds. Next, she helped Poppa into a velvet emerald green dress specially made for this occasion. The neck traveled low on Poppa's chest and came to a sharp point just beneath her breasts. The gossamer sleeves felt light on her arms in this heat. They flowed down over her hands and came to a point at her wrist. The dress hugged her hips and moved in rich waves down to cover her feet.

"No jewelry," Poppa instructed. "Rollo gets annoyed with the hindrance."

Mrs. Laurent smiled slyly at her. "You're radiant this evening. Glowing, to be sure. I haven't wanted to ask, for fear of speaking it out of existence, but I've noticed that you've not had your moon's blood for some time."

Poppa smiled brightly and nodded her head yes. Tears filled the aged woman's eyes as she embraced Poppa and kissed her on both cheeks.

"Go! Or you will be late."

The citizens of Rouen made way for Poppa as she joined them on the docks. She went to the edge and could see the ships make their way up the river. She could feel the excitement radiate off the mixed group of people around her. It was an eclectic selection of the different varieties of Norsemen and Franks, together as one, anticipating the appearance of the leader who united them. She studied their faces as they followed the ships into the harbor.

Poppa locked her gaze on Rollo as the ships drew in closer. His ship led the fleet. He looked dark against the fading sun, wearing all black. He had pulled his hair back to keep it from the wind at sea. Regal and handsome, he stood at the bow of the ship so he could be the first to leap onto the dock. Poppa's heart swelled with happiness as she watched him, aglow with the knowledge of his child growing inside her.

Indeed, he leapt off the ship first. Poppa prepared to wait her turn while he greeted his gathered chieftains, but he surprised them all by walking past them straight to her. His bearing felt intense as he pulled her into his arms and kissed her deeply. When he pulled back, he smiled at her and then inquired, "What is it, wife? You've changed since I left."

"Improved, I hope." Poppa smiled as she stood confident in his appraisal.

"I had not thought it possible," Rollo wooed. Then, turning to his officials, he said, "I'll meet with you all on the morrow. Come to my house by late morning. For now, I take my leave to bring my wife home."

Hours later, they faced each other in bed. Rollo tugged lightly at the waves of her dark hair, gently weaving it between his fingers while his eyes, heavy from travel and exertion, slowly began to close. Poppa smiled and kissed his lips gently.

"Rollo, I've something to tell you before you drift off to sleep," she whispered.

Rollo regarded her dreamily.

"The time we've waited for has finally come."

In his tiredness, Rollo felt confused and inquired, "What time has come?"

Her heart aflutter, Poppa gave a soft smile as she leaned in and whispered into his ear, "Rollo, I'm with child."

Rollo's eyes flew open as he jumped up from the bed in a fluid motion and at a speed Poppa didn't think possible. By chance, she'd moved out of his way.

"With child! Are you sure?"

Poppa bit her bottom lip and smiled brightly. "I'm sure."

He grasped his hand behind her head and pulled her into a deep kiss. Tears spilled down her cheeks and onto his.

"We must celebrate!" he yelled as he stomped into his clothes haphazardly. He shouted down the hall for all the servants to gather in the main room below and then instructed her to ready herself as quickly as she could. A burden Poppa hadn't known he carried lifted from his face. He smiled brightly and looked more youthful than she had ever seen him. He threw her nightclothes at her, and she laughed.

"Rollo, I can't wear this." Poppa rose from the bed gingerly and chose the dress she'd worn to welcome the ships. She turned her open back to him and said over her shoulder, "Help me."

His hands moved clumsily over the same clasps they'd recently worked deftly. In his haste, he misjudged the pairing of clasps and gave a frustrated grunt when he had to start again. He kissed the back of her neck. "I'm well pleased."

That evening, Rollo had flagons of wine and food passed around for them and all the servants as they celebrated the promise of new life and the continuation of a legacy.

JUDGMENT

MONTHS LATER, A FEAST OF CELEBRATION was held for all of the people in Rollo's territory. A small city of tents formed outside Rouen as more people arrived than the town could hold. Performers played and sang for coin in the streets. In the open air, shopkeepers bartered their wares up and down the narrow streets. Colorful banners danced upon the wind; their sigils identified the different family groups. Merrymakers flooded the city's bars and brothels, filling coffers and purses with coin. Visitors and townsfolk alike viewed melees and contests of strength in squares throughout the city. All the while, more people arrived.

Norsemen and Franks crowded together in the giant room of the main hall on the night of the celebration. Poppa, swollen with child, stood as the guest of honor. Raucous laughter and loud chatter chorused in harmony around the room. The sound of the revelers spilled out into the night. A fire burned brightly in the center of the hall, where meat roasted on spits. Young serving boys turned the long poles in a slow rhythm. The meat spat out its grease and the fire below sizzled in response. This communication continued until the meat was fully cooked. Those gathered passed around horns of ale and flagons of wine as they feasted. They danced and sang in merriment.

On the dais, Rollo sat on his faldstool speaking with Barri, a new chieftain who wore the clothes of a Norseman. Rollo had granted lands to Barri after the attack on Bayeux. Barri had returned to Rouen with Rollo to gather more men to help work and settle the area. Young and handsome, with his head shaved and tattooed, Barri had his gray eyes locked on Rollo as he spoke. Occasionally they both turned their attention to the young girl who danced before them.

Mercifully, the sickness had recently left Poppa. She glowed in her second trimester. She rested her hand protectively over the round bump in her midsection as she studied the dancer. The red-headed girl moved sure of herself and seductively before the men. Poppa felt discontented with the girl's presence before her husband. It went against what they'd agreed, but Rollo made no motion to remove her. Instead, he allowed his hands to wander from time to time. He was drinking heavily and enjoying himself.

Poppa sipped her horn of ale as she stood off in a corner of the dais with Ragnhild and Herleif. "You should put up your feet, my lady," Herleif suggested. "Would you like me to walk you home?"

Poppa's attention left her husband and she forced a smile as she replied, "I'm fine, thank you."

She turned her attention back to the stage. Out of the corner of her eye, she saw Ragnhild and Herleif share a questioning glance. The girl sat in Rollo's lap, her long pale fingers tracing the tattoos from his arm to his neck. Poppa's anger caused her face to flush. She felt a soft hand on her arm; it squeezed in warning. Poppa glimpsed over her shoulder to see Ragnhild behind her with a knowing look. When Poppa's eyes traveled back to the dais, the girl had pressed her lips upon Rollo's.

Poppa's temper flared. She turned to Ragnhild and spoke in an authoritative voice. "Give me your sword."

Ragnhild tried to protest. "Poppa—"

"It wasn't a question," Poppa asserted as she narrowed her eyes. "Give me your sword."

Ragnhild unsheathed her sword and handed it, hilt first, to Poppa. Then Poppa turned to Herleif. "Now yours."

Herleif, about to protest, saw the resolve in her eyes and placed his sword in her outstretched hand. Poppa turned her back to them and walked toward her husband and the redheaded girl, who still sat proudly in his lap.

"Get up," Poppa's eyes narrowed at the young girl.

The girl's eyes widened in fear, but she didn't move. She turned to Rollo for deliverance.

"Don't look to him. I said rise!" Poppa's voice carried throughout the hall.

An audible hush fell over the crowd as conversations stopped and heads turned toward the angry voice on the dais. Rollo flinched at his wife's anger, but he said nothing as the girl bashfully rose from his lap and stood before Poppa.

Poppa squared off and stared down at the girl, who stood a heard shorter. She was thankful the girl had enough smarts about her to keep her eyes cast downward. Poppa lifted Ragnhild's sword and offered it to the girl, who took it on reflex. The girl let the point fall to the floor while maintaining a weak grip.

"Come," Poppa instructed. She glared at her husband as she passed him on her way to the other end of the dais. The girl reluctantly followed.

"My lady, I—"

"I didn't instruct you to speak. Lift up the sword."

The girl did as Poppa ordered.

"Good." Poppa nodded once in affirmation. "Now fight me for him."

By this time, Poppa's shield-maiden training was well-known throughout the territory. She held Herleif's sword easily at the ready and stared down the girl who shook before her. Purposefully, she didn't do the girl the decency of asking her name. The girl meant nothing to her.

The fire to Poppa's right cast shadows that danced across her face as a crooked smile appeared there. "If you best me, I'll allow you what your heart desires."

Behind the girl, Poppa saw Rollo turn in his chair. He scanned the crowd before his attention returned to Poppa. An amused grin played on his face. He placed a finger over his lips and itched. He leaned to the right, his arm covering the carved lion as he crossed one leg on top of the other.

"You know I cannot." The girl shook her head fearfully, her eyes wide.

"Fight for him!" Poppa cried loudly. "You want him, but you won't fight? Do you think love comes for free? I had to pay with my home and with the life of a friend. You won't take what belongs to me without payment."

The girl before her teetered on her feet. Aware of the attention of everyone in the room, she shyly turned to them, but no one moved to save her. The girl's eyebrows knit in concentration as she thought through her options. The girl looked ethereal and young in the dancing flames. Poppa let out a sigh of frustration. If she allowed this girl to linger too long, she may change her mind.

"You're a Dane, yes? Norse by birth?"

The girl nodded shyly.

"Do they not teach you to fight? Fight for my husband's affection and for my approval. All his people gathered here serve as a witness to my promise. Best me and you've earned the right to be his mistress."

The girl let out a desperate wail and charged at her. She came faster than Poppa had calculated, but it wasn't quick enough. The girl clumsily swung the sword. Poppa caught it deftly with a hard-left blow, causing a clank and swoosh as metal sang against metal. Poppa forced Ragnhild's sword from the girl's hand and across the dais. The girl, disarmed, cried out in fear and surprise. Poppa wasted no time as she kicked her in the stomach with a gentle but strong force. The kick would hurt but not harm the girl as she fell to the hard boards of the dais. The sound echoed across the silent room. Gasps rang collectively throughout the crowd. Poppa stood over the girl and turned her onto her back with a shove of her foot. She looked down her sword as it pointed in the girl's frightened face. The girl shook as Poppa leaned in and spoke in a harsh whisper meant only for her: "If I see you or hear of you kissing my husband again, I'll cut out your tongue myself."

She kept her sword pointed at the girl's throat. She ignored her whimpers as she turned to the crowd, and shouted, "Where's her family? Who will speak for her?"

A rustle started in the crowd. A few hands were slowly raised at her right. She should have guessed. The family stood out with their shared ruddy coloring. Their bodies also mirrored the girl's delicate thinness, pointed nose, and crystal-blue eyes. Not one of them stood out as a great warrior or farmer. Poppa wondered what profession they offered the community. They looked around and at least had the decency to look embarrassed. Not one of them moved to defend the girl or speak on her behalf.

"You jest and make merry while a daughter of your house moves to seduce my husband right before my eyes! What have you instructed her to do? What favors are you looking to gain?"

The family remained silent, but Poppa thought she caught malice behind their crystal blue eyes.

When Poppa spoke next, she turned toward the whole of the crowd. "Let this be a lesson to you all. Don't push your daughters on your jarl. He will take no mistresses. I alone will bear his children, his legacy. They will have no competition from bastards."

The crowd stood enraptured by her as she stood before them, radiant in her pregnancy.

She lowered the sword and handed it back to Herleif. Poppa fetched Ragnhild's sword and returned it to her while the girl slowly rose. Then Poppa went to Rollo, took the horn of ale from his hands and downed it in one long pull. She sat in her husband's lap, the empty horn outstretched in her hand. She turned to the redheaded girl who still stood on the dais. "Now come fill my husband's cup. He's thirsty."

Poppa turned back to Rollo and kissed him deeply. The girl had no choice but to fill the cup in her hand while the couple kissed.

Poppa pulled from the kiss and peered at Rollo with hooded eyes. She quietly placed the horn of ale in his hand and rose from his lap. Ragnhild stood close to his chair as she watched Poppa gracefully step down from the dais, walk through the parted crowd, and depart into the night without uttering another word.

Ragnhild smiled proudly as she mused, "I wonder, Rollo, if not your wife has become more Norse as you've become more Frank."

Rollo turned to her, an amused and nervous grin upon his face. Around them, the room remained quiet following Poppa's departure. They looked to Rollo to cue whether or not the celebrations would continue. Rollo stood, outstretched his hands, and yelled, "We will drink to strong women on this glorious night. May that warrior spirit follow my wife to the birthing bed!"

Cheers rang through the hall.

"More ale!" Rollo shouted. The cheering grew louder. The family of blue eyes and red hair refrained from the cheering as they chided one another in hushed whispers.

"You should go to her," Ragnhild whispered when he sat back down. "I'll stay here in your stead. No one will mind if the girl dances for me."

Rollo nodded in agreement and gave over his seat to his kin. He quietly left the hall and went out into the darkness of the cool evening. He felt the weight of drink upon him as he rushed through the streets to catch up to his wife. He found her standing still on the path that led to their home. Two guards stood waiting at a respectful distance. They tensed when they heard Rollo's footfalls, and one grabbed his sword hilt before he recognized his jarl.

Poppa didn't turn to acknowledge him. She stood with her gaze pointing toward the full moon. Its bright light bathed her face in a haunting radiance, and for a moment Rollo stood basking in her as she basked in the light of the heavens. In the clear night, stars twinkled and danced, suspended and trapped in their formations.

"The sky shines beautifully this night," Poppa spoke into the silent darkness.

"Does it?" Rollo smiled at her. "I hadn't noticed."

Poppa gave him a sly smile over her shoulder and mused, "Charming, but it'll do you no good this night."

"Poppa," Rollo started as he moved closer to her. She took one step back, and he stopped in his tracks.

"You broke your promise."

"I did noth—"

"Yes, you did nothing. That's the problem."

Rollo hung his head. He didn't like her reprimands, and he felt his anger grow. His pride took hold of him and he snarled, "It's not our way, Poppa. You can't change me."

Poppa's lips formed a grim line. Her eyes narrowed and set as she explained, "You must find a way to change yourself. Rollo, our marriage is *more danico*. By right you can put me aside or take another wife at any time."

Rollo gave her a crooked smile and moved toward her again. "Is that what you fear? That I'll put you aside? Poppa, my child grows within you."

She raised one palm before herself to signal that he should go no further. Rollo swallowed hard but didn't advance.

"As a child could in many other wombs. Then what? What happens if others come along to seek claim of your inheritance? The heavens gave you a promise." Poppa's long arm waved above her as she motioned to the stars. "I won't have my children's future challenged by their own blood."

"I've already said I wouldn't enter into another engagement such as that of which you speak. I've kept that promise."

"And you promised you wouldn't parade your distractions in my face. I understand you're dumb with drink, but what I did this night won't be a lone event if I witness something like that again."

Rollo laughed, "I don't think you need to worry much about that, my wife. You made your feelings quite clear to all those in the room, and those absent will hear about it on the morrow."

Poppa sensed his need as he once again stepped closer. "You may walk me home, but I won't share your bed this night. I'll see you in the morning. I've much more to discuss with you."

◇◇◇◇◇

He found her in the morning walking among the flowers in the garden. He paused at the gate and watched her. Poppa had donned a fine ivory lace gown that hugged and flowed around her curved belly. Her hair was pinned in a mass of curls upon her head with soft tendrils cascading around her face. She turned to him and gave him a small smile as she placed a handful of small white flowers in her basket.

"Your head aches, jarl," Poppa spoke as she drifted toward him.

She stopped and turned to smell a yellow flower. She smiled as she picked a few of them to place on top of the others in her basket. Rollo rubbed his temples. Poppa smiled to herself. She walked over to the herbs, smelled one, then crushed it between her fingers. She went to him and rubbed the crushed herbs onto his temples. Rollo closed his eyes. He enjoyed her touch as his temples instantly cooled. The smell that reached his nose reminded him of a brisk winter's day.

Poppa smiled at him and handed him more of the herb. "Peppermint. It relieves the aching of the mind. Chew some and it will freshen the breath."

Rollo contemplated her as she turned again and entered the garden. He eyed the lace upon her back as she pondered different flowers, smelling them before continuing on her journey. The sun shone warmly down upon the garden, casting a halo of light that traced the outline of her frame. When she caught him looking, she smiled and rubbed her stomach reassuringly.

"How is my son this day?" The question left Rollo's voice in a croak of emotion.

"Active as always," Poppa smiled. "I believe he likes the warmth of the outdoors, for he has settled down in the womb after a morning of movement."

Rollo smiled at the thought of his growing child as he entered the garden and trailed behind her. She picked at the flowers. He noticed her movements became more sporadic and nervous. He waited for her to speak, but she didn't. "You wanted to discuss a matter."

"I have another favor to ask of you." Poppa glimpsed him over her shoulder.

Rollo swallowed hard. He couldn't allow Poppa, well versed in her wiles, to spin him about so easily. One thing remained about which she hadn't yet inquired. It surprised Rollo that it had taken her this long to ask him. He turned away from her and pruned withered leaves off a nearby plant in an effort to look busy.

"It's a small favor." Poppa came up behind him. She stood close, her swollen belly just brushing his back. "Only information."

Rollo breathed deeply and held it in before turning around. He knew what she sought. She'd certainly waited for an opportune moment. Now here she stood secure in his love and glowing in her pregnancy. His heartbeat picked up in pace. Alas, the one thing she craved was the one thing he couldn't and wouldn't give her. He didn't reply as he waited for her to continue.

He watched her muster her strength before she spoke. "Did you give the order to have those fleeing Bayeux murdered?"

Rollo let out his breath. He leaned his head toward her, and in his deep voice, he affirmed, "You know I did."

Tears spilled over and followed silent tracks down her cheeks. Her voice sounded hoarse as she struggled with her next question. "Why?"

Rollo turned away to collect himself so her emotion wouldn't affect the truth he had to explain. He sniffled and turned to her. His eyes darkened as he apathetically shared his reasoning. "I don't have the patience to rule over cowards. The people who inhabit my land will face their consequences and fates with courage. If, in their fear, they choose to flee rather than fight, it's a weakness. I won't tolerate it. The majority of them were men who had fled their posts and left their stations unguarded—including your guards, as you remember. We met very little resistance as we climbed the stairs toward your lady's room."

Poppa nodded once. As she'd suspected, many had abandoned their positions. Rollo waited for the question he knew would come next.

"I need to know who's responsible. I need to know the names of the men who killed Myra."

Rollo's face grew hard. His eyes narrowed as he studied her carefully for a moment. His lips set in a firm and uncompromising line. "I won't tell you that."

"But you know?" Poppa moved closer and pleaded. "I don't understand. Why not?"

Rollo rubbed his palm over his mouth and regarded her. Though it pained him, he couldn't shield her from his thoughts. "It doesn't matter. She's dead, Poppa. Knowing her murderers won't bring her back, nor will it give you peace. It'll do you no good. She was a casualty of the siege. Many women before her have shared the same fate. I won't seek punishment for her death, because it was done on my orders."

Poppa's tears flowed freely as she argued. "I need to know her last moments. I need to know what happened."

"It would only haunt you."

"But if I just—"

"No, and you will leave it at that. I don't wish to hear about this matter again."

He turned his back to her and all her splendor as he walked the path back to the front door. He stopped, turned, and called over his shoulder, "Nor do I wish to hear that you've asked others. It's finished."

Poppa considered him with frightened eyes. He'd once said he would grant her anything she wanted. She only needed to ask. Nonetheless, she could see he wasn't going to yield on this matter. She heaved a frustrated sigh but resolved to comply.

Later that evening, Poppa arrived late to a gathering of Rollo's area chieftains. They sat around the table in the living area. A warm fire crackled in the hearth. Laughter boomed from Rollo as he watched Herleif reenact a clumsy battle move. Poppa couldn't help but smile as she observed her husband. His large grin, with teeth of white, brightened his eyes as he watched Herleif. He still wore a grin when he turned to her.

"Poppa, join us," he called to her. "Herleif was just reminding us of his amazing feat in the attack on Paris." Rollo reached for her, and she went to him. She stood next to him as he wrapped an arm around her. He leaned in to kiss her belly before he pulled her to rest on his leg. He smiled at Herleif. "One more time for the lady."

Herleif pretended to climb a ladder, stumble over his own feet in his haste, lose his grip, and fall backward. His face a mixture of silly faces throughout the mime. Rollo's laugh rang out the loudest among them all when the man crashed to the floor in an exaggerated slam. The babe inside Poppa leapt at the sound. She started and put her hand to the swell. Rollo jumped and asked, "What is it?"

She smiled at him. "Your son likes the sound of your voice." Poppa took his hand and put it over where the baby moved within her. The baby kicked and turned under Rollo's palm. Rollo smiled widely and then softly kissed the back of her neck.

"I still remember him splashing around in that moat and cursing the Franks behind the wall as if they were responsible for his clumsy feet," Sigrid laughed. Sigrid, a seasoned shield-maiden, had sailed with Rollo when they first attacked Francia. She was mother to the Sigrid who had helped to dress Poppa on her wedding night. She had long black hair and brown eyes. A fierce scar ran from her forehead to chin, but it didn't make her ugly. If anything, it made her more terrifying and strangely beautiful. Legend held that she'd slayed more than one hundred men in the battle for Paris, where she'd received the scar she wore like a badge of honor.

As the chieftains laughed, servants started to remove the empty dishes that remained from dinner. When the table cleared, Poppa noticed a hazelwood tally stick laying before each chieftain. Each tally stick had varying numbers of lines carved into it. The lines recorded the debt that each chieftain owed Rollo. In front of him lay eight matching sticks Rollo had broken from their siblings in order to have his own record of the tallies. His carved wooden lion ring moved in circles as he fingered one absentmindedly. He laughed along with his chieftains. Poppa guessed that they'd settled debts over dinner. Judging by his light mood, it had gone well.

Poppa took note of those around the table. Of Norse birth and battle worn, all of them. They looked a fierce company. Poppa felt out of place as a Frank. Ragnhild and Herleif sat on either side of Rollo. Next to Ragnhild sat Barri, the young chieftain from the night before. Next to Barri sat Anlaf, an older warrior who wore a black slip of cloth over an eye he'd lost in the attack on Rouen. Last on that side of the table came Vogg, the trader from the beach who had long, matted hair and piercing blue eyes. Poppa remembered seeing him next to Ingmar at the celebration of their wedding. She wouldn't forget the haunted and sullen looks the pair had shared as they drank from their horns. She noted that his tally stick had the fewest number of carved tallies. Next to Herleif sat Sigrid. Poppa wasn't sure if Rollo noticed, but from her vantage point on his lap, she often saw their hands move under the table to find one another. On Sigrid's right sat her son Thorid—blond and comely, like the god he was named after. On Thorid's other side sat Ivar, Ingmar's brother. He shared his brother's cold eyes and piercing stare as he spoke over the laughter. "I don't mean to darken the lively mood, but if we could address one of the matters we came here to discuss this night . . ."

The laughter stopped, and a solemn mood descended upon the gathered crowd. Poppa looked around uncertainly at those assembled. Anlaf lowered his head, and Vogg stared across the table, a sinister approval in his nod. Sigrid's attention stayed focused on Rollo. Poppa felt him shift beneath her.

Poppa was grateful Rollo didn't ask her to leave when he spoke of his affairs. He wanted her to witness his rule—not only to understand him and his wishes for his part of West Francia but to understand the true cost of leadership and what it took to keep the peace. As a mother, the job of educating their children would fall to her. She would help shape the leader their son would become. For these reasons he kept her at his side and allowed her to stay perched on his lap.

Rollo adjusted to ensure comfort for them both. "In a moment," he replied. "I'll have updates from those who haven't yet shared them before we get to that matter. Herleif, it would please me for you to keep notes."

Rollo waited while Herleif produced a scroll and quill. He dipped the quill in a horn inkpot before he nodded to his jarl, who returned the nod and continued, "Thorid, last time we spoke you informed me of the overpopulation of your area."

Thorid's handsome face smiled at his liege lord. "It has improved with the acquisition of the Bessin area. I've expanded. Nevertheless, the women in my area are as fertile as the land they live off of."

"And how many of those pregnancies are of your own doing?" Ragnhild lifted an eyebrow and smiled at the young man across the table.

This caused an uproar of laughter, Rollo's loudest of them all.

Thorid smiled at Ragnhild charmingly. "Jealous, my lady?"

Ragnhild raised an eyebrow but laughed along with the rest of them at the jest.

Rollo turned to Sigrid. "How's the training of your troops progressing?"

"Well, with my son's problem of overpopulation, I've taken in many new recruits that I wouldn't normally choose to teach battle maneuvers to. Their progress is slow, but we will persist."

"Good," Rollo smiled. "Barri, I heard from you last night. You will continue to update me on the reconstruction process as it progresses. Vogg, we haven't talked much since the siege of Bayeux. I've heard that you've taken a Frankish wife since then. My wife and I look forward to meeting her soon. Do you have anything else to note?"

Vogg shook his head as he continued to pull chicken from the bone in his hand. Poppa thought the action disrespectful, but Rollo appeared unbothered as he moved on to the next.

"Anlaf, what's the word on your expected harvest?"

Excited for his turn to speak, the elderly man perked up. "Jarl, it'll please you to know that we expect an abundant harvest this year. Praise be to the Lord Jesus Christ."

Poppa smiled at him. A Norse believer. The man caught her stare and gave her a grandfatherly wink with his one good eye as he continued. "Because of that, I'd offer to take as many of working age as you deem appropriate. I could use the extra hands in the coming seasons."

Rollo conferred with Herleif and then turned his attention back to Anlaf. "I'm sure we can arrange something. Thank you, Anlaf."

"Finally, Ivar, I'll return to you." His voice sounded deep and authoritative. "I assume you have a confession from the wife?"

"I do, jarl," Ivar confirmed. "My men followed your orders and she confessed without the need of a serious beating, but there's more to the story."

"Proceed," Rollo encouraged. Poppa could feel his body tense beneath her.

"The husband confessed he knew all along what his wife had done. He watched it all happen but did nothing to help or hinder his wife from ordering the servants to hide the farm equipment."

Rollo's fist slammed on the table. Poppa, the only one around the table not to flinch, had felt his anger grow. Though she didn't understand the whole story, she understood enough. Rollo perceived the couple had taken advantage of him.

"And they took my money for the replacement of the equipment *and* said nothing when we held two innocent men suspected of the robbery!" Rollo's frustrated fury encircled all around them.

Ivar nodded. Rollo clenched and unclenched his fist. He waited to speak until he'd calmed. Then his voice came in a familiar low rumble. "What of the innocent men?"

"Unharmed. You were wise to have the wife interrogated before we acted rashly. I took the liberty of letting them go once she confessed."

Rollo approved as he added, "Award the wrongly accused men the farmer's lands and equipment for their troubles."

"This will raise their rank," Ivar noted.

"So be it. I'd rather have honest people rise than see deceivers rule over them."

Those gathered around the table shared a genuine murmur of approval before Ivar inquired, "We still hold both husband and wife. What's to become of them?"

"The ruse was orchestrated by the wife to deceive you and, in effect, myself. They had us believe that the equipment had been stolen. Indeed, she knew her servants had stored it, because she ordered it so. Her husband's failure to bring the deception to light even after they received repayment from me was theft twice over. They will both pay with their lives. My law is clear when it states the punishment for robbery."

Poppa gasped and then bit her tongue to stay silent.

Rollo went on. "Do it publicly. Cut out their lying tongues and then hang them. Don't let them die—lower them, disembowel them, and then allow them to bleed to their deaths as their innards are cooked over a brazier."

Poppa swallowed hard. She looked down at her hands as she tried to hide her emotion. A dizziness came over her as she struggled to force the images from her mind.

She was thankful when Ragnhild spoke first to contradict him. "Disembowelment? Rollo, does the punishment have to be so cruel?"

Rollo gave her a dark look, but she didn't shrink under it. "The people will understand that I don't tolerate deception of any kind in my lands. Furthermore, I'll make a decree ordering farmers to keep their equipment outside rather than stored away in the evening."

"I think it a just and strategic punishment," Vogg agreed as he leaned his head toward Ivar. "I'll help Ivar arrange it."

Rollo clapped his hands in gratitude. They had come to a decision without argument. He took a long pull from his horn of ale as the others started up conversations. Poppa caught the glance of Ragnhild, who gave her a subtle shake of the head. Poppa understood that she shouldn't challenge his decision further.

A crack of lightning and a following boom of thunder surprised them all.

"Thor approves," Rollo affirmed as he lightly removed Poppa from his lap and stood to stretch. "I've sat too long. Who wishes to spar with me as we wait out this storm?"

Ivar and Thorid lifted the heavy furniture to the edges of the room, creating a large open space in the middle. Vogg and Barri chose weapons that hung on the wall. Rollo favored two axes, one for each hand. Poppa admired him as he removed his shirt, revealing his tattooed and scarred chest and back.

Sigrid whistled at him. "If I was twenty years younger . . ."

Rollo smiled. "For that comment, you're first."

Sigrid smiled wickedly and bowed as she raised her sword.

They sparred amidst the backdrop of the storm raging outside. The lightning brightened the room from the west windows. Rollo caught blow after blow with his axes, spinning and moving so deftly and swiftly that the older woman had to back up and watch him before making a strike of her own. Ever the warrior, he didn't let up until she yielded, flat on her back, her sword flung to the corner of the room. Rollo extended his hand. She accepted, and he embraced her fondly when he brought her up. He kissed both of her cheeks and walked her to the edge of the crowd with his arm around her shoulders.

Poppa felt Herleif's presence at her side as Thorid and Barri moved to the center of the room to spar with one another. She smiled at him warmly, and he returned the gesture. "It was an amusing story of your mishap in Paris," Poppa commented.

"Já, and one the jarl likes me to recount often."

Poppa giggled "I'm sure he does," then paused and grew serious. "I've watched you for a long time, Herleif. You serve my husband well."

A light flush grew on the older man's cheeks from the compliment. "I have all his life, my lady."

"All his life?" Poppa turned to the man with questioning eyes. "Tell me."

The older man scanned the two fighters in the middle of the room who had abandoned their weapons and engaged themselves in a wrestling match. They wrapped their arms around each other, each trying to bring the other to the floor, but neither one gave any ground.

At length, Herleif spoke. "Rollo has told you of his lord father Rögnvald?"

"You knew him?"

"Já. He was my dearest friend, and I was his most devoted servant. My father served his house, as did his lord father before him. So you see, our blood has been tied together for generations. His family was one of the most distinguished families in our area—equally respected and trusted by the king above him and the common folk below him. Though I was five years younger, Rögnvald and I grew up together. He took me under his wing when my father died. I looked up to him as my brother. Neither of us had any male siblings, and it was a small community in those days. He was kind enough to allow me to tag along with him and teach me all he knew. We trained and raided lands side by side. Years later, when he became Jarl of Møre, it was an honor for me to serve him and his house. I did so for many years. I watched the rule take hold of my friend and change him. Power made him draw inward, and he became a hard man for many to love. I stood by as he favored his younger son, Thorir. Even Ivar was put above Hròlfr, your Rollo. I saw the boy's potential over his brothers. He alone was born to rule, but Rögnvald wouldn't listen to me."

"Why?"

"I believe he saw too much of himself in Hrólfr. The two of them shared too many similarities, and tensions between them boiled over many times. His lord father's mind began to darken to madness when Hrólfr left, or so I am told. When Hrólfr told me of his plans to leave, I pledged my loyalty to him and sailed with him over the waters, never to return to the land of our birth. Together we raided the lands of England and Frisia before we came to Francia."

Poppa smiled as he finished his story. "I understand your devotion better. My husband is blessed to have you and your confidence. I pray your sons will continue to serve ours."

Poppa took Herleif's hand, placed it on the swell of her belly, and smiled at him as he felt the boy within respond with a kick. Herleif agreed silently as he became overcome with emotion.

The men in the middle finally called a draw and walked to the opposite ends of the room to retrieve a horn of ale. Ragnhild came to Poppa's side and reminded her, "We never did show him how much you've learned."

"He won't allow it," Poppa argued. "Besides, I'm big and clumsy."

Ragnhild smiled deviously. "His own lady mother went to battle when she carried him in her womb. You just have more to protect."

Ragnhild handed Poppa a round shield that had rested on the wall moments before. Then she took out her sword and grabbed a second shield from the wall. In the meantime, Poppa took her own sword out of its sheath.

"What do you two think you're doing?" Rollo followed behind them as they armed themselves.

"I promised we would show you what she has learned. Get out of the way or you'll be knocked over." Ragnhild's chin went up in defiance of her jarl. He was not to question her in this.

Rollo crossed his arms but stood on the edge of the circle as they made their way to the middle of the room. "She's in a dress and with child!"

Ragnhild rolled her eyes at him. "Again, do I need to remind you of your own lady mother? Also—"

A loud ripping noise interrupted her speech. All heads turned to the sound. Poppa had torn the white lace of her dress in a long line up the thigh. Her bare and shapely leg shone starkly against the darkness of the room. Again, lightning cracked and thunder boomed outside, closer this time.

"Thor approves," Poppa shouted devilishly to Rollo as she raised her shield to protect her stomach. She spun her sword in a wide arc at her side.

The laughter in the hall thundered louder than the storm outside. Rollo reluctantly moved to the side with the other men.

The women squared off in the middle of the room. They had practiced this routine many times before, though never with any other swords but the blunted practice ones. Poppa could do the dance in her sleep. Ragnhild led with a slope that Poppa met with a deflect before she pivoted to the right, raising the shield to cover her left side. Ragnhild's sword crashed into the shield and gasps went up from the crowd, but Poppa's feet held firm. She absorbed the shock of the blow and channeled it into a twist of her body so that her sword raised again to meet Ragnhild's. Though she had the extra weight, she was light on her feet as they danced about the room.

Whether on purpose or by accident, Poppa would never know, but Ragnhild made a mistake that ended the dance. Early on in her training, Poppa had discovered a weak spot in Ragnhild's movements. Time and time again, she would leave a small area on her left hip unprotected by either sword or shield. It only appeared when she spun to the right, which didn't happen often. Poppa had checked her once or twice before Ragnhild had acknowledged the weakness. Ragnhild looked intensely at Poppa and then turned to the right. Poppa, as quick as a viper, pointed her sword in the spot. She didn't thrust hard enough to puncture the skin, but all of them understood the consequences of the deadly check. Then Poppa raised her right leg and kicked before Ragnhild could move to ward off the blow. Ragnhild fell, defeated, to the floor and raised her hands to yield.

A cheer rang up from the onlookers, but Poppa only looked to Rollo, who clapped and smiled at her. Pride shone across his face, his smile large and bright. She returned his jubilant approval and grinned at him before she offered her hand to her opponent. Both women breathed hard. With sweat upon their brows, they hugged. Ragnhild left one arm around Poppa's shoulder and beamed at her with pride. She took Poppa's hand in her own and lifted it above their heads to more cheering from the crowd.

Poppa felt a draft flow up her dress. She looked down to see that during the sparring she had ripped her gown further. A little pink crept up her cheeks, but before she could excuse herself, Rollo had pulled her into his arms. He drew her into a kiss of approval and then excused them both while he offered the rest of them the space to stay, eat, drink, and spar as long as they wanted.

In their room, Rollo slowly removed Poppa's dress while he lamented, "It's a pity. I enjoyed that dress."

"I'll have another made," Poppa replied as she kissed his chest.

Rollo took her to bed, and they clung to each other as Thor's storm raged outside.

ATONEMENT

As the days neared the birth of his son, Rollo's mood grew more anxious and broodier. He had a short temper with the servants, as though nothing could please him. He became impatient with his chieftains when issues arose that required his leadership. He didn't like when Poppa, larger in her last month, strayed too far from the house. He demanded that the midwife travel with her when she left and remain within earshot at all times.

He'd act beastly with Poppa and then continue on as if nothing was amiss. With little over a month left, he announced he would no longer make love to her, for fear of hurting the child or inducing premature labor. This only served to worsen his mood and eventually caused a rift between them. At a loss for how to handle him, Poppa sought help from the archbishop.

"Père, I don't know how to handle his moods. Each day, my belly grows bigger and so does his agitation and irrational requests. Do you think he doesn't want this child anymore?" Poppa worried as she wrung her hands and looked over toward Edda, the midwife, who sat patiently in a pew a few rows back. Edda, of Frankish decent, had the rich golden hair of many of the natives of the area. Her tan skin, littered with freckles, told the story of a woman who spent many hours in the garden planting and collecting herbs. Edda was the age of Poppa's mother, had she lived. This comforted Poppa, and she'd grown accustomed to the woman's presence.

"I think that's the opposite of what he wants. Though, he may not even know why he's acting the way he is. From all you've said, it sounds like fear is getting the best of him at the moment. Remember that his last experience ended with both wife and child dead upon the birthing bed. He has more to lose now. It's my belief that he's working through these thoughts and emotions."

Poppa realized he was right. "What do you think I should do?"

Père Guillaume smiled reassuringly at her as he gently instructed, "I think you should be obedient to his wishes, though some seem irrational. Perhaps with your submission, his anxiety will ease and he will open up to you. You've only a short moon's turn left. Surely you can bear this."

"I was afraid you'd say something like that. Yes, I can do that, but there's more I've neglected to tell you."

Guillaume made a motion for her to continue.

"He talks to himself. I only catch snatches of what he mutters under his breath. But from what I've heard, I fear he means to perform a pagan sacrifice to Freya."

Guillaume sighed. "That's concerning. Can you be sure?"

"Of course, he wouldn't admit to it when I asked him, but he did tell me that Freya is their goddess of fertility, life, and death, among other things. It's not a small jump to think that's his intention."

"We will pray for him and for his warring soul. He has fought many battles, Poppa, but I fear the one he fights within himself will prove to be his greatest. He will need you as a pillar of our Lord to always lead him back. We will pray for wisdom and discernment for you as well."

Poppa had never left the church without her burden lifted until this day. She walked home in silence with Edda at her side. As they walked, the rickety noise of wooden wheels over packed dirt clanged through the air. The hunched elderly man leading the donkey-drawn cart didn't meet Poppa's gaze as he passed. The two women stepped off the path into the tall grass to allow the cart to pass. As it went by, Poppa peered into the cart to see what it carried. Inside she saw a shapely statue of a woman about half the size of herself. An expert hand had carved and detailed the wood. Poppa followed, perplexed, as the cart made its way up the hill.

She arrived at the house to a commotion of activity. Servants pulled on ropes and slowly raised the statue in the front yard before the garden. It took two men to balance and place her. Several female servants milled about in the garden on the right picking herbs and flowers. Movement to the left, by the stables, held Poppa's attention. Rollo led a beautiful white horse out of the stables. The equine had crystal blue eyes with a long, flowing white mane and tail.

Poppa rushed over to them but then slowed herself as not to frighten the horse. "Rollo, she's beautiful!"

Rollo looked at her despondently for a moment, then at the horse. "She's fitting for her purpose."

Poppa read his expression and didn't need to ask. Her heart sank. "Rollo, you cannot."

"I won't be lectured by you. It's our custom. I didn't have the rites performed last time for fear of the Church and the people's perception. You know what happened then."

Poppa saw his squared shoulders and resolved expression and knew she couldn't change his mind. "If you do this, you know I can't be a party to it."

Rollo seemed to grow taller before her as he glared down upon her. "I don't need your permission, nor do I need you to be willing. Your dress is hanging in our room. I expect to see you down here in an hour. The ceremony starts at twilight."

Poppa glared at him as she spoke harshly, "This is heathenism, Rollo. This is putting idols before God, and I won't take part in it! You cannot ask me to do this."

"You carry my child. You've no choice, and it's not a request."

Rollo held the reins of the horse and led it over to the garden. He handed the lead off to the lady Ase, the woman who had married them in the old tradition. Poppa's stomach churned. She felt too frustrated to cry. She marched into the house and had to step aside as servants brought out two large chairs. The white cotton dress waited for her, as promised, when she entered the bedroom. She stared at it for a long time but made no preparations to undress.

Rollo came in as the night watchmen's bells rang in the valley below. Rouen's workers would be closing their shops and heading home for the night at this call to curfew. The night watchmen would soon take to the streets with their lanterns and keep Rollo's peace as the rest of them slept. Rollo said nothing to Poppa as he replaced his clothing with all white linens. He picked up the dress and handed it to her silently. Poppa pulled it from his hands in haste and grumbled as she put it on. She looked at herself in the leaded glass mirror. The dress stretched tight over her belly and at her widened hips, but it fit. It had a simple, modest neckline that cut just under her shoulders, leaving all above it open and bare. Rollo came up behind her and brushed her hair. He pushed some of it to fall over her shoulders.

"Leave your hair down and no jewelry. We're to come to Freya humbly and without decoration."

"I don't understand why you're making me do this."

Rollo sighed heavily and then tenderly picked up a tendril of her hair and twirled it through his fingers as he surveyed her hair and not her eyes. "I won't lose you too. Nor will I lose this child. I must do all I can to—"

Poppa took the hand that fingered her hair and covered it with her own. She brought his hand to her lips and kissed it gently, leaving her lips to rest on his worn knuckles. She looked up at him with her big brown eyes and reassured, "You won't lose us, Rollo."

"You can't be sure."

"I don't want our children to grow up knowing the heathen ways. Rollo, I want them to know and love our Lord. He will govern their rule."

Rollo's tender face grew stoic and he pulled his hand away from her. "They're waiting for us. It's time we go."

Poppa followed behind him feeling as though she was the one being led to slaughter. The atmosphere felt solemn when they arrived outside. The sky hung heavy in periwinkle blue and wrapped the garden in a haunted embrace. The crowd of chieftains and their wives stood in a large circle on the grass; every few feet, an iron brazier flamed tall between them. All of the invited guests wore black, as if in mourning, while Poppa and Rollo clad themselves in white. Rollo took her hand and led her to the faldstools in front of the statue of Freya at the center of the ring. Poppa stared at the carving of Freya, with its cold wooden eyes. The chiseled grooves in the wood ran deep. The shadows cast from the fire shifted sinisterly upon the face and crept into the carved hollows, making them appear black and empty. A young serving girl came before Poppa and placed a fresh crown of white flowers upon her head. In any other situation, Poppa would have enjoyed their smell, but on this night, the thick, sweet smell nauseated her. She placed a hand protectively on her belly and stared straight ahead into the large fire burning in the middle of the circle.

A woman sang a sad and mournful song nearby. A deeper baritone hummed along as drums kept a steady beat. Their words sounded foreign and ancient as their voices rose and fell to an entrancing melody. Poppa couldn't see where the singer's voice came from. The song seemed to flow from all around them as it enveloped the scene in a lament. As the woman's voice grew, the beat of the drum became faster to match Poppa's beating heart. The mixture of the sounds blended into a trancelike hum. Poppa felt light-headed as she swayed to the waves of the woman's voice. She tried to make out the faces of those standing around the circle, but on a night like this the light only cast shadows.

Rollo's low voice rumbled in her ear. "It's the story of Víðbláinn, the place that will serve as a refuge for all those lost in Ragnarök, the final battle of the gods. We bless the sacrifice with this song as her soul passes into the realm."

A tear trailed down Poppa's cheek as Ase slowly led the horse to the middle of the circle. The white equine was stark and enchanting against the world fading into darkness. Poppa gripped the arm of her chair where wood carvers had fashioned the body of a lioness. Ase lifted up a small sword and showed it to the crowd. The drumming intensified. The deep baritones matched its pace. The woman's voice reached a crescendo. The beautiful and doomed horse pawed nervously at the ground as the beat increased in speed.

All at once the music stopped. Silence hung around the yard and those gathered.

Poppa gazed at the light of the fire as it reflected off the metal knife. Time slowed, so when the swift cut came, she didn't even realize it until the horse had knelt in the dirt. Then it laid down completely. Ase held a large basin out to catch the lifeblood that flowed from the horse's neck. Poppa was vaguely aware of the tears streaming down her cheeks, but she didn't cry out. Beside her, Rollo took her hand in his and held on tightly as they witnessed the horse's final moments. It didn't seem to suffer, although it kicked helplessly in its final throes of death. Rollo's hand trembled, and

Poppa turned to him. She caught a glimpse of something she hadn't expected to see in his eyes: regret.

Ase stood behind the statue with two of her priests behind her. They held the basin full of blood, which looked black in the fading light. The priestess put a stiff ceremonial brush in the basin and then flung the blood onto the statue. She repeated this action eight more times before standing before Rollo. She bowed and then flung the blood so it dropped onto his head, face, and clothing. Nine times as well. Then she moved to Poppa and did the same. The blood felt warm when it hit her, it's smell metallic and meaty. Droplets landed on her dress, in her hair, and on her face. Nine times, Poppa noted. When the priestess finished, she took the basin and dumped it over the statue of Freya.

That's when the gathered group murmured an approving prayer and the singers began a new mournful song. Poppa sat wide-eyed and confused as those around her celebrated. A few of the men had come and hauled the horse to the outside of the circle. Immediately, they began to carve it. Next to them, servants tended to large cauldrons filled with steaming water atop a large cookfire.

Rollo stood and raised his arms. "Stay and eat with us as we continue to bless the goddess Freya. We will have ale and mead and feast until all the meat is devoured!"

He took Poppa by both hands and kissed her and then kissed her belly. Poppa wanted to get away—wanted to flee into the house so she could remove the soiled clothing and clean herself, but Rollo held her fast in his arms. One hand was around her waist, and his grip offered no yield.

"You must stay until it's finished. You must eat of the sacrifice, or it's all for naught."

The singing sounded different, yet still the ancient words surrounded the night in haunting tones. The light sound of wood pipes encircled the lively group as they spoke and laid offerings of money, herbs, and food at the feet of the statue. Those gathered began to dance and flow to the tune. As the meat boiled, the horse's carcass stripped to the bone, villagers arrived to await the meal. The Franks, having missed the ceremony, walked with confused expressions past the statue in the garden that dripped with the horse's blood. They crossed themselves when they witnessed Rollo and Poppa covered in the dark stains that appeared black in the light of the fire. They had expected to partake in a midsummer eve's feast and didn't understand the ritualistic nature behind the celebration.

A serving boy served Rollo and Poppa the heart of the horse. He had boiled the meat and charred it over the flame, but still the four chambers remained intact. Poppa's stomach churned. Rollo cut into the meat and made small pieces for her to chew. Poppa shook her head in refusal. Rollo glared down threateningly at her as he picked up a large chunk and put it into his mouth. He chewed with an open mouth and then swallowed before taking another large piece from the tray. She noted that he took the bigger pieces, leaving the smaller pieces for her to finish. He would do most of the work in devouring the cooked heart. Reluctantly, she placed a small piece of the meat in her mouth. Though she found chewing the meat tough, it was deliciously flavored with herbs and oils.

Rollo gave her a small grin of proud approval.

They took turns sharing the meat until they finished it entirely. Poppa's stomach rolled. She had to make a conscious effort not to recoil. She glanced around at the thinning crowd. They had devoured the sacrificial meat and slowly left. She noted that the villagers walked warily around the statue. Even more so, they cautiously took their leave from Rollo and herself. Poppa casted her eyes down in shame. When she could bear it no longer, she left and headed for the tepidarium.

The blood had dried on her skin and started to itch. She considered the droplets on her arms and dress. Her stomach still rolled. She felt a familiar hand on her back and turned to peer over her shoulder. Rollo had entered the room silently. Slowly he unhooked her dress with deft movements. Poppa rubbed and itched at her skin. The blood flaked and left reddish-brown stains. Poppa let her silent tears fall freely.

"You must understand this was necessary," Rollo pleaded in a low voice.

Poppa let the dress fall from her and removed her smallclothes before entering the pool. She didn't speak as she lowered herself into the water under Rollo's watchful glare. She submerged herself under the water and swam before reemerging at the opposite end, placing distance between them. She narrowed her eyes at him and raised an eyebrow as he entered the pool.

"You forced me to participate in a ritual that goes against all I believe in," Poppa spat. "That was. I don't know. It was . . . you asked me to go against my God!"

Rollo contemplated her grimly. He hadn't given thought about what the ceremony would look like to someone who hadn't seen the likes of it before. He had participated in this custom several times before. Though gruesome to behold, it no longer shocked him. He considered the horror Poppa may have felt or possibly still did. In his state of mind, he had overlooked her well-being. He felt ashamed. The customs of his youth constantly warred with the new faith of this land, but he had to remember that it wasn't so for others. He sighed heavily as a wave of the guilt he had felt during the ceremony overcame him again. "I've asked too much. Please forgive me."

"I'll go to the Père and ask for forgiveness on the morrow, but Rollo . . ." Poppa paused. "I'm concerned for your soul."

Rollo thought of the stories of the God of the Bible and all His vengeance when His people put other gods before Himself. Hadn't all the priests said that that was the number one commandment? He remembered a battle a small time ago when his enemies had laid holy relics before him. At the sight of them, momentarily blinded, he had lost his will to move. Rollo thought of the life of his wife before him and the babe she carried. A powerful God held them both in his hands. The familiar fear, his constant companion these past weeks, flooded his being. He had tried to abate his anxiety by going back to the customs familiar to him. He'd made a foolish mistake, and he needed to make amends. Rollo jumped from the bath. His naked body dripped water over the floor as he grabbed a long thick purple robe. He moved in frantic motions as he called for a servant and then turned to Poppa. "We won't wait until the morning. I'll call for him immediately. We'll both confess, and I'll make this up to you and to your God."

Poppa didn't have time to argue as Rollo fled from the room, following the servant. She sat in the pool for a moment to collect herself. She made sure she had washed off all of the blood before she followed after him.

Poppa, still wearing her robe, greeted Père Guillaume when he arrived. He set his mouth in a grim line, but his blue eyes twinkled with the familiarity of friendship as he embraced Poppa and then Rollo. He listened as they confessed and then offered them the Holy Communion. Rollo went through the motions along with Poppa. Though the hour was late, she felt a resurgence of energy and affirmation when they finished.

"Before you leave, Père," Rollo spoke as he handed him a bag of coins.

Guillaume took the offering with humility. He confirmed he would put the gold to use in furthering the Lord's work.

"There's more," Rollo explained. "I'd like to send more funds to Mont-Saint-Michel Abbey. I know the rebuilding has continued for years, but I'd like to expedite it. I'll also send capable workers. The common folk in that area will benefit from having a place of worship and study. I'd like your assistance in finding the monks that were displaced. They should know it's safe to return."

Guillaume bowed his head low. "A rich donation. Thank you, jarl. The church will not forget your indulgence. And of the other matter?"

"The ships are expected within the week," Rollo confirmed. "I had planned that monks would carry the relic to the chapel, but now I think it best that I carry it myself. At least for the last part of the journey."

"The relic?" Poppa looked to both men in turn for clarification.

Guillaume gave her a knowing grin before explaining, "Months ago Rollo arranged to have the relics of the virgin Hameltrude brought across the waters from England and transferred to the chapel of Saint Vedast."

Poppa smiled and tried to catch Rollo's eye, but he wouldn't meet her glance. A reddish flush crept onto his face under her stare. She gently placed one hand upon his arm and acknowledged, "Rollo, that will give the people great hope and encouragement."

"It will also help affirm your faith. People will travel many miles to witness the relic's journey to the chapel," Guillaume remarked before he blessed them both and took his leave.

It wasn't for some time after the door had closed that Rollo turned to Poppa, who smiled at him proudly. "Don't look at me like that."

"Like what?" Poppa took a step backward from Rollo and his harshness.

He felt conflicted and bitter again. His head was dizzy with the burden of all those he felt the need to please: the gods, Poppa's

God, Poppa herself, the common folk both Norse and Frank, and his chieftains.

"Like I'm the prodigal son that has just returned home. I am not that man." Rollo paused and then narrowed his eyes at her as he explained further. "I had meant this gesture merely as a gift to you and our unborn son. I knew that honoring the relics would please you. Now I'm taking that gift and I'm using it to my advantage. I didn't think about the effect the sacrifice to Freya would have on the Frank population. If I want to rule them and gain their respect, I need them to see that I honor the Church and their customs."

"So that's all this was this night? A show? For me? For the Père?"

"It wasn't a show. I understand the power of your God, and I understand the vulnerable state we're in as we await the birth of our son. On this night, I sought the approval both of my old customs and of the faith that's new to me. Nevertheless, Poppa, I must explain to you my motives so that we don't continue to have conflict over it," Rollo divulged seriously. "My power balances on the tip of a sword. One side is the people of my homeland, and the other side is your people of Francia. I must please them both in order to gain their approval as their liege lord. It's a constant act of righting my footing as I try to unify them. When I carry the relics to the chapel, I'll give the Franks what they long to see, and the Norse that haven't converted to the faith of this land will understand my appeasement. Don't fool yourself that this act is anything but that."

Poppa hugged her swollen belly between her arms and focused down upon it. She slowly shook her head. "Our children will worship the Christian faith, Rollo," she affirmed. "And I'll hold to the faith strong enough for us both until you realize that your own is more genuine than you allow yourself to believe."

Poppa turned her back to him and left him by the fire. She walked slowly up the stairs to the bedroom carrying the heavy burdens laid upon her, both spiritual and physical. Though weary, she felt a resolve of perseverance grow within her. If Rollo felt the burden of balance, she would carry the burden of holding the scale.

◊◊◊◊◊

The clouds moved in soft rolls across the brilliant blue sky. When they covered the sun, they cast shadows upon the land. Then they would roll on, and the brightness of the sun would shine upon the people again. Poppa sat upon a large oaken chair that monks had brought for her to rest on. She could witness, in comfort, the movement of the relics of Hameltrude along with the crowd that had assembled. It stretched out for miles along the road toward where the Seine met the sea. Père Guillaume stood on her right. A burly young Norseman was stationed on her left; his hand never left his sword's hilt as he scanned the crowd. Nearby, Edda stood amongst some of the other servants who had traveled down the Seine with them.

Poppa breathed in the salty air, and memories of her voyage to Rouen returned to her. She could almost feel the rocking of the ship beneath her. Her body began to sway at the memory, rocking the child within slightly. One hand rested upon her belly and the other shielded her eyes from the sun so she could see the progress of the relic's approach. Rollo had left before she arose that morning, and if it weren't for his size, she wouldn't have thought it him when she caught her first glimpse.

She saw the white of his simple robe first. It fit loose upon his skin. His long hair was pulled back from his face in a knot behind his head. Propped on one shoulder and tucked into the crook of his arm rested a long wooden box that carried the holy bones of the virgin nun. It didn't look heavy so much as awkward to carry. Six monks, in their familiar brown rough-spun robes, walked closely behind him. Poppa could hear the people cheering as Rollo and the holy relic he carried passed them. As he neared, she noticed his feet, bare and dirtied from the dust of the road. She would check for cuts later that evening in their tent. He wore a solemn expression as the crowd cheered around him. He made the hill's climb at a measured pace. Soon he reached the top, where he stood humbly before her and the clergy. He broke face and winked at Poppa before he handed the relics off to the waiting monks.

The nobility that had witnessed the event entered the chapel for a short service. Behind them, the common-folk filled in the empty seats. Rollo's people praised his name as the orchestrator of the day and for delivering the relics. Afterward, they held a feast outside. The mood felt light and gay that night as the crowd drank to the tunes of the lyre. Poppa brought Rollo to their tent early in the evening as the sky turned to twilight.

"Sit," she instructed him as she pointed to the bed.

On her orders, a servant had filled the basin with warm water and sprigs of fresh lavender. Poppa carried it to the edge of the bed where Rollo sat. She kneeled before him slowly and carefully in her heaviness. Gently, she set about the task of washing his feet with the perfumed water. He let out a small moan of pleasure as she skillfully massaged the aches. The calming fragrance of the lavender washed over them and made them breathe more easily. When she finished, she softly kissed his feet and laid her head in his lap.

He wouldn't admit that this day meant more to him than a political show, but she could feel it in his touch as he stroked her hair gently, putting her to sleep. She could see it in the following days when his mood became lighter and calmer than before. He smiled widely at her in the morning before he kissed her, and he didn't treat those around him with the impatience of a burdened soul.

Guillaume

THE PAINS CAME TO HER AS SHE WALKED in from the garden, the basket forgotten in her arms as she folded over her belly. Small pains had plagued her all morning, but the one that attacked her presently clawed from the inside out. Absently, she cried out, stumbled over to the table, and held on with all her might to brace herself and to keep from falling over. Her whole body tensed as it reacted to the pain. When it ceased, her breath heaved as she remained bent over the table. Edda flew to her side within a heartbeat, soothing and cooing in a soft voice.

"The master! At once! It's time," the midwife cried out.

A young serving girl, swift on her feet, went flying from the house. Rollo had left early that morning to survey work in the nearby fields, but how long it would take him to return, Poppa wasn't sure. She hoped he wouldn't take long.

"Ahh!" Poppa screamed as another pain gripped her and pulled from within.

"Breathe. That's it. Exhale. Breathe through it. You will have a babe in your arms before the day is done."

When the relief came, Poppa smiled and chuckled at the promise.

"Come, walk in the moments of relief. Rest on me. There, that's it."

Poppa leaned on the woman and held her hand, anticipating and fearing the next pain. It took hold of her at the bottom of the stairs. Her head spun from the intensity. She felt unsure whether or not she could go any further. She held onto the stone wall, her fingers gripping so hard she could feel pain in them. The next agony hit.

"They're coming fast, child. How long have you been having them?"

Poppa spoke through gritted teeth. "Little ones. Most of the morning."

The midwife breathed out a hiss, but she stayed calm as she slowly guided Poppa up the stairs. She called out orders for water and clean linens as they went. Poppa felt grateful when they reached the room, and she crawled slowly onto the bed as pain took her again and lasted longer. She thought she might split from the inside. She couldn't keep the scream from her lips.

Rollo entered the house and heard the unearthly scream come from upstairs. He flew two steps at a time and arrived just at the moment Poppa received relief. Poppa, her hair scattered around her, sweat upon her brow, smiled at him before another cramp gripped her and her face contorted in pain. She clenched her teeth to keep from crying out, but she couldn't stem the flow of tears upon her cheeks. She breathed heavily between the contractions, and Rollo was at a loss for how to help.

Behind him, serving girls entered with clean linens and a basin of water. Rollo's heart skipped in its racing as he remembered a familiar scene not so long ago in this very room. Gisela cursed him upon the bed. He left, preferring to hear her screams from the room below. He returned when the screams weakened and ceased—and was greeted with a bed bathed in blood.

Now he watched his new wife, young and vibrant upon the bed. She squatted and rested on her heels, hunched over her belly. Her brown hair waved and flowed around her, peaceful in all the turmoil. Her eyebrows knitted in concentration as she focused on her primal task. She resembled a goddess. He went to sit behind her and took one hand in his as she screamed through the pain and squeezed with a strength he didn't think possible. With the other hand, he rubbed low on her back.

Edda eyed him suspiciously.

"I won't leave her," Rollo spoke with authority.

Poppa leaned back into him and rested her head on his shoulder, enjoying the few moments without pain. The midwife helped move her legs out from under her and open them. She used her trained fingers to check how much progress Poppa had made. Poppa's dress, drenched with sweat, stuck to Rollo's chest. Suddenly, her whole body tensed and she whimpered as another pain rocked through her.

The midwife frowned when she looked up at them. "The pains come close together, but there's much progress still to be made. She must push with the pain." Then she took some rose oil and rubbed it generously over Poppa's swell and thighs.

Rollo whispered in Poppa's ear, "Do you hear that, love? You need to push. Use that same strength you used when you fought off my men and push, Poppa."

Poppa nodded in understanding as she took in a deep breath. Then, just as she felt another pain begin, she screamed—not with pain, but with determination of battle as she pushed.

Outside, the sun left the windows to favor the other side of the house, and darkness slowly crept into the room as the hours passed. Servants came to stoke the fire and take away soiled sheets and rags. Still the labor wore on. Poppa's flesh felt clammy. Her dress clung to her as her body rocked and she hummed through the pain. Her eyes grew heavy-lidded, and exhaustion hit her. Rollo wished he could take the pain from her.

She leaned back against him after a long, hard push and whimpered like a wounded animal, "Rollo, I'm so tired. I can't—I don't think I can—"

"Shhh," he whispered in her ear. His voice sounded deep and soothing as it resonated through her body. "Shhh."

The baby kicked within her and she gave a small smile. "Your son leaps to hear your voice."

Rollo smiled into her hair and kissed her head. "And I long to meet him, wife. You're doing beautifully, but you have more work to do, Poppa. Bring our son into this world."

Poppa's vision of the tall, handsome man with fierce brown eyes flooded her mind. In the vision, she'd stood next to him with pride and love overcoming all thought. "Mother," he had whispered as she'd gazed, then fell, into eyes of deep brown.

Poppa felt a resurgence of strength, and with the next push, she felt a pressure so great that pushing against it felt like the only natural thing in the world.

"That's it!" the midwife exclaimed. "I see the crown. Keep pushing."

Poppa, with one last primal scream of victory and a clenched smile on her face, pushed against that pain. She marveled as the head escaped from within her. She mustered enough strength to give one final push as the midwife pulled gently until the child broke free.

"A son," she smiled at them.

In a haze, Poppa followed Edda's movements as she cleared the mouth and nose. Immediately came the sound all in the room awaited. He wailed with all his might, a greeting to his new world.

Behind her, Rollo laughed at the sound of his son's first cry. Gently, he laid Poppa upon propped pillows and went to the baby. He took a knife from his side belt and cut the cord himself and then washed and wrapped the baby in a blanket. His eyes clouded with tears as his large hands moved across the tiny form of his son. Rollo placed their son in Poppa's arms and kissed her forehead as he complimented her. "Well done, Poppa. Well done."

Poppa studied the babe in her arms. A shock of thick, dark brown hair covered his head. The boy's eyes slowly opened and he blinked up at her for the first time. His lips mirrored hers and his nose his lord father's. His skin felt fuzzy and soft. She rubbed her fingers over it in a slow caress. Tears welled in her eyes. She smiled down upon him as she counted his fingers and his toes. So tiny and fragile between her fingers.

"Guillaume," Rollo whispered as he bestowed the name upon his son. "I've long waited for you."

Rollo kissed his wife again and studied the child as the boy's eyes fluttered closed and then opened again. He kissed Poppa on her lips, salty with the sweat of effort. Then he kissed the babe before he instructed her, "Rest now."

Exhaustedly, Poppa grinned up at him as satisfaction and relief coursed through her body. Her eyes slowly fluttered and closed as Rollo proudly lifted the babe in his arms, a permanent smile upon his face. She went to sleep with the peaceful knowledge that she had borne a healthy son. She had succeeded in her duty.

Outside, a crowd of people, Norsemen and Franks alike, had gathered in the cool night air. They drank and feasted in the yard as they waited for the news. Rollo, with joy in his heart at the renewed promise of his line, took his son to them. He held the babe close to his chest as servants opened the oak doors. All that gathered stopped in mid-action before him as he slowly raised the child and bellowed, "Guillaume Rolloson!"

The crowd roared so loudly that their cheers reached the sleeping mother upstairs. An old Norse song of celebration rose up from all who knew it. The babe began to cry, and Rollo brought him into the protection of his chest once more. Rollo smiled at his people as they celebrated. Some shouted cheers of blessings to him, the new baby, and the mother. Others praised the gods of old, and still others praised the One and Only God. Rollo left them to their celebrations as he brought the babe back into the shelter of the house.

NORSE ATTACK

THE FIRST ATTACK CAME A WEEK LATER. Poppa sat in the great room, nursing Guillaume. Always hungry, he fastened to her breast with ease. She marveled in the tiny squeaks of his swallows as he suckled, his eyes slightly closed in the pleasure of his feeding. Rollo stood by the table across the room, pouring over maps and comparing notes, when Ragnhild ran in breathless and unannounced. Her eyes were wild as they roved over the nursing mother and then the other side of the room, finding their target. Rollo looked up, surprised, from his work.

"Norse ships. Moving swiftly toward the mouth of the Seine," Ragnhild breathed out the words in a rush. "Word just came."

"How many?" Rollo straightened from his task. He stood calm and regal in the morning light.

"Five," Ragnhild informed.

"Only five?" Rollo searched the maps before him. "They are probing. They seek to learn our defenses."

Ragnhild agreed. "We should meet them with all of our forces, leaving no survivors but the few to return home and bring the message that this area is well defended."

Poppa joined them. She burped the baby over her shoulder, slowly pushing the air bubbles up and out with her pointer fingers. Rollo's eyebrows knit in concentration as he thought on his options. The oaken door flung open once more. Herleif walked hastily through. He saw them around the table and came to them in haste.

"Ragnhild suggests we battle," Rollo spoke to Herleif.

Herleif nodded. "It'll not exhaust many of us. There are very few of them."

Rollo thought to himself before he gave a firm no.

The three around the table focused on their jarl with questioning and expectant expressions. He gave them a sly grin and continued, "We'll only raise our arms to defend. We won't engage in a battle. Let them think we're weak."

"What?" Ragnhild shook her head in confusion and disagreement.

Rollo smiled at her lovingly as he chided gently, "You're always quick to pick up your sword, Ragnhild. No, we must appear weak at first."

Herleif nodded in understanding and approval while Ragnhild shook her head. "What do you mean?"

"They're here to probe. They may raid, and we will protect our churches and homes, but their main goal is information. Let the message they bring back to their king be one of apathy and weakness. When they return, they will expect to swiftly defeat us. We will train—and we will train *hard*—while we await their attack. When they arrive in full force, we will decimate them in one fell swoop."

"They won't expect it," Herleif agreed. "Jarl, your people will expect your protection from this first attack. Some are going to die. They will carry off some of our women and children."

"I know the sacrifice I ask. Either way, they will return with greater numbers. If we first appear weak, they will not expect to be met with fierce opposition the second time."

Ragnhild grinned before she cleared her throat. "There's one more thing."

Rollo motioned for her to continue as he began rolling up one of the maps before him.

"Your brother's sigil was spotted on the sails."

Rollo stopped in the middle of his rolling. His face snapped to attention as a shadow passed across it. His thick brows furrowed and his eyes darkened. His lips formed a scowl. Though he didn't voice his displeasure, Poppa could see it written all over his expression.

"Perhaps they aren't here to fight. What if it is a friendly visit or an offer of peace?" Poppa offered in her naivety. She immediately regretted her words.

The three Norsemen watched her with amused expressions. Rollo gave her a sympathetic smile. "It's not our custom," he stated simply.

Herleif nodded in agreement with Rollo and then asked, "What will you have us do?"

"Ride as fast as you can. Take with you about fifty of your men. Join the forces there and keep them from killing, raping, and pillaging as best you can, but don't form up. I'll stay here with my wife and child. Let them think I've grown soft and comfortable in my marriage and fatherhood."

Poppa didn't say it out loud, but she was glad he wouldn't ride out to meet them. Guillaume, full on milk and properly gassed, slept in her arms. Rollo came to her and took the baby, cradling Guillaume in his arms. He looked down proudly.

"And what task would you assign to me?" Ragnhild shifted impatiently on her feet, ready and expectant of his orders.

Rollo sighed in annoyance at having to leave his reverie. "This isn't the time to divulge the strength of our shield-maidens. You will stay here. Recruit more fighters and continue training."

Ragnhild pressed her lips into a firm, disappointed line, but she didn't argue with her jarl. Her fists clenched at her side and Rollo took pity on her. "Ragnhild, the time will come when I'll need you and your maidens. Today's not that day."

The five ships carrying Norsemen from afar met little resistance on the beach before the mouth of the Seine. Herleif's men allowed the foreigners to pillage the coastline but kept them from going any further inland. The invaders mocked them and accused them of growing weak like the native Franks. When they had filled their ships with loot, they left for their homeland, full of tales of the weaknesses of Rollo's defenses.

◊◊◊◊◊

It was a gray spring morning more than a year later when the watchmen spotted the ships far in the distance, cutting through the early fog. Knowing the invaders would eventually return in greater numbers, Rollo had ordered his men to build beacons along the river, reaching from its mouth to Rouen. The signal passed up the line within an hour of the longships appearing, proving the work successful.

Poppa had just arrived outside with Guillaume toddling at her side when she saw the light of the beacon fire in the distance. Her heart skipped with both fear and excitement. Another fire, closer this time, sparked and lit as she picked up her son, much to his protest. She turned and watched the last beacon, located to the left of the stables, light in colors of orange and red. The heat from the inferno kissed her cheeks. She hugged her son close as she retreated into the house.

Guillaume had grown into a vibrant young boy over the last year and a half. He brought joy and laughter to the home. All in the household took pride in his accomplished milestones. All in the household found frustration in his fierce temper. His face turned the brightest shade of red when his incessant wail carried throughout the house. Everyone agreed he had the warrior battle cry of his lord father. Only under Rollo's stern stare would the child silence himself. Currently, the boy used this cry to voice his displeasure at losing his playtime. He had learned to walk and then run in the long, cold winter. He took much joy out of movement and enjoyed his morning playtime above all else. Now all would suffer his temper.

Rollo, wrapped in a cape and donned for battle, stormed into the room from outside. Recently, Rollo sensed that the return of his brother neared, so he clad himself for battle daily. Standing in all his regalia, he focused on Poppa and spoke darkly, "It's time."

"I know." Poppa nodded her head. The threat of this day had hung over the both of them this last year, even as they'd relished their son's toddler achievements.

Rollo gave his crying son a thunderous look filled with warning. True to form, the boy hushed in the middle of a wail. Through his tears, Guillaume, along with his lady mother, watched Rollo hastily pack. Though Rollo tried to hide it, Poppa could feel the energy of his excitement radiate off of him. He moved swiftly about the room, checking his inventory. He was light on his feet and confident.

Poppa had to remind herself that he was a warrior first and foremost. For long years, he'd kept that part of himself resting while he busied himself with decision-making, politics, and rebuilding. Over this past year, the lion within had awoken. With his warrior nature set loose, he felt free to sate his appetites at will. He trained for battle daily. The exercise didn't tire his body. Instead, it fueled him. His need for Poppa had grown along with his stamina. She could barely keep up with him when he returned in the afternoons and took her to the bedroom. He seemed to grow younger before her eyes. He smiled more and laughed heartily and often.

Despite the distractions, he'd remained a good father to their son. He took time to play with the young boy and didn't falter on discipline or expectations of behavior. At night he would place the young child in his lap by the fire and regale him with tales of battle and legend in his deep, soothing voice. Often the boy would fall asleep in the middle of a story. Rollo would carefully rise from the chair and bring him to his bed, flinching with every squeak of the floorboards as he carried his sleeping son.

Poppa anticipated his next need and called for Mrs. Laurent to take the child and prepare him to watch the longships leave Rouen. When they left, Poppa glanced at Rollo over her shoulder as she ascended the stairs to their bedroom. Rollo followed silently afterward. They reached their pleasure quickly, and Poppa prayed this encounter would give her another babe. Despite the increase in their lovemaking this last year, they'd had no success. Poppa had begun to worry. Rollo kissed her forehead; reading her mind, he spoke gently, "Don't be anxious, Poppa. I'll come back to you, and we will continue to try. It's not so bad trying, is it?"

Poppa laughed at his jest and teased, "Yes, it's such a chore."

Rollo smiled, his white teeth gleaming. "Well, then maybe you will enjoy this time of rest until I return."

Poppa glanced down. She felt his hand in her hair, pulling slightly. He pulled her into an embrace and held her to him. She relished in the familiar smell of him: cedar, woodsmoke, and sweat. He kissed the top of her head. "Come, I expect the ships to pull out soon."

The Seine flowed dark and gray as it reflected the light of the dreary day. The rain that the clouds threatened would create a nuisance, but it wouldn't slow the ships down as they sailed to the mouth of the river. Poppa watched them depart down their windy path only until she felt sure that the ship's occupants could no longer see her or the dock. For she had plans of her own.

BATTLE AT THE MOUTH

While Rollo had trained and prepared for the pending battle, Poppa had done the same. She'd kept her body lithe, quickly working off the weight she'd gained in pregnancy. With the help of a reluctant Ragnhild, she'd prepared to attend the battle as well and fight alongside the shield-maidens. She'd kept those preparations secret from Rollo, naturally. Her heart thudded at a rapid pace as Ragnhild stood rocking from side to side next to her.

"You don't have to go through with this," Ragnhild informed. "No one would think any different of you. Rollo will find out, and when he does, his punishment will be swift and harsh."

"I'll suffer it," Poppa said decidedly.

Ragnhild inspected her skeptically. They had danced through this argument many times before. Ragnhild knew Poppa had proved herself a great asset in training. She felt happy and willing to have her fight alongside them. She had always disagreed with Rollo, who treated his Frankish wife as though she were made of glass, but this plan, if discovered, was folly. Ragnhild thought Poppa relied too heavily on Rollo's love for her. Poppa took advantage of that love now. If Rollo discovered Poppa, it would wound and infuriate him; this she knew. Still, she accepted the risk.

Ragnhild let out a heavy sigh. "We must leave as soon as possible." She stood by as the young mother hugged and kissed her son goodbye.

Poppa passed Guillaume to Mrs. Laurent, who feigned ignorance of Poppa's plans. With the conflicting emotions of a mother's heavy heart and a warrior's anticipation, Poppa followed Ragnhild to the stables along with the other fighters who would journey on horseback. If they traveled at a good pace, they would arrive at the camp in less than four hours. It would take the longships traveling down the Seine longer.

With the river on their right, they rode out of Rouen and into the surrounding countryside. It wasn't long before they overcame the longships. A collective cheer went up as the men on the ships saw the riders along the road. Poppa carefully hid her face beneath the hood of a cloak. She fought the urge to search the ships for her husband. Thankfully, the road didn't follow the curves of the Seine after that and instead went straight through the flattened country of farms and small establishments. The path met up with the river again as they neared camp, but Rollo's longships would still take hours to travel down the river.

Rollo stood on the bow of the ship and thought of his plans for the battle to come. Herleif estimated that Thorir's ships, still a distance off, would arrive on land by morning. Lighting the beacons had been a risk. Rollo assumed Thorir had seen the fires from far off. He hoped that because Thorir's first raid went unopposed, his brother would expect the same circumstances the second time. Rollo remembered Thorir as a child, spoiled and impulsive, if what he wanted wasn't given to him, he waited until the opportune moment to take it without opposition. It wasn't in his nature to strategize and plan for all outcomes. No, Thorir wouldn't be prepared or numbered for battle. Rollo took a deep breath of confidence and set his sight towards the mouth of the river.

Poppa stayed hidden inside Ragnhild's tent, though she heard the cheering rise up around the camp when the longships arrived and she longed to make her presence known to her husband. Would he still allow her to fight, or would he keep her under guard in his tent while the battle raged around her? Most likely the latter, and so she stayed hidden until morning.

The morning weather was much like the day before. Dreary and gray. Rain had fallen the night before, its soft patter incessant upon the canvas of the tent. Poppa tried to rest, but the nervous excitement of the pending battle overcame her every time she drifted off. In the cool light of the morning, she donned the same clothes she'd trained in so many times. The leather and weight were now familiar. For battle, she wore the new addition over her leather bodice of a finely woven mail tunic. The metal wove tightly together and would stop a blade from piercing her skin. Though it could save her life, she wasn't fond of the new weight that she had to adjust to. She pulled her hair back from her face in several loose rolls and then joined them together at the back of her head. This would give no one the advantage of taking hold of it. Ragnhild rimmed Poppa's eyes with kohl, dark and thick, the rings almost touching each other over the bridge of her nose. Then she made small dots across Poppa's nose and a symbol between her brows. Ragnhild did the same to her own face before they set out, carrying both sword and shield.

The battle would take place on the beach. Rollo would lead the vanguard charge. The shield-maidens, positioned in the middle behind him and on both his flanks, would cover the retreat. They would push forward swiftly and cut down anyone who managed to pass the front lines, making the battlefield smaller and more lethal. Poppa carefully planted herself to the right and as far from Rollo as she could. She could see him running down the line of his men, shouting and encouraging a chant. Behind her loomed a small wooded area that would provide cover if the need for retreat came, but as she looked across the beach at the unformed and confused Norsemen exiting their ships and forming up in haste, she didn't think that likely.

The invaders, surprised at meeting such numbers when they arrived, were flustered and disorganized. Several boats tried to bypass the beach and work their way up the river. A massive chain wall spanned the width of the river and prevented the ships from going any further. Rollo had anticipated that some of the ships would try to escape upriver unscathed. He'd ordered his best blacksmiths to create the marine fencing with great haste. Poppa could hear his laughter ring over the crowd when he saw what he'd envisioned come to fruition. In their haste, the longships tried to paddle back toward the mouth, but they ran into the rest of their fleet that had already moored. Confusion arose amongst the attackers. The fleet, clustered and crowded at the mouth of the river, had no choice but to moor their ships or head back out to sea. Rollo waited for them to flood their men onto the beach and into the jaws he'd created. He knew his brother wouldn't retreat.

Poppa looked on with excitement as more Norsemen exited the moored longships and waded to the edges of the beach to join their men already in formation and clad for battle. Their weapons were at the ready. A fierce call went out among Rollo's army. Then, for a single moment, everything remained eerily quiet and still. Poppa turned to look at Ragnhild on her left and smiled before the screaming started. From her vantage point on the right side of the horde, she could see Rollo lead his men in the charge. She heard the ring of metal clashing upon metal as they clashed with their targets. At that moment, fear for her husband's safety took hold. She shook her head in an effort to clear the feeling. She couldn't allow herself to entertain those thoughts.

Ragnhild screamed orders and their line began moving forward. A wall of shields united before them. Everything within Poppa told her to run and join the battle on the beach, but that wasn't their way. They moved as one at a methodical pace. Her line would move south, with the river on her right, toward the opposite shield wall moving north. Additionally, a third shield wall moved in the middle, effectively enforcing the sea as the only retreat. Behind the wall, more men and women waited in lines and hid in the woods should any foe get through the walls of shields.

A massive man covered in tattoos broke through the vanguard first. His battle wail, wild and savage, shrilled around the beach. Ragnhild shouted orders down the line, and the wall of shields stopped as they waited to see where the man would choose to attack. He slowed and scanned the line before him. Behind him, another man, his hair matted and long, broke free and didn't wait to assess. Instead he ran straight into the wall. The blow came off to Poppa's right. A redheaded shield-maiden sunk her sword into his shoulder. More men broke free and charged the wall.

The woman next to Poppa had no time to process before the attacker crashed into her shield. Poppa braced the impact with her feet in the sand. She screamed as she thrust her sword through a hole in the shield wall. Her strike came swift and lethal. Then, quickly, she pulled her sword back behind the wall. The attackers came at them in hordes, but Poppa and Ragnhild let no one through their section of the wall. In the confusion, Poppa couldn't see where Rollo had gone or how close to the other shield wall they'd gotten. Her whole world had shrunk to the small area in front and beside her. At that moment, her neighbor, a younger shield-maiden, fell to a blow.

Poppa cursed out loud and stepped around her before joining up with the next shield-maiden. She could hear the girl whimpering, but she had no time to stop as more men broke through their wall at an alarming rate. A wave of tiredness overcame her. Then an odd dizzy feeling took its place before she felt her energy renewed. She couldn't and wouldn't give up. She moved in unison with her line, filling holes when her comrades fell. To her left, Ragnhild remained a beacon of strength.

Minutes later, a call rang out from in front of their wall. The men who prepared to charge stopped and looked behind them. Several longships regrouped and started to flee. The invading Norsemen who weren't trapped on the beach ran for the ships. The ones trapped between the shield wall and Rollo's men either chose Valhalla or fell to their knees and surrendered. Poppa discovered later that the ones who made it to the woods shared the same fate as those on the beach—Valhalla or surrender. Not one made it past Rollo's men and women in the woods.

Ragnhild wailed in a victory cry, and Poppa followed suit.

Poppa allowed the other shield-maidens to fight the remaining men who hadn't chosen surrender while she went behind the line and ministered to those who had fallen. When she found women still alive and able to move, she lifted them up and shared their burden. They stumbled to the edge of the woods, where others with makeshift stretchers waited to carry the wounded to camp. She must have done this a dozen times before Ragnhild found her.

"You must go," Ragnhild cried hurriedly. "He's approaching."

"Just one more. I heard a cry from over there," Poppa said desperately as she pointed.

"I'll take care of it. You must go." Ragnhild smiled at her then. "You fought well today, Poppa."

Poppa ran back toward the camp as fast as she could. Her adrenaline coursed as she flew through the woods. She barely noticed the bodies of the fallen invaders as she went. When she reached the tent, she could finally catch her breath. As she breathed heavily, she noticed a stinging pain at the base of her neck. At some point in the battle, she had suffered a blow. A steady stream of blood flowed from the wound. It pooled and seeped into her linen tunic. She felt light-headed when she saw the bright red, and she shook her head to clear her thoughts. As she assessed the long gash in Ragnhild's mirror, she found it wasn't as deep as she'd feared. She grabbed a towel and pressed it into the cut to staunch the flow of blood. The black kohl on her face mixed with blood that didn't belong to her and sweat that did. She wondered if Rollo would've even recognized her if he'd seen her on the beach. She barely recognized herself.

◊◊◊◊◊

Meanwhile, Rollo, covered in the carnage of battle, made his way back to camp from the beach. Just as the Valkyrie retrieved the souls of the dead and brought them to Valhalla, the shield-maidens retrieved the wounded and helped them back to camp. He walked past several of them and saw Ragnhild in the distance as she made her way back to camp. The sight of her made his heart light. He would visit her tent later and see how she had fared. For now, he made his way to his own tent along with several of his men. He would have to wait for the final count, but he felt confident that most of his men and women remained unscathed.

"By my count, fifty captives, jarl." Herleif came up beside Rollo to answer the question in his head. "We have erected a tent to keep them in until they're ransomed."

Rollo placed a bloody and dirty hand on Herleif's shoulder and shook. Though stained and in need of a cleaning, the rings of wood and bone on his fingers remained intact after the severe blows they had dealt. The men shared satisfied smiles of victory as they entered the camp. On the edge of camp, Rollo heard a name that stopped him in his tracks.

"Praise be to you, and praise be to Poppa! She saved me this day!" a voice called to his left.

Rollo spun and faced the voice. A young shield-maiden sat in a chair outside a tent and nursed a wound on her shoulder. Rollo went to her and kneeled down before her as he asked, "What did you say?"

"During the battle, jarl. I fell and it was Poppa who came for me after victory was announced. She helped get me to safety. I was bleeding horribly from my shoulder and from my head. I don't think I could have made it on my own."

"Poppa?" Rollo squinted at the woman, not sure if he had understood her correctly.

The girl smiled at him. "Já! She fought bravely, m'lord. M'lady wouldn't leave the beach till she knew we were all safe."

"She fought bravely," Rollo said quietly under his breath and then turned to glare at Herleif.

Herleif shrugged and shook his head.

"You're mistaken," Rollo said to the girl.

"Forgive me, jarl, but I'm not. Poppa, she's very beautiful and a fierce warrior. I've trained with her many times. I'd know her anywhere."

Rollo glared at her and then turned toward his tent. The woman's face was pale from loss of blood. She was probably mistaken and confused. He had almost reached his tent when the chatter of a nearby couple stopped him again.

"Did you see Poppa fight? I stood just two people down from her and Ragnhild. They held the middle of the line. No warrior could pass through them."

Rollo gave a roar of frustration as he searched the crowd. That's when he saw Ragnhild coming toward him from her tent.

She matched his stare as she continued to move closer. He could read the guilt even from afar. She slowed her steps toward him. He walked with heavy steps in her direction, closing the distance between them.

"Where is she?" Rollo's face was covered in the dirt and gore of battle. His voice boomed.

Ragnhild winced and raised her palms in an effort to diffuse him. "Rollo, wait."

He looked past her, searching the crowd, before turning back to his cousin. The full weight of his anger fell upon her with his condemning look. She flinched and instinctively moved her body into the ready position, though her sword still hung fastened at her side.

"I'll know your role in this."

Ragnhild lowered her eyes in respect. "Her mind was made up. She wouldn't listen to me. The best I could do was keep her as safe as possible."

"Where is she?" Angry spit flew from his mouth with the repetition of the question.

"Rollo, wait," Ragnhild pleaded. "She's here, and she's unharmed . . . mostly. She fought bravely today. We couldn't have held the line without her. Afterward, she rescued handfuls of women from the battlefield who would have bled out in the sand. You would've been proud."

"Don't you dare speak to me of pride!" Rollo towered over her. He couldn't remember a time he had been angrier than this moment. His heart, still racing from battle, beat hard against chest. Blind rage filled his core. A long-forgotten instinct crept in and begged to be let loose.

Ragnhild nervously searched the dozens of faces observing their argument. The anger emitting off of Rollo was so palpable she felt as though she could grasp it in her hands.

"No one knows, Rollo," Ragnhild reasoned quietly, her voice just above a whisper. "No one knows you didn't know she would fight. To many of them, she's a hero this day. You can't punish her. They'll hate you for it."

Rollo looked around at the people and took a deep breath. "I can't punish her publicly."

"That's not what I meant."

"I see that she has sent you to try and soften the blow. Don't deny it. I know the way women connive and deceive with each other. I assume she's in your tent?"

Ragnhild wouldn't meet his eyes but gave a slight nod.

"See that we aren't disturbed. That will count as a small form of payment, but you're still in my debt. Don't think that you've escaped my judgment."

Rollo stormed past her, bumping her shoulder as he made his way toward her tent. Along the way, he grabbed two men and ordered them to follow him. Before they arrived, he instructed them that under no circumstance should they let anyone get within several yards of the tent. He also ordered them not to enter under any circumstance and no matter what they heard. They nodded their heads in understanding and stood sentry outside as Rollo entered.

Poppa, in the midst of washing, jumped when he entered. She gave a startled cry when she saw his reflection in the mirror. She turned around and backed against the table as she gripped it for support. His frame seemed to fill the tent. The shadow behind him loomed and grew as it encompassed the walls of the tent. His fierceness and hollowness reminded her of the time they first met. When he'd burst through the door of Myra's chambers, lifted Poppa by the throat, and slammed her into the wall. Again he stood before her, his chest bare and covered in blood and sand. His wild hair surrounded his face. His hands fingered the battle axes hanging at his thighs. The axes were stained with gore that dripped on the furs covering the earth. Absently, Poppa's eyes flicked to them and back to his handsome but fearsome face.

He breathed heavily in his anger. His eyes burned beneath his sinister eyebrows. She didn't think she'd ever seen him this angry. Not even on the day they first met, when he'd held her throat as he pressed her to the wall. She swallowed hard and scanned her surroundings. Rollo blocked her only exit. Her sword and shield lay carelessly on the ground and out of her reach.

"Rollo, I—"

"I don't wish to hear it," Rollo bellowed. "You deceived me, Poppa. You must have been planning this for months. All the time we shared together, and you kept this from me."

Poppa observed the change in his expression as his rage turned to hurt and then back again.

"Where's our son?"

The question took her by surprise. Did he think her stupid enough to bring Guillaume here? Her voice cracked when she replied, "He's at home. In safe care."

Rollo took a step toward her. Poppa's heart started to race. Her chest rose and fell heavily. She tried to plead with him silently as he slowly advanced toward her. She tried to reach the tender heart she knew he possessed, but his distant eyes burned with vengeance and savage need.

"Stop that!" Rollo yelled at her. "Stop trying to make yourself into a wounded deer. You're not weak, and you're not going to escape so easily. Your doe eyes awaken the predator in me."

Poppa tried to steel herself as she watched him. She slowly inched herself to the other side of the table, instinctively moving to put an object between them. That's when he flew at her. She only had time to move a few steps around the table. He grabbed her neck and spun her around so her back faced him. He bent her at the waist and lowered her to the table. He stood behind her and braced her between his legs as he continued to put pressure on the back of her neck. The wound on her neck burned under his hand as he pressed her into the hard table.

She cried out and then stayed silent as his grip on her neck tightened. He used his other hand to pull down her pants and smallclothes. She could feel their weight on her leather boots as they pooled around her ankles.

The crack of the belt came without warning. Three hard strikes on her buttocks. She raged in surprise. A short pause came. In the quiet, she instinctively knew that six more would follow. Nine in all. She clenched her muscles and braced herself for the impact. Though they stung, she could tell that he hadn't put his full force behind the leather. This served as her warning. A precursor of what would come next. She whimpered beneath him as he kicked her legs apart with his foot.

He leaned over her and whispered a threat into her ear. "I don't want to hear a sound from you. Do you understand? This is purely for my enjoyment. It won't be over quickly. I'll have your consent, lady wife."

Poppa gasped. *Is consent under force even consent?* Nevertheless, as silent tears fell down her checks, she nodded once. She understood and tried not to cry out in her own pleasure as he took her from behind. She could feel the cut on her neck reopen as her body moved back and forth upon the table. She clenched her teeth and tried hard to keep her mouth closed. A sigh and whimper escaped. The hand on the back of her neck tightened, but he continued. He was right. It wasn't over quickly.

When he finally finished, he backed up and straightened himself while she continued to rest upon the table. The hair covering her face rose and fell with her deep breaths. She felt his eyes roam over her before he instructed, "Clean yourself up and get to my tent. I expect you at my side when I negotiate with my brother."

Poppa rose with fire in her eyes and made contact with his. She made a point to pull her breeches up slowly. She picked up her belt—the one he'd used on her in his anger—and stoically fastened it around her waist again. She never turned her face from him through all her movements. For a fleeting moment, she recognized the familiar look of his guilt as he watched her. Then he turned and left her to do as he instructed.

That moment she would attribute to the creation of their daughter. Not all the countless times they'd made love tenderly before or after, but the moment he took her in the lust of battle rage and the throes of wounded pride. The moment she learned how much she'd risked, how badly she'd hurt him, and how fiercely he could retaliate.

THORIR, JARL OF MØRE

POPPA WAS CAREFULLY DRESSING HER WOUND when Ragnhild rushed into the tent. Ragnhild looked wild with concern as she scanned the room. Poppa stood facing away from the door and shaking before the looking glass. Poppa made eye contact with her in the mirror and then, with trembling hands, continued to place the last bit of linen on her cut. Outside the tent, the victors celebrated with raucous laughter as they passed around the mead. The joys and the horrors of battle had left Poppa, replaced by a hollow ache.

Ragnhild came to her and covered her shaking hands with her own. "Allow me to help."

Poppa, numb, didn't acknowledge Ragnhild as she began to wash the kohl, blood, dirt, and tears off of her face. Poppa stared over Ragnhild's shoulder, seeing nothing as her mind replayed images she wanted to forget. Rollo's wounded anger and the heat of battle had caused the merciless attack. She shook with the memory of her own defenselessness.

Ragnhild studied Poppa with concern as she began to repaint her face. Poppa didn't need to tell her what had happened. Ragnhild, a warrior familiar with the aftermath of battle, had seen it all before. The lust that overcame men after slaughter was almost as dangerous as the battle itself. She'd seen Rollo take a slave girl once after a battle. That was years ago, but she still blanched at the memory. Ragnhild shut her eyes. When she opened them, Poppa was watching her inquisitively.

Ragnhild leaned forward and embraced her. Poppa didn't cry as she leaned into Ragnhild. It felt good and safe. Poppa felt relieved that someone else knew. She didn't have to relive her embarrassment in the retelling. Ragnhild handed her a horn of mead and waited while Poppa drank it down.

Poppa allowed Ragnhild to help her remove the mail and change her tunic, but she continued to wear her leather battle clothes. Ragnhild brushed and twisted Poppa's hair in the same battle fashion. Then, instead of tying it back, she left the rest to fall loosely over Poppa's shoulders. When they finished, Poppa looked beautiful even though her eyes looked haunted. She had stopped shaking—thanks, in part, to the mead—and instead stood still and calm. She was numb.

Ragnhild accompanied Poppa to Rollo's tent, and they entered in solidarity. Rollo sat at the table along with Herleif and Ingmar. Their eyes were focused on an unrolled piece of parchment as the women entered. Rollo glanced up and his stare roved over Poppa, who stood at the edge of the tent. She would come in no further. Ragnhild left her side to embrace Ingmar and glance at the parchment on the table.

"We're looking over the list of the captured," Rollo explained. "Take a seat."

"It's more comfortable to stand, my lord," Poppa said. Her words were cold and full of meaning.

Rollo had the decency to wince with guilt before a small smirk twitched on his lips. He beckoned her to his side. She obeyed and came to stand next to his chair while he sat. One hand held the parchment and the other gently caressed the small of her back. The tender affection surprised Poppa. It didn't repulse her like she thought it would. After all that had happened, she needed the reassurance of his touch. In the comfort of his embrace, she felt the tears well in her eyes. She kept them at bay by studying the names on the list, but her tears blurred the writing. She blinked to clear the water and then swiftly wiped them away with her finger. She looked back to the list, which totaled more than fifty men and women.

"Is the final count recorded?" Rollo's eyes roamed over the list, recognizing several familiar names from his childhood.

"Já, we're all accounted for. They took not one of ours," Herleif confirmed.

"Most of the ships have retreated. Only ten or so remain. Your brother and his men hide in them like old women waiting for their people to be returned," Ingmar sneered. His white-blue eyes sparkled in the firelight. He noticed Poppa's glare and sneered at her hungrily. She turned her head quickly back to the parchment.

Rollo nodded in understanding. One side of his mouth rose in a smirk before he addressed the room, "I'll have your opinions on what to do with the captives."

"Obviously we could ransom them back to your brother. As Ingmar has said, it seems they're waiting for this decision," Herleif offered.

"They could be sold into slavery," Ragnhild suggested. "Ships pass this port frequently. We wouldn't have to wait long."

"We could have them executed on the beach before the ships. It would be a powerful statement of our supremacy and might," Ingmar suggested.

Poppa's face, quiet but firm, looked intent as she cleared her throat. "You have enough riches. Do you really need to trade for more?" she asked. "The last option is brutal and could cause a blood feud. The point of your dominance in this area has already been made clear by the victory of the battle today. Surely there has been enough bloodshed."

Rollo turned his head and glanced up at her as she scanned the list. The fates of the men and women played out in her mind as she continued, "You could offer them incorporation."

"Incorporation?" Ingmar scoffed. "A woman's answer."

Poppa shot Ingmar a scathing look. Rollo's lips twitched in a smirk, but he held up a hand for Ingmar to remain at peace and then turned back to Poppa. "Explain."

"You could offer your brother parley. Allow him to partake in this discussion. Let the offer for reconciliation remain on the table. These men fought well today. Your army outnumbered theirs. Defeat was inevitable. You said once that you've no time for cravens who flee from battle. These didn't leave on the ships. They're still here with your brother. Give them the option to stay along with the captives. If they kneel before you and swear fealty to you, these men could be of great use. More use than riches and beheaded bodies feeding the crows on a beach. Rollo, I've seen you unite Franks and Norsemen and rule them equitably. Power isn't all might. It's also mercy."

Rollo knew they talked not solely of the hostages and his brother. Her words chided him, and it cut deeply. He hung his head for a moment. Only Poppa could see his shame. When he looked back at his advisors, his face was resolute. "As she says. Herleif, send word to my brother. We will host them this night and dine on meat and mead as we discuss the terms of their departure."

Ingmar's fists hit the table, and Ragnhild placed a hand upon his shoulder to calm him. "This is a mistake! Rollo, they foolishly attacked you—and we've beaten them. They have nothing to negotiate with."

Rollo stood, his presence once again commanding the room. The eyes of those gathered moved to look upon him, and their mouths, respectfully, stayed silent as he spoke. "They have their lives and their fealty. He's my brother."

Ingmar's eyes flashed with anger, piercing Poppa with a look of blame before he turned and left the tent.

"He'll be fine," Ragnhild comforted. "I'll see that he has a woman and a large horn of ale that doesn't go empty." Her eyes found Poppa's and asked a silent question of confirmation. Poppa gave her a discreet nod before Ragnhild took her leave.

Rollo stopped her on the way out. "There's one more thing, cousin."

Ragnhild winced. With balled fists, she turned to face her jarl.

"You will travel back with my brother."

"Rollo!" Poppa protested. He shot her one dark look that stopped her from saying anything else. She realized she wouldn't suffer alone for her decisions. Ragnhild had kept her secrets, and for her part in the ruse, Rollo would have her exiled.

"You have not seen your lady mother in some time." Rollo's voice cracked with emotion as he spoke. "And I long to have news from my homeland. You will stay as long as you wish, but I do expect you to return. All the better if you bring more Norse with you to help settle this land."

Tears built behind Ragnhild's eyes. It was the first time Poppa had seen the Norse woman cry. She lifted her chin and replied, her voice thick with emotion, "It's an honor, jarl, to serve you in this way."

Rollo gave her a nod of approval before she left without looking back.

Poppa let out a shaky breath that she hadn't known she'd held onto. Beside her, Herleif swallowed hard before he changed the subject.

"It's a good option, the parley," Herleif confirmed. "I'll go myself to talk with Thorir. It has been a long time since I've seen him last."

Herleif departed, leaving the two of them alone in the tent. Poppa walked to the bed and sat down gingerly. She studied her hands and let out a long sigh. "I'm sorry, Rollo. I'm sorry for planning behind your back, and I'm sorry for lying. Yet I cannot be sorry for coming here. These people belong to me as well. My training started when I was young, with my father. I have to believe that was for a reason. I fought well today. The victory feels right and good. I'm proud I was a part of it. Please, don't punish Ragnhild on my account."

"I'd always planned to send someone I trusted back with Thorir. It was just a matter of whom. Ragnhild is young and will journey well. I'll hear no more of this matter," Rollo explained as he walked over to Poppa to kneel before her. He placed his hands on both sides of her head. He couldn't bear to hold her eyes, so he bowed his head in shame. "I was so angry, Poppa. I was . . . I *am* so upset with you. What I did was wrong. I was overcome by the spirit of battle and my pride, but as you can't be fully apologetic, I can't be free of my disappointment in your choices."

Poppa held his head and kissed the top and then gently placed it in her lap to rest. "Then we will have to find contentment in the impasse."

◇◇◇◇◇

A large tent, erected in the camp's center, served as the hall where the feast took place. Revelers stumbled about inside and outside the tent at will. Outside, fires burned and the victors danced in celebration as they mocked the captives. Haunting music played and varied from celebritory melodies to mournful laments for those who had gone to Valhalla. Though their enemies this day, those fallen were still Norsemen and they received the necessary tribute. The guards placed around the captives playfully shooed away the revelers. In a show of good faith, Rollo didn't deny the captives meat and mead. The revelers heard the collective intake of breath from the captives as their jarl passed them on his way from the moored ships to the large tent to decide their fate.

They waited under the canopy for his arrival. Poppa stood behind Rollo's faldstool, which sat by the fire. Both were still dressed for battle, but they had washed and cleaned their wounds. Poppa added a wolf skin that she wrapped around her shoulder. The flattened and eyeless head fell over her left breast. One hand held a horn of ale; she kept the other on Rollo's right shoulder. She could feel the tension under her hand, and she ran her thumb slowly back and forth. None could see the small gesture, but Rollo felt it deeply within him. He kept his eyes fixated on the door to the tent. He didn't react when his younger brother entered, flanked by two of his men.

Poppa studied him. The difference between the two siblings surprised her. Though similar in size and build, Thorir's features contrasted Rollo's dark complexion in their fairness. Thorir wore his long blond hair tied in a bun behind his head. His eyes, a deep blue the color of the ocean, reflected the firelight and shone with a flash of brilliance as he looked about the room. His easy and carefree manner would make no one suspect he'd just lost a battle. When his gaze fell upon Rollo, he grinned amusedly. When he smiled, Poppa saw the familiar grin of her husband.

Rollo rose to greet him. He offered his right arm and his brother took it in his. They clamped forearms, and then, with their other arms, they embraced for a long time. Rollo pulled back and placed his hands on his brother's shoulders. He stared at him and then knocked his forehead against his and chuckled. If Poppa hadn't known better, she might have thought she was simply watching two brothers reunite after a long absence. But a palpable heaviness hung in the air between them and surrounded their greeting. It was the tension of two brothers—one the victor and the other the vanquished. Together they would have to forsake their pride and decide upon acceptable terms after the battle.

"Sister." It was the first word that Thorir spoke to Poppa. He took her hand in his and smiled at her as he gently kissed her knuckles. "Tales of your beauty have reached us far across the sea, but we didn't expect to be greeted by the fierceness of a shield-maiden as well."

"It's a pleasure to meet you in both ways, my lord." Poppa's eyes sparkled in the light of the fire, the brown irises lit with honeyed flecks. She watched her brother-in-law carefully. He was handsome, with an innocent face and ease about him that made her think of a spoiled young boy. She guessed he only needed to smile and whatever he wanted he received. She sensed another expression, similar to her husband's, a calculating shrewdness that hid beneath the guise of goodwill. The twist of his lips and the darkness behind his eyes matched his older brother. He hid the darkness better with his youthful and angelic good looks.

Rollo smiled at her before ordering a servant to bring them meat and mead. Poppa left the brothers to talk together about their terms. She wandered around the tent and celebrated with the people. Many wished to share mead with her and embrace her as she slowly made her rounds. Her head felt light with drink when Rollo finally stood up and clapped his hands together for attention. Thorir rose on his right side, his mouth still in an amused smirk. Poppa wondered if he wore that look as a permanent expression.

"All will join me today in welcoming those of today's foes who choose to offer me their fealty. We will welcome them into our society, and we will live in peace with those who choose instead to sail over the waters with my brother." Rollo's voice boomed around the tent.

Those standing near Poppa quickly offered their affirmation of support and agreement. She did notice some of Rollo's people left the tent quietly. She hoped this wouldn't cause a lasting rift amongst Rollo's people. She went to his side and congratulated the brothers. "We never know when we or our children will have need of your aide." Poppa lowered her head before her brother-in-law.

He respectfully bowed lower before her, and she allowed him to kiss her ring. Rollo didn't miss how his brother's lips lingered. He clapped Thorir hard on the shoulder and then embraced him. Herleif led a short ceremony while more than a hundred of Thorir's men and women kneeled before Rollo and Poppa to swear an oath of fealty. The rest chose to leave on the ships in the morning, vowing only to return to Francia in peace or to come to her aide.

Not all of Thorir's men who chose to leave seemed at peace with the new pact. Poppa noticed a handful of them spit upon the ground as they left the tent and went into the cover of night. They had just bowed before the victor brother in their defeat. She saw that the gesture hadn't escaped Rollo's calculating glance either. His hand clenched and unclenched at his side, but he made no move to deal with the disrespect. Instead, he chose to walk amongst his people, recounting tales of the battle and thanking them for their part. Poppa sat on Rollo's regal faldstool. Thorir had a chair brought for him so he could sit at her side while her husband roamed the room. He leaned on the arm of his chair toward her and followed his brother through the shrewd eyes she had recognized before. This time, she thought she noted a hint of jealousy.

"My brother's gaze rarely leaves you, no?" Thorir smiled coyly at her through his observation.

Poppa turned to discover his face was quite close as he leaned over the arm of his chair. A crooked grin still graced his lips. "Do you not notice how he walks about the hall but keeps his watchful gaze upon you? He has the look of a blackbird. Our lady mother always said so. No, I don't mean a hawk. Hawks see to hunt. Blackbirds see with an intelligent and calculated knowing."

Poppa nodded in understanding as she looked toward her husband. She smiled when he noticed her looking at him. He had pulled his hair back into a bun like his brother's, which offered a full view of the handsome features of his face. His scarred eyebrow raised when their eyes met, and he returned her smile before turning to Vogg, who had just come in along with Ingmar from outside.

"I had a mind to bring you back with me over the seas after I won the battle," Thorir teased. "I suppose I can't add that into the negotiations."

Poppa smiled at him in his jest. "Are you not married?"

"Já, but it's our custom to take more than one wife, and I've heard of the nature of your marriage."

Poppa's smile turned into a frown at the mention of the *more danico* arrangement that made Rollo free to dismiss her or take another wife.

"Oh dear, I didn't mean to offend. Take it only to mean that I could easily take you as a wife if I didn't think my brother's love for you was true." Thorir took a long sip of his mead and continued, "The princess Alof was given to me by her lord father, King Harald. I had to accept the gift, you see, but she doesn't please me. She's not comely, and she squeals like a pig beneath me when I mount her."

Poppa choked on the mead she had swallowed and tried to stifle a laugh. Thorir enjoyed her reaction and smiled at her. His amused grin only widened.

"Go ahead, it's all right to laugh."

He laughed along with her and mimicked the noises of his wife, which made her laugh all the more until Rollo stood between the two of them, a strong hand placed on each of their shoulders. "Do I dare ask what's so funny?"

Poppa, in a fit of laughter, couldn't make eye contact with her husband. Thorir smiled up at him innocently before he charmingly said, "I'm simply getting to know my new sister."

Rollo's eyes narrowed as he looked over his brother, but he didn't push the matter. He took a large bite of the charred rib he held in his hand and then a long pull of his ale before sitting on top of Poppa, who still occupied his chair. He wiggled upon her in play. She laughed and smacked his back hard as she pushed with all her might to move the heavy weight from her lap. Rollo leapt up, and in one fell swoop he scooped Poppa into his arms, sat down, and placed her on his lap. His greasy hands left marks on both linen and leather. She kissed him then, enjoying the smoky taste of meat on his lips. Thorir laughed, taking the point.

◊◊◊◊◊

Poppa woke in the morning naked beneath the furs and cradled against Rollo. Facing him, she held tight with her arms wrapped around his body. She snuggled her face against his chest, breathed in his smell, and kissed him. She could feel his hand in her hair as it softly ran down the length, from crown to end. Last night, they had reconciled beneath the furs. In the light of the morning, she longed to see and hold their son.

Dreamily, Rollo kissed her forehead, his eyes still closed as he woke to the world slowly. "Guillaume will be happy to see us this evening." Rollo's voice came out heavy with sleep as he turned in bed and slowly sat up.

"It's as if you can read my mind."

Poppa watched as he clothed himself and admired his tattoos as they moved with the muscle that rippled under his skin. She sat in the bed and hugged her knees to her chest. Her milk had dried up months ago, and she ached for another baby at her breast. She had vehemently refused to hire a wet nurse. Instead, she preferred to do the work herself, longing for the bond with her baby. Daily she felt that need grow, and she grieved each time her monthly moon's blood came.

"I'll take another stab and guess you're hoping for another one."

She smiled prettily at him. "How do you do it?"

"You wear your thoughts on your face, Poppa. That or I've become very good at reading you."

"When do you think it'll happen? In my vision . . . I never told you, but as we stood on the hill next to our son, I felt—no, *I knew*—there was another. A boy or a girl, I couldn't tell. I just knew. Do you think that odd?"

Rollo kissed her forehead. "I don't. Visions don't tell us everything, and often much is left to interpretation. Come now, we must see off my brother's ships before we head home ourselves. I have much work to do. I have to find new lands to satisfy Vogg. I have to—"

"To satisfy Vogg? Whatever could you owe the man?"

Rollo gave her an exasperated huff. "I shouldn't have said anything."

Poppa jumped from the bed and donned herself hastily. "You look burdened. Tell me and maybe we can come up with a solution together."

Rollo sighed as he sat on the bed again. "Do you know the work that Vogg manages for me?"

Poppa remembered the time on the beach. It felt so long ago, but she could still remember the screaming mother Vogg separated from her son. Poppa hadn't known a mother's love then, but she had known mercy. As the scene replayed in her mind, her heart ached even worse. She knew what it felt like to carry, birth, and raise a child. She could not process how she would feel if someone ripped her son away. She sighed and spoke quietly in an effort to convey her disapproval. "He's in charge of the slave trade."

Rollo nodded.

Poppa's mouth hardened into a thin line. "And he hoped to have some captives to sell after the battle."

"Já, and now that he doesn't, I'd like to give him something. He performs his job well. I can't afford to lose him."

"You said you wanted to meet his new wife. That was more than two years ago. We'll invite them to dinner. He's a man of few words, but hopefully he or she will say something that will give you an idea of how to appease him."

"At least it's a start. The trade brings in a good profit for him and I."

As heart-wrenching as it was for Poppa to accept this side of Rollo's management, she knew it was the way of things. She couldn't ask him to put an end to this part of his business. She kept her silence and took peace in that she had at least saved the invading Norsemen from this fate. She turned quietly and began to ready herself for watching Thorir and his ships leave.

Many gathered on the beach to watch the remaining ships hoist their sails. Poppa held fast to Ragnhild, who returned her hug and whispered in her ear, "This isn't your fault. We all choose our paths. We each chose the right path, Poppa."

Ragnhild's eyes and cheeks were wet when she broke from the embrace.

Rollo also took Ragnhild into his arms. He embraced her fiercely, and then he kissed both of her cheeks. Before letting go, he whispered in her ear, "May Odin give you wisdom on your path, may Thor give you courage and strength, and may Loki bless you with laughter wherever you go."

She gave him a small smile and turned to walk toward the ship. Her blond hair whipped in the wind behind her. She walked confidently upon the sand, with her shield strapped to her back and her sword buckled to her side.

"Are you sure I cannot take you with me?" Thorir teased Poppa as he came to stand before her.

"I think one of our shield-maidens is enough for you to handle," Poppa replied as she nodded toward Ragnhild, who had just reached the ships.

Thorir turned to follow her gaze and laughed heartily. "I believe you're right."

After he kissed her cheeks, he turned to his brother. They stared at each other for a time before they hugged, and Poppa had to turn her gaze to the ship to keep from feeling the emotion of the moment. Her long dark hair danced upon the wind and blew before her face as she pondered the odds that they had arrived as enemies and left as allies. Rollo had explained to her that this happened often in their culture. Mercy had been the correct choice. Both sides became stronger for it. Poppa felt confident they would find a way to unite the people again. When the ships had sailed well out to sea, they gathered their things and walked the short distance upriver. They passed where Rollo's men had lifted the chain fence before the battle. The woven metal still hung obstructively over the water, glistening in the sunlight. Finally, they came to the spot where Rollo had moored his longships. Poppa felt reluctant to get on the boat again, but she wanted to stay by Rollo's side when they returned to Rouen and their son.

ADÈLE GEIRLAUG

IT TOOK ONLY THE SLIGHTEST AMOUNT of sickness to confirm Poppa's suspicion. She hadn't bled for two turns of the moon. She had just bent over to retrieve one of Guillaume's wooden horses when a wave of nausea washed over her. She breathed hard and grasped the back of a chair. She closed her eyes until it passed while Guillaume regarded her quizzically.

"Mama! Mama! Horse!" He cried with outstretched hands.

She smiled down at the young child. The rich brown of his hair matched hers and reached past his shoulders. Today she had it pulled back from his round face and tied at the back of his head with a thin strip of leather. His brown eyes shimmered up at her as he reached for the toy.

"Oh." Poppa gasped as she remembered the sickness from her first childbearing. She handed the toy to the child, and he ran about the room making the horse gallop and prance over every surface he could reach. Instinctively, she placed her hand over her belly. Throughout the day, she caught herself smiling at odd moments as she busied herself around the house and garden. As she cut flowers, her thoughts would stray. Then she'd remember the joy that grew inside of her, and smile.

Later that evening, as a storm blew in from the sea, a frustrated Rollo returned home from errands. He mirrored the stormy energy and wrath when he stomped into the house and shouted orders for food and for messengers. He walked past Poppa with a cursory glance. She had taken great care with her appearance that evening. Wearing a fine dress of dark purple lace and satin, her hair fell freely, the way he liked. It shimmered in the fire as the tendrils waved down to her stomach. The neckline plunged in a V-shape down past her breasts and seduced the eye. He took little notice as he passed her and fumbled through the shelves of scrolls that lined the walls.

He mumbled to himself as he searched for the item that plagued his mind. Disgruntled, he tossed scrolls to the table, unrolled one, sighed, and reached for another. Poppa waited patiently as she watched him fumble around. She knew better than to insert herself. If he needed her help, he would ask. Again, he boomed for something to eat, but this time he demanded a drink as well. Outside, the wind picked up and howled as it slammed into the panes of glass. The first flash of lightning cracked, and Poppa could see the night sky light up over the valley from the large viewing window. Shortly after came a boom of thunder that brought Guillaume screaming into the room.

He took one look at his lord father and then another at the rain falling hard outside. His stare went back to his father as the man shoved scrolls around on the table and muttered under his breath. The young boy jumped when Rollo's fist slammed onto the table, and then his face turned back to peer at the storm outside. His eyes widened as he decided which of the two scared him more at that moment. Then he found his beacon of calm. His lady mother stood quiet and unfazed in the midst of it all. He went to her, wrapped his arms around her legs, and held tightly. Poppa placed a protective hand over him and continued to consider her husband. Nothing could shake her this night.

Rollo finally took notice of the two of them, and then he glared down at his son and growled, "Don't be afraid of the storm. It's only Thor. He has come to protect us and water our fields for the harvest."

Another boom of thunder came from outside, and this time it shook the house. Guillaume startled and closed his eyes as he tightened his grip on her.

"You look beautiful this night, Poppa," Rollo said absently and without glancing up.

Poppa took this as his invitation. She sighed heavily as she scooped up their son and walked to the table to see what had him so enraged. Just as she arrived at his side of the table, a serving boy brought in a plate of cold meat, bread, and fruit. Rollo took the horn of ale first. He gulped it down and ordered another, then paused with thought before deciding he wanted a whole pitcher brought instead.

"What is it, Rollo?"

Rollo narrowed his eyes at her in his familiar fierce look. She had come to enjoy the fierceness of his look and didn't balk under it. Instead, she remained patient as she leaned into him and searched the contents of the parchment that lay on the table. Another boom of thunder caused Guillaume to hide his face in the crook of her neck. Rollo rolled his eyes and grabbed the child from his lady mother.

"Come here, son. I'll tell you about the storm and why we shouldn't fear," Rollo said as he carried his son to the window to watch the storm beyond. He turned to tell Poppa, "I was looking for an account on the holdings around Bayeux. The king has requested I present them personally."

"Personally?" She couldn't keep the disappointment from her voice.

Rollo ignored her question, already deep into the story of Thor throwing his great hammer, Mjölnir, and creating the lightning they had just watched light up the valley. Poppa listened absently as she searched through the parchments with a much more careful hand than her husband. She found the scroll causing Rollo so much distress, carelessly hidden under others he'd discarded. She carefully spread it out and weighed it down, preparing it for when he sought it again.

"Thor is a great warrior. The strongest of all the gods of Asgard. He has long hair and a beard, which shine in their ruddiness. He wields his mighty hammer forged by dwarves in the mines of Svartalfheim, and all fall under it. He comes to us upon the storm riding his chariot pulled by goats that can never die. They're reborn from their own bones. Thor comes to remind us that he's here and that he will protect us always. He blesses our land with the rain and his lightning. That's why we shouldn't fear the storm."

Outside came another flash of lightning that lit up the room for a heartbeat. Poppa came up behind Rollo and pressed her body into him as she wrapped her arms around his waist.

"For!" Guillaume screamed excitedly, not yet able to make a *th* sound.

Rollo smiled, and Poppa rested her head upon his back silently. She couldn't keep her husband from sharing the stories of his youth with their son, no matter how hard she tried. She would have to trust that in the end, faith in Christ would win out over Rollo's pagan stories of old. She prayed silently to herself that they would remain stories and not become religion for her children. Her children. She'd almost forgotten the news she'd held onto all day.

"The scroll you've been searching for is waiting for you on the table," she spoke against Rollo's back.

Rollo peered over his shoulder and down at his wife with his scarred eyebrow raised. "You're in fine clothes this evening. Is there a reason why?"

Poppa smiled slyly and walked slowly across the room, looking over her shoulder. The back of her dress opened to the small of her back. She let him enjoy the view before she spoke again. Rollo put down their son, who went running around the room using his fist to mime a hammer as he screamed Thor's name. Rollo smiled at Poppa and rubbed his hand over his mouth as he studied her. His stress and bad mood were forgotten as he appreciated his wife.

She waited until his eyes found their way back to hers before she smiled and said excitedly, "I'm with child again."

A quiet moment hung between them as her words formed their meaning in his mind. Then suddenly Rollo shouted a hoot of excitement that startled the boy running around the room. He dove for his son and brought him back into his arms. He spun him in a circle before going to Poppa and kissing her fully. Little Guillaume clapped his hands. He didn't know what they were celebrating, but whatever made them so happy, he wanted a part of it.

"You're going to be a big brother!" Poppa told the boy excitedly. He didn't know what that meant either, but he did understand the joy on his parents' faces and knew "big brother" was a good thing to be.

◇◇◇◇◇

Their daughter, born while Rollo visited with the king in Paris, came healthy, stout, and screaming into the world on a wave of pain and blood. The labor, shorter than Poppa's previous, had its complications, leaving her weak long after. She nursed the baby from her bed, where she stayed all day and all night long, only getting out to make water and occasionally take a soak in the tepidarium when her strength would allow. News of the birth hadn't reached Rollo in time. It wasn't until he returned home and was greeted by the distinctive cry of an infant that he knew his second child had come.

The baby wailed as Rollo rushed up the stairs only to find his wife struggling to hold the baby to her breast. Her hair looked unwashed and disheveled. Her complexion appeared pale and clammy.

"She won't eat," Poppa said desperately as he entered the room. Beside her, the midwife slowly and cautiously helped Poppa. In her calm, trained hands, the baby began to suckle from her lady mother. Poppa gave a cry of relief and then turned back to Rollo. "You're home."

Rollo went to her and kissed her forehead, wet with the sweat of frustration. As she stared listlessly up at him, he realized her eyes had lost their luster. Dark hollows around them caused ghastly shadows that made her look wraithlike. A shade had come over her while he was away. He was careful not to show his surprise. He turned to admire their daughter. She nursed hungrily, a shock of golden curls upon her head. She looked plumper than her brother and, over time, would prove wilder in nature.

"She's beautiful, Poppa. I'm sorry I wasn't here."

"She awaits a name." Poppa's voice came out quiet and hoarse, as if each word took effort.

Rollo waited until the baby finished, and then he softly lifted the child from her mother to get a better look at the newborn. She had pudgy cheeks that held her lady mother's smile. The babe shifted in his hold. She fit in the palms of his hands and looked upon him with dreamy deep blue eyes. He couldn't help the tears that flowed down his cheeks. "Geirlaug," he called her—a name from his homeland

Poppa gave a weak smile and then closed her eyes to rest. Rollo motioned for the midwife to follow him out the door. "What's wrong with her?"

Rollo braced himself for the worst.

"I cannot be sure, m'lord. It's been almost a moon's turn since the birth. It was swift, but it was hard on her. She suffered greatly from the loss of blood. Yet she persevered. We did invite an expert of medicine to examine her. He told me in confidence that he doesn't think her womb will hold another child. I didn't tell her, m'lord, but I think she knows. Mothers always know."

Edda paused and took one of his hands in both of hers. "Don't look too downcast. We can rejoice that we didn't lose her and that her heart is strong, though she grows weary and takes to the bed most of the day. We can find nothing physical that would cause this. We've tended to the damage in her womb. She doesn't complain of pain, though her head hurts at times and she cries. She's easily frustrated and flustered with the baby. It's like—" The midwife paused. "It's as if she has given up. She says she doesn't have energy and that she's tired, but all she does is lay in bed. Perhaps she will improve now that you're here . . ."

Edda paused.

"If you could get her to eat, m'lord. She needs to take food if she's going to continue to nurse the baby. You've seen the babe. Your daughter is strong and thriving. Poppa's stubborn, if you don't mind my saying so—she won't let anyone else nurse the child, though it takes too much from her. We have tried, m'lord, but she won't see sense."

Rollo nodded. His eyebrows knit in concentration. "Where's my son?"

"He's in town with Mrs. Laurent. Some days, my lady refuses to see him. The boy is confused. He doesn't understand this change—the baby, his lady mother's aloofness . . ."

"Bring him to me when he returns. Thank you for your service."

Rollo pressed two bags of gold coins into the woman's hands. Her eyes widened at the weight of the gold. He asked her to take the baby outside for some fresh air and returned to the room. In his initial surprise, he hadn't noticed the sour smell hovering over the room. He lost his patience.

"Get up," Rollo spoke to Poppa.

"I'm tired," Poppa refused as she rolled on her side with her back to him.

"The room stinks and you're filthy. I'll take you for a bath, and then you will eat some dinner."

Poppa didn't move.

In a frustrated huff, he went to her and kneeled by the bedside. Her open eyes stared back, empty and hooded. "Poppa, tell me what's wrong."

"I don't know! Nothing. Everything. Everything hurts. All the time. It's as if a shadow has settled over me, Rollo. All day it claws for my attention. It's hungry, but I don't know what it wants to eat. Père says I should pray—and I do, but it doesn't work. The shadow keeps clawing and growing. Always hungry."

Rollo pushed back the hair clinging to her forehead and looked at her with concern. He'd seen this before. Women would give birth and then for no reason at all would wither afterward. Sometimes they would improve over time, and sometimes they would die. He couldn't allow the latter. He left her and came back a few minutes later with peppermint sprigs from the garden.

"For your head," he said as he smiled. He rubbed the crushed leaves against her temples, and she gave him a slight smile at the memory. When he spoke again, his voice sounded low. The voice she enjoyed so much rolled over and through her. "This will take time, Poppa. But I need you to try every day. I need you to act like you do when you're training. I need you to push through the pain every time you feel like giving up. Can you do that? Can you act a warrior in this way? I won't leave you. You won't be alone, but the work will be your own. Do you understand, Poppa?"

Poppa stayed silent as she watched him. A tear escaped down her cheek and then onto the pillow. She gave the smallest of nods and then allowed him to help her up. She was weak and dizzy. Her bones ached. He helped her walk all the way down to the tepidarium, where he entered with her and washed her body as she sat on the steps. Her body had become frail, and she had lost the extra weight she had gained from carrying her child. Now her bones poked out at sickly and sharp angles. When he finished, he allowed her to save her strength and carried her back up to the bed. Changed sheets made the bed look welcoming. New flowers sat in a pitcher by the bedside. The windows, opened, let in the fresh spring air. He laid her down and fed her a thick brown stew and warm bread.

When she closed her eyes to rest, he took the baby in his arms and carried her down the stairs to meet his son. "Yord Father!" Guillaume screamed in surprise when he saw Rollo enter the room. He sat on the floor playing with wooden blocks. In his excitement and haste, he knocked the tower over and ran to his father. Rollo knelt down and opened his free arm. He allowed his son to fall into him and kissed him on the head. Then he pulled the boy back to get a better look at all that had changed in his absence. His big brown eyes reminded Rollo of Poppa's, as did the twist of his mouth. The square of the boy's nose matched Rollo's, as did the arches of his thick eyebrows. Mrs. Laurent had bathed and brushed him. His long and wavy brown hair was pulled back into a bun. He had the earthy smell of grass, dirt, and sunshine upon him. Rollo breathed deeply.

"Son," Rollo smiled at his boy. "You've grown taller since I saw you last."

"Já, yord father! Tall yike you!"

Rollo laughed. The boy had celebrated two name days and spoke more each day. "I believe someday you will be."

"Mama sick," Guillaume spoke. His face grew sad, but then his expression turned hopeful as he looked into his father's eyes. "Better. Yord father home."

"I hope so."

Then Guillaume gave the baby a side look and made a face of disgust. "She come. Mama sick."

"No, son," Rollo spoke firmly. "You sister, Geirlaug, is a gift from the gods. A gift from God. She didn't make your lady mother sick. You must love her, and you must protect her all of your life. Will you do that, son?"

The boy examined his father with wide eyes. He understood by his father's expression the seriousness of the matter. He craved Rollo's approval above all things, and so he nodded his head in agreement. Then he kissed the small baby in his father's arms. He thought she smelled strange and cried too much, but he would do as his father said. She was very little and helpless, and he was big and strong. He could feel the duty in his father's words.

Rollo smiled at the gesture. "Come and let me tell you a story of the land I lived in when I was a boy and how the gods would give us the gift of peace."

Guillaume clapped his hands once. He loved his father's stories, even if they made him sleepy as he listened to the deep voice and the rolling of Rollo's tongue over the funny words and names of people from far away.

Rollo sat in a chair by the fire with a child in both arms as he spoke. Geirlaug woke with big blue eyes to the sound of his voice. She stared in wonderment as did her brother when their father began his story.

"On cold and clear winter nights, when it felt as if the air was biting your skin, you could look up into the starry sky and see green fire dance and ripple upon the blackness. Some thought it expressed a warning, but others believed they represented the souls of the widows whose husbands had gone to Valhalla that year."

"Val-halla," Guillaume spoke. He had heard this word many times before.

"Valhalla," Rollo echoed as his eyes bathed in the glow of the warm fire before him. "Now, these souls would dance for us and wave down to all that still remained on the earth. They meant to encourage the men and women to fulfill their roles in battle. Still, others thought they shone as the Valkyries escorting the fallen warriors to Valhalla. I believe, my son and my daughter, that it was a mixture of the two. The green fire as it rippled upon the sky was the souls of the widows meeting the souls of their husbands. Together they met and danced upon the brilliant emerald waves across the night sky."

Rollo looked down upon his children and came to terms with what the midwife had said. Poppa could bear him no more. Despite the grief that crept in, he smiled in his thankfulness for the two beautiful sleeping children in his arms. He kissed each and then he too let his eyes slowly close before the fire as he dreamt of the green lights that lit up the night sky of his homeland.

Each day Poppa seemed to brighten more, though, at times her attention would leave the present and she would close within herself. In those moments, Rollo left her to rest, but always came back and offered for her to try again. Rollo found those days the most difficult. He had to tame his impatience and frustration, though he knew she could feel it.

"Come back to me, Poppa," Rollo whispered in her ear one night. He cradled her small frame in bed as she lay with her back against his chest. He propped himself up by pillows and ran his fingers through her hair as she fell asleep. He wasn't sure she had heard him until ever so slightly her fingers in his hand tightened.

She held fast to him as she adjusted her body against him and drifted off to sleep.

◊◊◊◊◊

The morning of the baptism was a bright spring day, but dark clouds billowed toward the sea. Poppa knelt before Guillaume, pressing the folds of his tunic and fussing over his long hair. She smiled as her son watched her. He spoke sweetly, "I yike your smile, mama."

Rollo walked in with baby Geirlaug in his arms. She wore a long white-lace baptismal gown. She would have seemed an angel if not for the red face and the shrill wails.

"I'll feed her before we go," Poppa said as she took the child to her breast. She gave a small smile when the baby started to feast. She took pleasure, as she had with Guillaume, at the squeaks of swallowing.

Rollo contemplated his wife as she slowly sat in a chair and allowed the baby to finish. Her color had returned to her in these last weeks. The shadows around her eyes had lifted and she had slowly gained weight. She wore a pretty and simple white gown embroidered with pink roses. In her hair, she wore more roses entwined in the dark plaited crown that circled her head. He remembered her in a similar color the day they had stormed Bayeux. He remembered the fierce look of determination in her eyes when he had stared into hers as he pressed her against the wall. Now, here she sat before him nursing their daughter, a small tendril of hair escaping and falling over her face as she contemplated their second child. Poppa's hand clasped Geirlaug's in her own. Gently she moved her fingers over the tiny palm before bringing it to her lips. She kissed the child ever so slightly. Rollo had studied the shape of those lips over many months, but never had they looked as beautiful as they appeared to him now.

Rollo smiled as he went to her and placed the hair back in place.

"What is it?" Poppa smiled innocently.

"It's nothing," Rollo denied as he kissed her forehead.

She peered at him skeptically. He returned her look with an innocent smile. She smiled back knowingly.

Père Guillaume baptized their daughter that evening, just as a storm blew in from off the sea. They gave her the Frankish name of Adèle, but her people and history would come to know her by both her names. A symbol of both her lord father's and her lady mother's heritage.

The family stood on the stairs of the cathedral in the city of Rouen. The people gave a cry of joy and a prayer of blessing. Little Guillaume smiled down on the people he would one day rule. The fiery Adèle cried at the noise of the crowds that would someday love her for her beauty and her fairness. Rollo and Poppa stood with their children, united in their destiny. They waved to their people and threw coins as they had the day Poppa first arrived in the city. They kissed, and the cheers reached a crescendo amongst the people—the Norsemen and the Franks, former enemies now united under Rollo.

◊◊◊◊◊

Rollo went on to rule his people until his death at the age of eighty. Then leadership passed to his son, Guillaume, known to history as William Longspear. When he was betrayed and murdered, his title and rule passed to his son, Richard I, at the tender age of ten. Still, the rule of Rollo's line held true. The area of West Francia entrusted to Rollo coupled with the lands he took for himself formed the territory we know as Normandy. Its united people of Francia and the North, known to history as the Normans, were a wise and hearty group. They worked hard for their profit while they sought to retain power above all else.

Years later a direct descendant of Rollo and Poppa's union, William the Conqueror (their fifth great-grandson), conquered and united England in the Norman Conquest, becoming the first of a long line of Norman kings. Their descendants grew in number and power throughout the world. From then until this day, two centuries have passed and their descendants still rule many European countries. For their lineage, the sun will never set.

AFTERWORD

I FIRST HEARD ROLLO'S STORY from the History Channel show *Vikings*. I found him fascinating. I had to know more, so I started my own research into the life of this enduring Norseman. I only became more intrigued. Not only did scenes of his life start to play out in my mind, but they started to line up with actual historical accounts. This patriarch of one of the most important dynasties is admittedly shrouded in both historical fact and legend.

Dudo of Saint-Quentin, a late tenth-century historian, was hired by Rollo's grandson, Richard I, to document the events in Rollo's life. Later historians suspect his account may have been commissioned to cast Rollo and his lineage in a more favorable and Christian light. Though notably romanticized and based more on oral stories than less historical documents, Dudo's *Historia Normannorum* (History of the Normans) makes Rollo look like a model Christian after his baptism. Other accounts weave a much more interesting tale of a man in conflict between two faiths and two cultures. This conflict lasted his entire life as he teetered between the pagan beliefs of his childhood and Christianity. Yet he still managed to bridge the gap between the Norsemen and Franks and rule in a holy unity that earned him the respect of his people.

What history is not always clear on is Rollo's actual origin. Some claim he is from Denmark, others Norway. I chose to go with the more widely accepted explanation that he came from Norway. What is clear is that Rollo had a considerably long life for the late ninth and early tenth century. He lived to his eighties. His remains now rest in Rouen Cathedral.

The term *viking* isn't found in the body of this work—less because I'm a Packers fan than because the term wasn't widely used until centuries after the events of this story. At the time these events played out, this ferocious and feared group of people were known as *Northmen* or *Norsemen*. I chose the latter for my tale.

I did take some timeline liberties with Poppa's birth and some other events. I felt I had a window of time to play with, and I opened up that toy box and went to work. Her upbringing and earlier life are lost in history. It's an invention to make her the handmaiden to the true young Lady of Bayeux. I imagined her to be fearless and strong in her faith. She had to possess the strength and spiritual maturity to curve and balance her husband's internal conflict, as ultimately their line would carry on the faith and lead with a heavenly purpose.

Nevertheless, paganism had to play a tangible role in this book. I took liberties with the rituals and sacraments, but I stayed true to the stories of Norse mythology. In his book *Norse Mythology*, Neil Gaiman encourages readers, "The fun comes in telling them yourself—something I warmly encourage you to do, you person reading this." I enjoyed bringing these ancient stories into the narrative. Though they weren't written down for many years after these events, they were the oral tradition of the Norse culture and surely familiar to all Norsemen.

On the cover of this book is the Norse symbol of nine intersecting lines known as the Web of Wyrd. It's the symbol of destiny and fate. Past, present, and future are woven into this shape. In it, every ancient rune can be found. The back cover features a peppermint plant. Not only is the peppermint plant in the story as a headache reliever, but it also symbolizes conscious thought. Above the plant is the rune *Sowilo*, which symbolizes healing and strength and is ruled by the sun. Not only does it tie into the title, but it is fitting for this beginning's tale of one of history's great dynasties.

Last, I took the advice of author Nayyirah Waheed: "The thing you are most afraid to write. Write that." There are parts of this book that were difficult for me to write. I was surprised by what came out when I just let my mind flow. One part in particular I tried to erase. I tried everything to wipe it out, but I couldn't make the story work without it. The intensity of humanity's failings is vivid and true—and there's no way around that truth, raw and painful though it can sometimes be.

In the end, whether grounded in myth or history, I'm telling the story of the patriarch and matriarch of the Normans as I imagine it. I hope you enjoy reading and imagining it as well.

ACKNOWLEDGMENTS

I HAVE TO START WITH MY FANTASTIC HUSBAND, DANA. Thank you for encouraging me to write this book and for supporting me every step of the way. Thank you for pretending to be excited when I went into dork mode and rambled about how cool it was that history lined up with the scenes in my head. Your enthusiasm as I rattled only further encouraged me. Thank you for still loving me on those long winter days when you would arrive home from a day's work only to find me glued to my screen, fingers typing rapidly but barely capable of more than a grunt, hair unwashed and tangled. My love and respect for you will only grow and will never cease.

To my daughters, Elaina and Evelyn, you will still be the greatest tale I will ever tell. Thank you for lending your mum to this book. Thank you for your patience during the countless times I was unavailable as I wrote. Thank you for your patience and understanding that, for a time, the words in my head had to flow first. Thank you for respectfully moving the Goldfish crackers into my sight line so I knew you needed me the next time I came up for air. You helped make this possible. I am in your debt. I love you fiercely.

To my original editor and coach, Renee Garrick, thank you for taking me on—and for getting to know my heart and my story.

Thank you for your suggestions and willingness to work with me. I can't wait to read your book someday soon.

To my team at Beaver's Pond Press: Lily, Alicia, Athena, Wendy, Becca, Paige, and Hanna, thank you for each of your individual roles at making this dream become a reality. Thank you for your consistent support and belief in this project and in me as a writer. You've maintained my voice, encouraged my steps, and helped me through each step of this process. I'm so grateful to you.

To my beta readers, Dana Borgschatz and Audrey Moon, thank you for your help and suggestions. You were the first to delve into this story, and I am awash in gratitude.

To my sister-in-law Gabrielle Marroquin, thank you for your beautiful cover design and for taking time away from the best and cutest boys in the world so you could dream it up. Thank you for your insight and creative vision with your artwork. I will leave you with some of the first words you ever spoke to me: "You're pretty. I like you. You should sit next to me."

To my *bestest* friend since kindergarten, Kelly Smith, thank you for the headshot. It has been a joy to watch you use your immense creative ability as a photographer. I am so proud of you.

To my parents, all of them, thank you for telling my story first. Thank you for letting me be wild in thought and action even as you guided me. I love you all.

Finally, thank you to all of you who have encouraged me and shared joy with me as I went through this process. Every time I was stopped on the street or asked how the process of this book was coming along, it made me feel wonderful. Thank you for sharing this exciting journey with me, and thank you for reading *The Sun Will Never Set*.